PRAISE FOR *SH...*

"Lily Meyer's *Short W...* ... felt portrait of youth and longing, and ... barnburner of a story that spans continents and generations, exposing US foreign policy on the scale of an intimate human drama. Meyer's prose is beautifully understated, conjuring up a style on her own. *Short War* is the most assured debut I've read in a very long time. This is the announcement of a major new talent."
—DWYER MURPHY, author of *The Stolen Coast*

"Lily Meyer has all the sensitivity to language and nuance that comes from being an experienced translator as well as a gifted writer, deftly alternating between lighthearted romance, life-or-death political intrigue, and literary mystery. A stellar roller coaster of a debut."
—MEGAN MCDOWELL, translator of *Seven Empty Houses*, winner 2022 National Book Award for Translated Literature

"*Short War* is extraordinary. Any debut novelist would be gratified and delighted to pull off a compelling love story or a propulsive mystery or a tangled family drama or a devastating political and historical novel—but somehow Lily Meyer manages to do all of that here in this ambitious, suspenseful, and beautifully constructed book."
—CHRIS BACHELDER, author of *The Throwback Special*

"This compelling mix of political thriller with bildungsroman cutting across generations and nations blazes a pathway for the contemporary novel. *Short War* is bittersweet and sexy, a melancholy fable of the trauma of fascism that is both an American story and a transnational grief. What a gift to have storytellers like Lily Meyer on the rise now."
—GINA APOSTOL, author of *Insurrecto*

SHORT WAR

SHORT WAR

A NOVEL

LILY MEYER

DEEP
VELLUM

Dallas, Texas

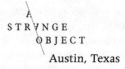
A
STRANGE
OBJECT

Austin, Texas

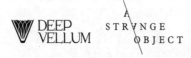

Published by A Strange Object, an imprint of Deep Vellum

Deep Vellum is a 501(c)(3) nonprofit literary arts organization founded
in 2013 with the mission to bring the world into conversation through
literature.

Library of Congress Cataloging-in-Publication Data

Names: Meyer, Lily, author.
Title: Short war : a novel / Lily Meyer.
Description: Dallas, Texas : Deep Vellum ; Austin, Texas : A Strange Object,
    2024.
Identifiers: LCCN 2023039417 (print) | LCCN 2023039418 (ebook) |
    ISBN 9781646053155 (trade paperback) | ISBN 9781646053308 (ebook)
Subjects: LCSH: Americans—South America—Fiction. | Families—Fiction. |
    LCGFT: Political fiction. | Novels.
Classification: LCC PS3613.E9735 S48 2024 (print) | LCC PS3613.E9735
    (ebook) | DDC 813/.6—dc23/eng/20231109
LC record available at https://lccn.loc.gov/2023039417
LC ebook record available at https://lccn.loc.gov/2023039418

Cover design by Emily Mahon
Cover art: *América Invertida (Inverted Map)*, courtesy of the Estate of
Joaquín Torres-García
Interior design and layout by Amber Morena
Printed in Canada

To my father, who is a real writer

It's complicated, being an American,
Having the money and the bad conscience, both at the
    same time.

—LOUIS SIMPSON, "ON THE LAWN AT THE VILLA"

CRISIS
\\\

Santiago, Chile, April 1973

A girl was walking toward Gabriel Lazris. A girl in a green miniskirt. She was across the packed basement, between the makeshift dance floor and the card table laden with booze, but he knew, with inexplicable, terrifying certainty, that she was coming for him. Faint light seemed to rise from her pale hair, illuminating her path through the human mass of Ítalo Ibáñez's seventeenth birthday. She held herself upright, like a dancer, but she moved toward Gabriel, who was folding himself into the corner of the tiny, tile-floored kitchenette, with determination rather than grace.

Nobody else was looking at her. His friends hadn't noticed her approach. Gabriel tried not to stare, but how could he not? She was glowing. Also, she seemed to have extremely important business to conduct with him, though realistically, her agenda probably involved not Gabriel but the beer-filled fridge. She probably didn't even see him. In the years he'd lived in Chile, Gabriel had spent a lot of time asking God to make him invisible. Maybe his prayers had been heard.

In the future, Gabriel would return often to this moment. He would imagine descending from the cloud of memory, elbowing his sixteen-year-old self, telling him how close he was to the true start of his life. He would never shake the belief that without Caro Ravest, he was less than his full self, though their relationship lasted less than six months. That September, the Chilean military, covertly backed by the United States, overthrew Salvador Allende's Socialist government. Before the coup, Gabriel was in love; he had plans; he had friends. After, he was a lonely American kid in a lonely American suburb, writing frantic letters to politicians who couldn't care less that his girlfriend had disappeared.

Party heat rolled through the basement. A Los Golpes song played, all jangled harmonies and rough, poppy guitars. Boys slouched in corners, sprawled on couches, straddled turned-around chairs. Girls filled the improvised dance floor, wiggling and tugging at their clothes. From his corner of the kitchen, Gabriel could hear Carlos Aldunante, his worst classmate, monologuing on the virtues of neofascism. He saw Ítalo squinting through the viewfinder of a boxy black camera. He smelled joss sticks smoldering on the kitchenette counter. Somebody had abandoned a school tie beside them, which seemed like a hazard. Those ties were 100 percent polyester and—Gabriel knew from a Hanukkah-candle incident—highly flammable. He moved it to safety, feeling pleased with himself. He'd contributed to the party now.

Nico Echevarría and Andrés Saavedra, Gabriel's best and

only friends, were bickering over their beloved soccer team, Colo-Colo, which had played like shit in Wednesday's championship qualifier. Andrés thought the problem was bad goalkeeping; Nico thought the problem was God. Gabriel thought the glowing girl was approaching swiftly. She was very pretty, and very much looking at him. He agreed with Nico, but more importantly, he needed his friends to quit play-fighting and help him out.

She walked into the kitchen, smiling. Up close, she went far beyond pretty, into the horrifying terrain of the legitimately beautiful. Maybe that explained the glow. Gabriel glanced away from her, just to confirm that he could, and took a slug of his terrible drink. Nico had decided the correct mix for the night was pisco, red wine, and Coke. A great experimenter, Nico Echevarría.

Andrés finally spotted the girl. "Hey, Caro," he said, lifting his chin. "How's it going?" Gabriel hadn't realized that his friend knew her. Absurdly, he felt a stab of jealousy.

"Fine." She shrugged and pushed her hair back, showing a hot, irregular birthmark climbing her neck. It was reddish-purple and rough-looking, like a dried pool of spilled paint. She smiled directly at Gabriel, which made a muscle in his jaw seize. Before he could unclench it, she said, "You're Gabriel, right?"

His first impulse was to deny. To say, What's a Gabriel? But she'd crossed the room to talk to him, and he, somehow, had known it. Surely this was his chance. Gabriel had been sixteen for half a year now, and he'd still never kissed a girl. Not for lack of wanting, either. He just had no clue how to act. His inner voices were not helpful. Right now, for instance, they were suggesting very strongly that he pretend not to speak Spanish, or maybe hide in the fridge. Anything to keep Caro from discovering that he was the human idiot: useless, hopeless, and thoroughly unworthy of her time.

She tilted her head. "The American friend?"

Nico reached over to ruffle Gabriel's curls. "You got it. Our quiet American."

"Good book," Caro said, alarming Gabriel still more. He didn't know what book she meant. "And sorry for ambushing you. My cousin Alejandra is Andrés's neighbor. She sent me to introduce myself."

Nico shuffled his feet. He'd dated Alejandra over the summer. She'd dumped him in January for sex reasons, or Catholic reasons, depending on your perspective.

"It wasn't an ambush," Gabriel managed. "I mean, not a bad one."

Nico winked at Caro. "See? He speaks!"

Amusement flickered in her eyes. "I've never heard of a good ambush."

"Surprise parties?" Gabriel offered.

"Ever had one?"

He shook his head.

"Alejandra threw me one last year." Caro wrapped her hair around her hand. "Not good."

"Why'd she send you over?" Gabriel asked, belatedly surprised. He and Alejandra weren't exactly close. In general, he was startled when she remembered he existed. He'd known her for nearly nine years, but he still had an impulse, every time he saw her, to reintroduce himself.

"Some guy we don't know was telling us about his trip to Miami, and I said I'd never even met an American, or any foreigners except the German nuns at our school. Alejandra thought I was complaining. She said if I was so sick of Chileans, I should come talk to you."

"Typical," Andrés said wryly. "I bet Miami Boy is Sebastián

Kahl. Caro, did he talk"—he slipped into an imitation of Kahl's braying voice—"like this?"

Caro giggled. "Maybe."

"I better rescue your cousin, then. Very difficult to shut Kahl up once he starts bragging."

"I noticed that."

"I'll come," Nico said. "I should say happy birthday to Ítalo." His mouth twitched with anticipation. They'd already greeted Ítalo, who'd insisted on photographing them with his new camera, but they hadn't lingered long enough to see if he had coke. He usually did, and Nico, of the three of them, was by far the best at drugs. Gabriel, though smallest by half a head, was best at drinking. Andrés could chain-smoke a whole pack of cigarettes and not puke.

"Nice seeing you," Andrés told Caro. Nico reached for the half-empty pisco bottle, poured a stream into Gabriel's glass and a splash into his own, then led Andrés into the party. Gabriel had to remind himself to stay behind. Talk to Caro. Keep her from wanting to dance. It was not biologically possible for him to be sober enough to converse but drunk enough to dance. It was only narrowly possible for him to dance while still capable of standing up.

He considered his newly disproportionate drink. It smelled like an enemy of self-control. "I think," he said, "Nico ruined this. And it was terrible to begin with. Would you like a beer?"

"Please."

Gabriel searched in the fridge, finding two Cristals hiding behind a girl's shoe. Why was everyone leaving their clothes in the kitchen? Should he ditch his sweater here to join in? He showed Caro the shoe, which made her laugh, then banged the beers on the counter to open them. Neither foamed too much, which was a relief.

"Short war," he said, lifting his bottle to hers. It was the

Lazris toast, adopted or created during World War II. Possibly imperialistic now, but Gabriel liked it. In Spanish, which he alone in his family spoke fluently, it felt like an invention of his own.

"Short war," Caro echoed. She didn't question the toast, which Gabriel later realized was highly uncharacteristic. She hated not knowing details. He would come to both envy her curiosity and love it. He'd dig for it in himself and, someday, teach it to his daughter.

Somebody put on João Gilberto, whose soft bossa nova made the whole party sigh and slouch. Caro took a step closer to Gabriel. "You seem less American than I thought," she said. "Not that I know what Americans are like."

"Loud and capitalist, I think."

"And you're quiet."

"Quiet and Communist."

She arched an eyebrow. "I thought Americans hated Communism."

Gabriel thought of his father. "Most do."

"I don't know." Caro's voice dipped, and her eyes took on a teasing shine. "I bet you're as Chilean as I am. I bet the real American Gabriel is halfway across the room."

Pride rippled through Gabriel, swiftly followed by fear. He didn't want to seem American—he'd devoted years of energy to sounding, looking, and thinking like a Chilean—but what if she decided he actually was an impostor? If she set off to seek the real Gabriel, she'd never come back. "I wish I were Chilean," he said. "But I can prove I'm not."

"How?"

"You speak English?"

"I take it in school."

Gabriel took a sip of beer. In middle school, before he got exempted from English classes, he'd often used the speed of his English to annoy teachers and make his friends laugh. Now he got to sit in the library while everyone else did languages. He always told himself he'd use that time to read about Socialism, but somehow he never did.

He took a deep breath. In his slowest English, he said, "I was born in McLean, Virginia. I moved to Santiago when I was eight." João Gilberto plunked and plucked in his ears. Gabriel sped up as he continued: "My dad used to be the Senate correspondent for the *Washington Courier*. After the Bay of Pigs, he started reporting on Cuba, but we couldn't move there, I guess. I was little. Anyway, when I was eight, he got made the *Courier* bureau chief here." He increased his speed to the pace at which he spoke with his parents. "We moved right before the '66 World Cup, and—"

"Okay, okay." Caro flapped a hand at him. "I believe you. I have no idea what you said."

Gabriel switched back to Spanish, relieved. "Just that I moved here eight years ago."

"I'm impressed you have no accent." She pressed a hand to her mouth. "Wait. Shit. Was that a bad compliment?"

"Not at all. I worked hard to get rid of my accent."

"Does it ever come back?"

"Only if I'm really mad. Or really drunk."

Caro grinned. She had a dimple in her left cheek. Somebody had switched the record back to Los Golpes, and people were thrashing toward the dance floor. "We better keep drinking, then."

They swiped a fifth of vodka from the freezer to supplement their beers, then settled on a rolled-up rug at the edge of the room. Andrés, who'd abandoned Alejandra in favor of smoking weed with a pack of soccer players, caught Gabriel's eye and grinned. Nico was busy flirting with a vaguely familiar-looking girl in bell-bottoms, but turned to do the same. Gabriel ignored them. He couldn't get distracted. Keeping up with Caro took all his attention. She could move a conversation anywhere: Chilean politics, American politics, Zen Buddhism, Colo-Colo's Primera División record, her lack of interest in playing team sports, her love of televised Alpine ski races and thwarted dream of learning to ski—lessons and travel would be too expensive—his recent Communist Youth–sponsored hiking trip to La Campana National Park, their shared desire to visit the glaciers in Patagonia someday. Halfway through a description of her fantasy backpacking trip, Caro paused and touched Gabriel's arm.

"I think I need a cigarette," she said.

Half the people in the basement were smoking, but she led him out to Ítalo's yard. The April air was thin and cold, and fog hung below the Andes, turning the sky a strange purplish-brown. There were no helicopters tonight, no old fighter jets dragging themselves westward to the Air Force base, no head-lights crawling past. Just the brown sky, the dark arms of ar-aucaria trees, the faint smell and sound of the Mapocho River five blocks to the north. The Mapocho separated their neigh-borhood from the slums in the Andean foothills. It smelled, to-night and every night, like fertilizer and dead fish, laundry soap and dumped-out diesel, duck and human shit decompos-ing together at the river's edge.

Gabriel suspected that he smelled too. His forehead felt greasy and his shirt clung to his back, but if Caro noticed, she didn't seem to mind. She'd shown no signs of minding a single thing about him. Gabriel took her free hand while she smoked, and she nestled into his side. The world whirred beneath them. Now, he told himself, not moving. Now, Gabriel. Kiss her now.

He didn't kiss her outside. Caro finished her cigarette and led him into the house, turning away from the basement stairs and into the Ibáñezes's guest bathroom. She shut the door and Gabriel's heart slammed. His first kiss. He had never imagined, in all his years of imagining, that it would come with this soft, cracked-open feeling, this total desire to please.

Expectation flickered on Caro's face. The mirror behind her showed Gabriel his own desire and fear. To escape his reflection, he guided Caro to the dry bathtub, which, once they were in it, seemed right. The confined space was calming. Gabriel had a brief, inexplicable urge to turn the faucets on, but Nico and Andrés would laugh for a month if he returned to the party soaking wet. Instead, he pictured Caro dripping, water rolling down her high cheekbones, pale hair stuck to the sides of her neck. He scooted closer, braced himself on the tub's side, and tilted his mouth to meet hers.

At first he felt nothing but clumsy. He didn't know where to put his free hand. Caro bit his lip, which he liked, but was it an accident? Was he supposed to bite back? Where did his tongue go? Was he drunk? Was he kissing like he was drunk? But he kept going, and slowly, he felt the barrier between them getting thinner. He wondered if it would dissolve.

Experimentally, he moved his mouth to her collarbone, then her neck, her jawline, the warm curl of her ear. Each time his lips touched her skin, a shock moved through him, as if the glow he'd thought he saw earlier were not only real but electric. He felt like he was on the verge of a significant revelation. His new life was in motion.

"Caro," he said softly.

"Gabriel."

"Do you like this?" he asked, or meant to, but the question that emerged, though different by only one vowel, was another one entirely. It was his first Spanish error in years. Not a mistake, really, so much as a lapse into helpless truth. He hadn't asked if she liked this. He'd asked, "Do you like me?"

GABRIEL SPENT ALL OF SATURDAY trying not to call Caro. On Sunday, they spent so long on the phone he got neck cramps. On Monday, he spent his first three class periods daydreaming about her, then lost three back-to-back Ping-Pong games at break out of distraction.

"What's your problem?" Nico asked, flipping his paddle. "Still hungover from Friday?"

Andrés glanced up from his book. "Lovesick. Look at him. The boy suffers."

Gabriel scowled at his friend, who wasn't wrong. Andrés was never wrong. It was one of his many infuriating traits, along with political perfection, goalkeeping ability, charisma, and height. Gabriel would hate him out of pure jealousy if they hadn't been friends since he arrived in Chile. Nico and Andrés had adopted him his first day at San Pedro Nolasco, when he was a monolingual eight-year-old terrified to make eye contact with the school priests or anyone else.

Now the three of them were an unbreakable unit. A package deal. Musketeers, or, if you asked certain priests, Stooges. They were unique at San Pedro Nolasco in that all three were white, with the minor caveat of Gabriel's Jewishness; all three lived in Vitacura, the city's richest neighborhood, and were rich even by its standards; and all three were ardent Communists. Generally speaking, those traits did not align, but Andrés's dad had politicized them. Dr. Lucas Saavedra was an ex-pediatrician and famous militant, a commander in the ultra-left Movimiento de Izquierda Revolucionaria, or MIR. He was in the news often, at home almost never. He had been in hiding since 1971, when the Santiago police—not part of Allende's government or friendly to the left wing—began to issue warrants for his arrest. As far as Gabriel knew, Andrés had last seen his dad in January, three and a half months ago.

Nico, like Gabriel, did not have revolutionary relatives. His parents, both descendants of Spanish nobility, were archconservative anti-Semites. Nico was neither. He disliked nobody and radiated kindness the way a cartoon skunk radiated stink. In recent years, he had acquired a laugh like an American mall Santa and a gigantic set of shoulders, which Gabriel envied almost as much as his friend's fundamental goodness.

"He does look bad," Nico was telling Andrés. "Weakened by love."

"That's right," Gabriel agreed. "I can barely move. I probably have to go home."

Nico waggled his eyebrows. "Oh, do you?"

Gabriel glanced across the courtyard. No priests in earshot. Ítalo Ibáñez was taking pictures of Mario Amengual tossing a flat basketball through the lone hoop. On the bench beside the court, Raúl Colinao, the class prodigy, smoked a cigarette— strictly forbidden on school grounds, but Colinao was exempt from all punishment, if only because he could talk circles around the priests. Behind him, Carlos Aldunante trailed a pack of assholes toward the rusted outdoor stairs, trampling Father Recabarren's beloved patch of bright purple lupines en route.

Andrés was looking at Aldunante too. In a low voice, he said, "I saw him showing Amengual a pair of brass knuckles the other day."

"You're joking."

"I wish."

Gabriel wanted to talk about Caro, not Aldunante. Ideally, he would have liked to never talk or think about Aldunante again. "Where'd he get them?"

Nico smacked his Ping-Pong paddle into his palm. "He says he's in Patria y Libertad. Guess he's not lying."

Patria y Libertad was a horrifying pack of soft-Nazi creeps who staged marches in jackboots. Gabriel chose to consider them comical, which worked if he looked at them as a Communist, not a Jew. "Did Amengual laugh at him?"

"I wish," Andrés said. "He seemed impressed. Wanted to try them on."

It was a worrisome answer. Mario Amengual was apolitical. Medium-rich, medium-dumb, interested mainly in sports and whitehead-popping. If he was drooling over Aldunante's brass knuckles, it meant either that he was drifting rightward or that he was stupid enough to be attracted to violence for its own sake. Gabriel looked at Amengual again. He was still mugging for Ítalo's camera. He didn't seem like a person able or willing to do harm.

"Now I really want to get out of here," he said.

Nico, who had been glowering, grinned. "You're not going home."

"No. I need to go to Santa Úrsula."

"Is that—"

"Caro's school."

Nico and Andrés hooted and clapped. "Gabriel!"

"Look at you!"

"Andrés, we've created a monster."

"A womanizer."

"A confidence machine."

"Have you talked to her since Friday night?" Andrés asked. Gabriel nodded. "Sunday."

"Good." Nico reached for him. "Now you just need——" He straightened Gabriel's school tie, tugged wrinkles from his blazer. Then he licked his palm and went for the cowlicks, but Gabriel squirmed from reach.

"What?" Nico said, mock wounded. "You want to show up looking like Bob Dylan?"

"I always look like Bob Dylan."

"True."

Gabriel wondered if Caro had registered that he looked Jewish. He hadn't mentioned his religion, which was potentially unwise. It was entirely possible that she'd never met a Jew. Santiago's Jews tended to be insular, which Gabriel couldn't criticize. Not all Chilean Catholics were fans of his people. Plenty of his classmates thought he'd killed Jesus or was doomed to burn in hell. A few had asked if his family's wealth came from moneylending. Paco Menjívar had once felt his head for hidden horns. Aldunante made a habit of drawing swastikas in the school bathrooms. Gabriel had caught him twice.

In fairness to the nation of Chile, Gabriel's own parents were not exactly pro-Semitic. Ray and Vera Lazris did not mix with their fellow Jews. Shamefully, Gabriel was grateful for his parents' commitment to assimilation. It was half the reason he went to San Pedro Nolasco, which was among Santiago's fanciest Catholic boys' schools. The other half was that his mother disliked the American wives she played tennis with. She considered them clubby, snobby, and terminally vapid and insisted—she had no evidence, but Gabriel thought it seemed perfectly plausible—that all their husbands were CIA. She forbade her husband to send Gabriel to the American school with their kids. Gabriel, privately, thought it was a little hypocritical for his mom to call anyone else a snob, but he appreciated the end result.

It wasn't that he loved San Pedro Nolasco. The school was right-wing and stuffy, and the administration seemed not to care that Carlos Aldunante was covering the walls with swastikas. But without San Pedro Nolasco, Gabriel would never have met Nico or Andrés. He might not have had a single Chilean friend. He would be another expat kid lapping up his parents' tales of life in the United States, convinced a better, realer self awaited him on the far side of the equator.

On the microbus to Santa Úrsula, Gabriel tried to persuade himself that he was adequate as he was. Caro seemed to like talking to him. She hadn't objected to his looks or personality. She'd kissed him in a bathtub. Still, he couldn't shake the thought that this bus trip was an awful idea. What if she refused to be his girlfriend? What if she laughed at him? If she laughed, he'd eat his own tongue.

The crowded micro was making him nervous. Sweaty too. He disembarked fifteen minutes from Santa Úrsula and walked with his head down, scanning the sidewalk for dog shit, bird shit, leaf mold, rotten fruit: anything that, if he stepped in it, would make him too smelly to kiss. Maybe he smelled bad already. Who really knew how they smelled? How they looked? Nico had misled him. Confidence was a scam. Confidence told him he looked like Bob Dylan on the cover of *Freewheelin'*. What if he just looked like he was twelve?

He turned onto Calle Alonso de Sotomayor, which was lined with sleek, glass-balconied new apartments that seemed designed less for Santiago than Miami or Barranquilla—some city with glittering beach views, not a brown, fogged-up river and Andean foothills covered in scrub and slums. Not slums. "Slum" and "shanty" were reactionary words. The proper choice was "settlement," but their Communist Youth leader, a burly art student named Claudio Aristeguieta, had brought up the vocabulary issue only a few weeks ago, and Gabriel hadn't quite retrained his mind.

Gabriel worried often that he had inherited reactionary thought patterns from his dad, who was a real live American conservative. He and Gabriel fought constantly. Their eternal argument was, Gabriel knew, torturing his mother and their housekeeper, Luz, but how could he not fight with his father? First of all, it kept his dad from picking on his mom, and second, his dad's opinions were terrible. Dangerous. As the Santiago bureau chief for the *Washington Courier*, Ray signed off on every word the paper's subscribers read about Salvador Allende, the world's first democratically elected Socialist president. In Gabriel's opinion, that meant it was both bullshit and unethical for his dad to hate Allende and irresponsible for Gabriel not to challenge that hate.

He wished he had a dad like Andrés's. A dad he could admire. Dr. Lucas had actual principles. He'd married a socialite and turned her into a Socialist. He had abandoned a lucrative pediatric practice to join MIR, which appealed to him on both personal and political fronts: not only was it a vanguard group that wanted to spark revolution, it had also been founded by a doctor, Miguel Enríquez. Dr. Lucas kept practicing medicine in MIR, but instead of prescribing pills to sick little rich kids, he stitched up wounds and delivered babies in Santiago's poorest settlements—and, according to his son, carried out various other operations so he could pay for supplies and lifesaving drugs.

Dr. Lucas was the reason Gabriel and Nico were real leftists, if not brave enough to want to run away from home and join MIR themselves. For a long time, it had taken all Gabriel's courage to keep going to Communist Youth meetings against his dad's wishes. He'd joined, at Dr. Lucas's invitation, during Allende's successful 1970 presidential campaign. Dr. Lucas drove Gabriel, Nico, and Andrés to their first meeting, which, now that Dr. Lucas was underground, had become one of Gabriel's most cherished memories. Andrés's dad had picked all three of them up from school. He had the radio blasting rock music, a fat bag of snacks on the passenger seat: salted pumpkin seeds, chocolate-filled cuchuflí cookies, a giant popcorn ball that Nico instantly cracked in half, sending shards of hardened caramel corn flying through the back seat. Dr. Lucas didn't mind. Of the four of them, he was the most excited. To this day, Gabriel had never encountered an adult who showed enthusiasm—or any positive emotion—as freely as Andrés's dad. He sang to himself while driving, roared and sometimes wept with joy at his soccer team's victories, never let Andrés walk by him without a hug. Gabriel imagined that Nico would grow up to be like that. He wished he could imagine the same for himself.

Their Communist Youth group met, then and now, at Claudio's squat in Almagro. Even its exterior walls smelled like mold. Dr. Lucas had parked in its driveway, then gotten out of the car and, solemnly, shaken all three boys' hands. You're doing a big thing today, he told them. A good thing. Especially you, Gabriel.

Me?

You. So few Americans have the guts to be Communists. You can set a powerful example. Scratch that. You're setting it right now.

Nearly four years later, Gabriel carried those words like a mantra. No matter how small he felt, no matter how useless, he could at least set an example. He'd been trying to set an example, he thought, when, for his thirteenth birthday, he asked his parents, who had no idea he'd been attending Communist meetings, to pay his Party dues. He'd hoped his dad might be proud of his courage, even if he disagreed with his politics. No dice. Ray was livid. He called the Saavedras' house to shout at Dr. Lucas. Gabriel still remembered the shame he felt listening to his dad's guttural, fragmented Spanish, his record-scratch repetitions. Eavesdropping on that phone call, he wished, for the first time, that he wasn't Ray Lazris's son.

Gabriel had left the phone call out when, on Sunday, he told Caro the story of his political conversion. She'd asked whether he thought he would have become a Communist if he hadn't had Andrés and Dr. Lucas to guide him. He told her the truth: he doubted it. Without the Saavedras, he probably would have accepted the toxic Lazris combination of Nixonian Red-bashing and bootstrap belief in the American Dream.

Granted, the family had experienced the latter. August Lazris, Gabriel's grandfather, emigrated from Berlin to Chicago in 1929. By 1939, he owned a massive tannery near Chicago's Loop, a clanking, belching, smoking two-block building that sucked in workers from the city's Black and Polish neighborhoods and spat out hundreds of hides every day. The tannery—Lazris Leather—had Americanized August fast. In a decade, it got him a native-born wife, a lakefront house in Glencoe, and a salary that more than covered three first-class tickets on the MS *St. Louis* for his parents and much-younger brother, who still lived in Nazi Berlin.

But the *St. Louis* never got past Havana. The United States forbade it to go farther. The Roosevelt administration denied the nine hundred Jews on the *St. Louis* entry. Some managed to find asylum elsewhere, but more than two hundred, Rosa, Abraham, and Sander Lazris included, were murdered in Hitler's concentration camps. Why should Gabriel have felt pride in his nationality, knowing that story? Why should he have wanted to be American at all? He saw no reason to side with the country he was born in. He sided with his poor dead great-uncle Sander, who, according to the letters Gabriel's grandfather had saved, wanted to live somewhere Socialist but knew better than to try Stalin's USSR. He sided with Luz, whose relatives had often gone hungry in the three years since Nixon slashed aid to Chile. She gave half her wages to her sister, who had three daughters, but, she said, it still wasn't enough.

Gabriel was nearly at Santa Úrsula. Time to stop fretting about his family. He cut through Plaza Turquía, passing the right-wing newsstand, the soft-porn newsstand, the candied-nut cart streaming sugary smoke. The nuts were tempting, but he didn't want Caro to catch him with a full mouth.

Her school was walled like a fortress. A Chilean flag snapped from its roof. Gabriel wondered what the gory-saint situation was like in there. San Pedro Nolasco was full of terrifying portraits: Sebastián spiked with arrows, Bartolomé with his skin peeled off, Lorenzo on the grill. After eight years, Gabriel still had nightmares about them—Bartolomé especially—at least once a month.

He settled on a bench across the street from Santa Úrsula and squinted upward, as if he could tell the time from the sun. It couldn't be later than noon, and presumably Caro's school, like his, didn't let its students out for lunch until one o'clock. He imagined Caro slipping through the gate in a flood of high-socked, uniformed girls, a few black-habited nuns mixed in. He remembered her feline face, her long hair, her birthmark with its ragged coastline. His heart sped, and some blood began making its way downward. To prevent an erection, he started listing and ranking the best plays Colo-Colo had made that season, replacing Caro's skirted legs with star striker Carlos Caszely barreling toward the Unión Española goal. Gabriel loved Caszely. He loved how unathletic Caszely seemed, with his bulldog cheeks, ham-hock thighs, top-heavy run like a tod-dler's—and a diagonal shot that could rip through a goal net. Gabriel had seen it happen. One perk of familial wealth was al-ways getting good seats at soccer games.

He looked over Santa Úrsula at the mountains. Flat light drained through the pearl-colored clouds. The trees in Plaza Turquía clacked their branches in the breeze. The school's high door creaked, then swung open to let Caro out.

She was alone. Her unbuttoned coat swung at her knees. She waved, and Gabriel, astonished, waved back. What was she do-ing? Had he conjured her? Was Carlos Caszely going to walk up to him next?

"I saw you out the window," she called, crossing the street.

Gabriel croaked. An actual croak, like a toad. Caro seemed not to notice. She sat beside him, then asked, "Why are you here?"

"I came to see you."

She nodded. "Thought so."

The trees shook harder. Caro scraped a line with her heel in the dirt. Her socks sagged at her ankles. The breeze picked up, carrying the smell of ozone. Over the Andes, white clouds min-gled with gray.

"It's going to rain," Gabriel said.

"You came to Santa Úrsula to tell me that?"

He swallowed. Reddish dust blew between them. Why had he wasted time thinking about Carlos Caszely? He should have been scripting his lines. "I came," he tried, "to tell you it's go-ing to rain. And"—what would Nico say? Something confident but also ridiculous; something that would make her laugh—"everyone knows the best place to wait out a rainstorm is in a fruit shop with somebody who wants to be your boyfriend."

She glanced down the street. "There's not much fruit."

There was, in fact, almost none. On the sidewalk, the grocer had set out a few cartons of withered citrus. Inside, there were tragically puckered cherimoyas and overripe cactus fruits with fat black pocks where their spines had once been. A crate of downy, bruised lucumas sat on the counter next to a radio tuned to the center-right station. A white fan turned slowly in the corner, moving the smells of mulch and decay through the store. The counter man, who had a sagging, purplish face and a thick, hand-sharpened pencil tucked behind his ear, looked at them sorrowfully as they approached.

"Hey, Tino," Caro said. "How're you doing?"

Tino rested his forearms on the counter. "No onions," he began. Gabriel couldn't tell if this was an answer or an automatic recitation. "No garlic. No lettuce, no carrots, no turnips, no parsnips, no beans. No potatoes. Sweet potatoes, yes. You want sweet potatoes?"

Caro was already shaking her head. "I would, but I don't have my ration book."

Gabriel never had his ration book. He barely ever saw it. Luz did all his family's food shopping, and she shopped on the black market only. Tino didn't bother looking at him, but to Caro, he said, "Your boyfriend either?"

Gabriel flushed, and Caro reached for his hand. The dry touch of her palm sent a skittering, sparking feeling up his arm. "My boyfriend either," she said, and the skittering feeling hit his chest and bloomed into the great heat of joy. My girlfriend, he thought, looking at her. From first kiss to first girlfriend in three days.

He pulled Caro close, wishing he'd found someplace more private. Rain pattered in the dust outside. Not nothing, but not a monsoon. He thought again of his impulse, in Ítalo's bathroom, to turn the taps on.

"How do you feel about getting rained on?" he said.

"I don't mind."

"Then I could walk you home."

Caro smiled. A new smile, Gabriel thought. Fuller, some-how, than the ones he'd seen. Maybe a little triumphant, which made him feel triumphant too. Even better: he felt confident. Not like the human idiot or the American friend. Like his own person, and one who had the potential—maybe, God will-ing—to be a good boyfriend. He couldn't wait to tell Nico and Andrés.

ONLY AFTER HE GOT HOME did Gabriel regret not mention-ing his religion. He'd wimped out. On their walk, Caro had said her parents were serious Catholics. Her mother, especially, con-ducted her life according to priestly instructions: prayed rosa-ries nightly, never cooked meat on Fridays, voted alternately for the conservative National Party and centrist Christian Dem-ocrats. Caro herself was further left on the political spectrum, if not entirely sure where she fell. Her indecision was excit-ing—maybe Gabriel could convert her to Communism!—but did not alleviate his concerns that she might reject him on re-ligious grounds.

He'd call her, he resolved, hanging his soggy blazer on the shower rod. The smell of wet wool rose from it, mixed with the tiniest hint of Caro's shampoo. He would call her, and she'd ei-ther dump him after less than two hours or laugh and tell him not to be absurd. If the former, he'd change his name and go live in the mountains. If the latter, he'd enter the realm of con-fidence for good.

First, though, he had to survive Lazris family dinner, a rit-ual to which his mother was devoted. She made Luz set the dining room table nightly. Starched tablecloth, candelabra, the works. Gabriel hated that candelabra. He didn't see why he had to spend meals staring at a foot-tall bronze antler. He'd rather have eaten in front of the TV.

Family dinner would have bothered him less if his mom cooked. He would understand the ceremony if it sprang from chef's pride, but in their house, only Luz touched the stove. She planned, made, and served every meal, then ate alone in the kitchen while Gabriel and his father dutifully praised his mom for the steak's scarlet juices or the fish's tender flesh.

Tonight was halibut, which was, in fact, delicate enough to flake beneath Gabriel's fork. It also tasted as if it had been caught last week. Hazards of the black market. Gabriel spooned tomato pebre over his portion, hoping to drown the thick fishiness in onion and spice.

He loved Luz's pebre. She made two batches a week, chopping as many tomatoes as she could get her hands on, then mixing in diced onion, green bell peppers, cilantro, garlic, and a quarter-bottle of red wine vinegar. During the truckers' strike, when not even dollars could buy produce in Santiago, Gabriel had missed pebre most. Now he ate it daily: on fish and meat, on scrambled eggs for breakfast, mashed into avocado and spread on toast for lunch.

He swiped up tomato juice with a piece of bread. His parents were fighting about his winter break, which was nearly two months away. Vera wanted to drive to Buenos Aires; Ray was refusing, seemingly out of spite.

"Black-market prices are getting ridiculous," she said. She rested an elbow on the table, which Gabriel was expressly forbidden to do. The cashmere fibers of her sweater shone dully in the candlelight. She reached for her water glass, then continued, "In Argentina, we can buy a wheel of Parmesan for the price of a tiny piece here."

"Why do we need a wheel of Parmesan?"

"Ray. It was an example."

Gabriel's father swirled his scotch, the same bronze as the candelabra. Its melting ice clinked and foamed. He'd always been a small man—shorter than his wife, and, as of four months ago, shorter than Gabriel—but recently he looked shrunken, crumpled, like one of his own balled-up drafts.

"Vera," he said. He was using his patient voice, which Gabriel loathed. If and when his mom divorced his dad, she could play a recording of the patient voice in court as proof that Ray was too condescending to live with. "I don't know what else to say. We can afford the black market, one, and two, I have to be in the newsroom. It would be irresponsible for me to leave."

Gabriel groaned. "It would not."

His father ignored him. "The political situation is extremely unstable. Allende barely has any military support left. Chances are, he loses the Army completely by winter, and then what? What happens if we're in Argentina and there's a coup?"

"There won't be," Gabriel said.

Ray glowered. "Don't interrupt."

Gabriel tried to make his face innocent. "You asked a question. I answered. There's not going to be a coup. And the commander in chief of the Armed Forces is in Allende's cabinet. I think that's plenty of military support."

The candles flickered between them. Their dog, Sammy, barked in the yard. Gabriel would have liked to trade places with Sammy. He'd rather have spent his nights napping and howling than debating across the perfectly set table with his dad, who had now abandoned the patient voice to say, "In your little youth-group fantasyland, maybe. But in the real world, Communists only hold on to power one way."

"Which is?"

"Dictatorship."

"So Allende's plan is to start a dictatorship by alienating the entire Army?"

"Gabriel," his mom warned.

Sammy barked again, louder. Gabriel knew perfectly well what his dad was claiming: that in order to prevent Allende, a constitutionally elected president who had devoted his entire career to advancing Socialism through democracy and coalition-building, from somehow transforming into a despot, the military was going to seize control of the country. He didn't doubt that the Army would love a power grab, but the rest was absurd.

"I don't think Dad's ideas make sense," he told his mother. "He's claiming there's going to be a coup against Allende, but also that Allende's going to turn into a dictator. You have to admit that's illogical."

"Right," Ray said. "You, Gabriel, my sixteen-year-old son, are the arbiter of logic. You know everything. More than me. More than the entire *Courier* bureau."

"Which is what? Six reporters who don't speak Spanish?"

"Don't be a smartass. We have interpreters. And sources."

Interest shot through Gabriel, competing with annoyance. His dad rarely mentioned his sources. According to Claudio, this was because the CIA had infiltrated the foreign press corps in Chile. Claudio was confident that the CIA fed propaganda to the *Courier*, the *New York Times*, CBS News, and so on, with the goal of making American voters fear Socialist leadership like a twentieth-century plague. Gabriel believed him in theory, but he wouldn't have minded finding out for himself.

"Who are your sources?" he asked.

"Nobody you know."

Gabriel shrugged. "I can still be curious."

"They're confidential."

"Who am I going to tell?"

His dad scowled. "Your Communist friends, presumably."

The answer stung more than Gabriel expected. "Trust me, they all know the CIA feeds you stories. Nobody needs to hear it from me."

Ray curled his lip. To Gabriel's mom, he said, "Isn't it fun when our only child spouts crap at the dinner table? Doesn't it fill you with pride?"

She didn't answer. Gabriel took a bite of fish. After a moment, Ray rose to refill his scotch. Gabriel wasn't sure who'd won this round of their argument. He had introduced the CIA question, which was good, except that he now felt like shit. His mother looked miserable. Briefly, he entertained the possibility that not only was his dad in fact serving some clandestine propaganda purpose, but also that his mom knew about it. Maybe she condemned the CIA wives so he wouldn't guess she effectively was one. A plausible theory for another woman, but he didn't think Vera would be willing to lie in that way.

"Sorry," he told her quietly.

She shook her head. "You're wearing me out."

"I could come to Buenos Aires."

"I need a second driver."

"So teach me how to drive. Or hire somebody to do it."

"No one's going to teach you by July."

Gabriel didn't want to admit it aloud, but she had a point. He was not, traditionally, a quick learner. At least, not in the physical realm. He'd picked up Spanish in a semester, but learning to dribble a soccer ball had taken a solid year of Dr. Lucas's backyard coaching. Tying his shoes had been a major challenge, as had buttoning the fly of his jeans. His Ping-Pong aim was not great, though he, Nico, and Andrés played at almost every school break. There was no reason to think he'd be able to drive across the Andes anytime soon. Besides, he'd already joined a Communist Party agriculture brigade with his friends. It was a terrific scheme. High school break started in mid-July, but Claudio had referred them to a university-student Trabajo Voluntario brigade that kicked off in June, which meant they got to skip two weeks of class.

Gabriel had not told his parents he was missing school to pick vegetables. Nor had he told his school. He had written and hand-delivered a letter to San Pedro Nolasco's administration explaining that the Lazrises would be taking Nicolás Echevarría and Andrés Saavedra on a monthlong trip to the United States. He signed it "Vera Lazris," of course. He did a very good version of his mom's signature. Meanwhile, he and Nico—Andrés had no need to lie—had explained to their parents that San Pedro Nolasco was recruiting upper-school students to do various repair and gardening jobs in the elementary school before and during winter break, and that Father Recabarren had strongly suggested they sign up. His parents disliked the idea, but, as expected, didn't interfere. Neither of them expended enough effort on parenting to genuinely forbid or prevent him from doing what he liked.

He considered reminding his mom of his made-up construction project now, but an irritable haze had settled over the table. Gabriel excused himself the moment he could. His parents murmured as he carried his plate into the kitchen. Discussing his antagonistic behavior or resuming their fight. Resolution seemed unlikely either way.

Luz was at the sink, washing dishes. The smell of lavender soap filled the room. She had the radio on, her apron tied loosely at her thick waist. In Spanish, Gabriel told her, "Good fish."

"A bit off, no?"

"Not too bad."

"I heard you fighting with your father again."

"Only for a minute."

Luz twisted to look at him. She'd recently started dyeing her hair back to its original black. Somehow, the color made her seem older, though maybe it was only the impact of change. "You know how it works," she said. "You fight with your dad tonight, and your mom shouts at me in the morning."

Gabriel lowered his head. "I'm sorry."

"Feel sorry for your mom."

Luz returned to the dishes, and Gabriel set his plate down beside the empty fish pan, which was lined with stuck scraps of halibut skin. He scooped a tangerine from the fruit bowl, listening to the radio—Luz had it on the Communist station, Radio Magallanes—crackle about the reactionary female vote. In last month's Congressional election, women had sided overwhelmingly with the right wing.

"Stupid," Luz said, shaking her head. "Stupid girls listening too much to their husbands."

Gabriel made a sound of agreement, though he wasn't sure he agreed. If husbands were the problem, wouldn't the male vote have tipped even further right? But he didn't like contradicting Luz, who had been a Communist for fifty years, and so he took his tangerine off to the living room to call Caro.

She answered on the first ring. "I hoped it would be you."

"You did?" Gabriel said, joy and nerves fluttering together in his chest. He channeled them into working the citrus skin free. If he could peel the fruit in a perfect, unbroken spiral, he decided, that would be a good omen. It would signal a perfect, unbroken future for his relationship with Caro. At minimum, it would point to Caro not minding that her new boyfriend was a Jew.

"I did. I meant to mention I wouldn't be here this weekend. Alejandra and I are visiting our grandparents in Quilpué."

The tangerine peel snapped. "Shit," Gabriel said. "I mean—sorry—that's great."

Caro laughed. "I'd rather spend the weekend with you."

Gabriel collapsed into the brocade couch. He felt himself beaming, and sweating. Heat surged over him from the woodstove, which sat opposite the sofa and gave off enough warmth for three houses. Luz kept its fire stoked from March to October, filling the living room with the pleasant smell of quebracho wood and keeping it roughly the temperature of Miami in spring.

"I get back Monday," Caro said. "We could see each other Tuesday, if you're free."

He split the tangerine in half. "There's a Unidad Popular march downtown," he said. "To celebrate May Day. But I could skip it."

"Or you could invite me."

Gabriel grinned at the woodstove. "Do you want to come?"

"I do."

"Have you been to a demonstration before?"

"Never."

"You'll like it," Gabriel promised. He thought it was a safe bet. Nearly everyone liked their first march.

He ate a tangerine section, which was juiceless and much too sour. Bitter pith caught between his teeth, and he moved the receiver away from his mouth to suck it free. Once he'd swallowed it, he said, "I meant to say earlier."

"That there was a demonstration?"

"That I—" He took a deep breath. "I'm not Catholic."

"You're Jewish," Caro said. "I know."

He stopped himself from asking if it was his nose. "Alejandra?"

"Alejandra."

Gabriel did not feel reassured. He popped three sections of

the third-rate tangerine into his mouth. Ray clattered at his typewriter, audible even though his study was all the way down the hall. Luz was still cleaning in the kitchen. His mom moved around upstairs. The fire popped audibly, and the phone line buzzed.

"It's not a problem?" he asked.

Caro sighed. "Not for me."

"Meaning?"

"Meaning my parents probably shouldn't know."

"About me? Or—"

"No, no, no," Caro interrupted, stumbling in her urgency. Gabriel imagined her blushing, waving a hand in the air. "Only your religion. They already know about you."

Every muscle in Gabriel's body relaxed. He was parent-official. If she was willing to tell her family he existed, and, even better, willing to lie to protect her ability to see him, then she must truly like him. For the first time, the realm of confidence swam into view.

Quietly, Caro said, "I wish I could trust them not to mind."

Gabriel shrugged, as if she could see him. "Parents are parents."

"Would yours care that I'm Chilean?"

Briefly, he wished he'd told them he had a new girlfriend, though, as a rule, he disliked telling his parents about his life. "I doubt it. My dad would only mind if you were a Communist. And neither of them would admit it, but they wouldn't be thrilled if you weren't white."

"Same with mine."

"We can't all be Dr. Lucas's kids."

Caro laughed. "I know. Speaking of parents, though, mine are going to kick me off the phone. I hogged it long enough on Sunday. What time's the demonstration?"

"Starts at four. I could pick you up if you want." ·

"Isn't your school downtown?"

"It is," Gabriel admitted. "Corner of Huérfanos and Mac Iver." He'd liked the idea of returning to Santa Úrsula, Caro kissing him at the school gate as her classmates watched—jealously, he hoped. Kissing her in front of his own classmates somehow wasn't the same. Nothing sexy about having Aldunante for an audience, or dumb Menjívar, or zitty Amengual.

"Perfect," Caro said breezily. "Meet you there."

IF GABRIEL HAD KNOWN that the May 1 march would be his last demonstration for a decade, he would have taken it more seriously as a political event, not just a date. He would have made signs. Bought an anti-fascism button or two. Originally, the march had been a standard May Day celebration of the working class, but, according to its Communist Party organizers, it was now doubling as condemnation of Patria y Libertad. Its leader, a thick-necked ideologue named Pablo Rodríguez Grez, had issued a formal call for a new government, which even the right-wing paper, *El Mercurio*, conceded was a poorly veiled effort to incite a coup. Gabriel's dad wrote a *Courier* column in which he agreed but added that Patria y Libertad was an essentially minor and powerless street gang. Later that year, the group would reveal its connections to the military; it would start attempting assassinations, blowing up transmission towers, and cutting fuel supplies from Santiago to Concepción. But in late April, Gabriel thought his father was right: Rodríguez and his little acolytes couldn't incite shit.

Unsurprisingly, Aldunante had a different interpretation. In geometry the day of the march, he proclaimed, "If we wanted a coup, we'd plan a coup." His announcement carried through the whole room, but deaf Father Ávalos knit at his broad desk, undisturbed. Blue wool snaked from his needles. Poor Father Ávalos. He was nearly eighty. San Pedro Nolasco should have already let him retire. He should be playing shuffleboard on a Caribbean cruise, not sitting in an icy classroom filled with assholes who took zero interest in calculating the interior angles of trapezoids.

"We certainly have access to firepower," Aldunante continued. "And manpower."

Gabriel tried to apply himself to his worksheet. If angle ABC measures 60° and angle ADC measures 80°, then—fuck it. He couldn't listen to this shit.

"Hey," he called, twisting. His uniform pants squeaked against his metal chair. "Carlos. Who's 'we'?"

Aldunante looked delighted. "Was I talking to you?"

"Seemed like it," Gabriel said. "Since I could hear you."

Nico leaned over. "I think they could hear you in Brazil."

Aldunante pressed his thin shoulders back. "I was talking to Facundo." Beside him, Facundo Solís bared his mossy teeth in an obliging grin. Gabriel thought of Aldunante flaunting his brass knuckles to Amengual. It was not good to see his classmates, even the ones whose lights had never quite come on, playing along with somebody who had been reviled for years as a loser and creep.

He wished he could do disdain better in Spanish. He tried to imagine his words passing through a thick pool of hate. "Were you?"

"I was."

"So you and Facundo personally have the firepower to unseat the president?"

Aldunante smirked. Gabriel was starting to regret this. He didn't need to waste his time getting sneered at by little fascist shits. Behind him, Andrés asked, "Why not? Carlos and Facundo are tough guys."

Nico gave Aldunante's skinny arm a squeeze, flexing his own considerable bicep as he did so. Gabriel could tell he was digging his fingers in hard enough to hurt. Clearly, Facundo could too; he returned to his trapezoids as Nico, eyes wide with fake awe, announced, "Very strong."

Aldunante jerked his arm away. "Don't bully me."

Gabriel burst out laughing. "Bully you? Is that a joke?"

"I have an idea," Andrés suggested. "You quit bragging about your fascist friends, we quit bullying you. Deal?"

"Sounds like a great deal to me," Nico said.

Gabriel nodded. "More than fair."

Aldunante scowled but said nothing. The plastic sheet taped over the classroom's broken window billowed. Cold wind gusted between the desks, ruffling worksheets and blank notebook pages. It lifted Andrés's unwashed hair—that was the disadvantage of blondness; you could always tell when he hadn't showered—and made the maps pinned to the corkboard crackle. Gabriel wrapped his arms around himself for warmth. Five more minutes till class ended. One more day in which he hadn't learned geometry.

The moment the bell rang, Aldunante fled. "What's he scared of?" Nico asked, gesturing at his retreating back. "Does he think we're going to beat him up in front of Father Ávalos?"

"We probably could," Andrés said.

"The Father would probably join in." Gabriel waved at the old priest, who gave him a kind, false-toothed smile. "Stab him with a knitting needle."

Gabriel had always liked Father Ávalos. He seemed to practice the simplicity all the priests preached. He knitted his own scarves and sweaters, always wore fat white tennis shoes and the same ancient robe. His perspective on Jews, also, was one of curiosity rather than hostility. He'd once asked, in a stage whisper, if Gabriel might be able to show him a yarmulke. Gabriel would have been glad to, but the Lazrises didn't keep such things in their home.

The priest headed to the door, sneakers squeaking. "Thanks, Father!" Nico called, loud enough to crack the classroom's last intact window. Then, in a more normal register, he said, "Snack before the march?"

Andrés rose instantly. He was always hungry. San Pedro Nolasco had a small canteen that sold a variable array of snacks—though lately the selection wasn't shifting so much as shrinking. It did provide free milk courtesy of Salvador Allende, but that program ended once you turned sixteen. Gabriel, whose capacity to digest dairy was limited, didn't miss it. He knew Andrés did.

As they descended to the canteen, it occurred to Gabriel to hope that Patria y Libertad wouldn't show up at the demonstration. It was an official, permitted gathering, which meant that the cops would be required to pen counterprotesters in some empty alley where they could flash their brass knuckles at one another to their hearts' content. Still, Gabriel would prefer that Caro not see them. He wanted her to feel safe.

It was breezy out, and the canteen was in a courtyard that was less than thoroughly sheltered. Gabriel jammed his hands into his pockets as he and his friends lined up behind a gaggle of younger boys awaiting their milk. Over their heads, he could see a promising quantity of bagged peanuts. If he was lucky, there would be candied ones too.

"By the way," he said, "we have a guest for the march."

Andrés cocked his head. "'We'?"

Gabriel drew a loose triangle between himself, Andrés, and Nico. "Caro's coming. She's meeting us outside in a bit."

"Nice work," Nico said. "Alejandra never would have come to a demonstration with me."

"Alejandra and Caro are different," Gabriel said, which was an understatement. Alejandra was the most adult-seeming person he'd ever met, including actual adults. Her attitude toward Nico had been equal parts animal trainer and tolerant aunt. It was inconceivable that she had ever let him kiss her, though he claimed—at length and in detail—she'd let him do more.

Nico shrugged. "So? Take the compliment."

Gabriel didn't know how. He turned to Andrés, who was examining a puffy red scratch on his right hand. It indicated an effort to corral a stray cat. Andrés was softhearted where cats were concerned, though cats didn't seem to reciprocate his affection. He was always getting hissed at, or bitten, or clawed.

"You should invite Caro to do Trabajo Voluntario in June," Andrés said.

"You think her parents would let her?"

Andrés shrugged one shoulder. "Are your parents letting you?"

"I thought our brigade was full," Nico said.

"It was."

"But?"

"But I have to drop out," Andrés said. "My mom's making me go to Bío-Bío."

Gabriel lifted his head. "Since when?"

"I thought you hated visiting your grandparents," Nico said.

Andrés stretched his arms overhead. His sweater released a faint cloud of wool smell that blew toward Gabriel in the wind. "I do. I told you, she's making me. Allende is finally expropriating the ranch at the end of June, and she wants to go say goodbye."

Nico clapped his hands. "No shit!"

"As of July 1, Hacienda Gibson belongs to the Chilean people."

Gabriel wished somebody would give his family tannery to the American people, who would, he assumed, transform it into a workplace less thunderous and horrifying than it was now. Four years ago, he'd gone to see his family in Chicago. It was an awful trip. Nothing about the United States felt right to him. Everything was too big, too loud, too on sale. His grandfather, who had yet to retire from Lazris Leather, had toured him around the tannery floor, which was dark, acrid-smelling, and unbearably hot. Surely if the hide scrapers and drum operators owned the means of production, they'd put some windows in. Ventilate the place better. Invest in chemicals that stank less, if that was possible.

"Never thought it would happen," Andrés was saying. He glared at the boys still collecting their milk before continuing. "I was convinced that old fucker would dodge land reform somehow. He's weaseled his way out of so much else."

"Like what?" Gabriel asked.

"Military service. Taxes." Andrés thought for a moment. "Mostly taxes."

Gabriel glanced at Nico, who looked embarrassed. His father took great pride in his tax avoidance. He didn't flash his wealth—not by Vitacura standards, anyway—but he loved to enumerate his international bank accounts.

"Where are your grandparents going to live?" Nico said.

"Here or Zapallar."

"So, Zapallar," Gabriel said. The choice seemed evident. Back when Andrés didn't fight with his grandparents, who considered Dr. Lucas both a deadbeat dad and a hazard to the nation, Gabriel had loved getting to tag along on their family's beach trips. The Gibsons' Zapallar house was palatial: four floors, three gardens, a pebbled path leading directly from the grill to the beach club, where Andrés could order unlimited fried shrimp on his grandparents' account. Gabriel remembered devouring those shrimp. He remembered climbing slippery rocks by the marina, watching fat crowds of pelicans spill fish from their accordion beaks. He remembered crabs for dinner and chocolate mousse for dessert.

Finally, the milk distribution ended, and Gabriel, Nico, and Andrés descended on the canteen counter. Between them, they bought sweet peanuts, salty peanuts, and a package of strawberry-flavored cookies that were objectively bad but better than no cookies at all. Once they had settled on a bench in the swiftly emptying courtyard, Nico asked Andrés, "Where's Marco going?"

Marco was Andrés's older brother. He had managed the ranch since graduating from university. He was Andrés's absolute opposite: he hated cities, hated Communists, and thought his dad was a dangerous bum.

"Moving to Miami."

Gabriel snorted. "Seriously?"

He'd been to Miami twice: once as a little kid, and once en route from Santiago to Chicago. His mental image was sparkling water, sparkling properties, a whole city built from sequins and gloss. It was a challenge to see Marco thriving there.

Andrés sighed and shifted. The pride on his face had faded. "Romina's pregnant. She and Marco want to have the baby in the States."

Nico beamed. "Uncle Andrés!"

"Uncle *Andy*," Gabriel corrected in English, leaning on the short American *A*. Nico laughed, but Andrés scowled through a mouthful of peanuts.

"If we have the money for plane tickets, I'm not wasting it on a trip to Miami."

Gabriel and Nico looked briefly at each other. Andrés rarely spoke of the financial difficulties he and his mom faced now that Dr. Lucas was underground and the Gibson fortune was off limits to them. Nico asked, "Where would you go?"

Andrés scowled even harder. He drummed his knuckles on the bench. It had long ago been painted forest, but the paint had flaked and faded to a miserable shade of sea green. He scanned the courtyard, whose only other inhabitants were the canteen ladies and a starved-looking bird. "Look," he said. "Promise to keep this secret."

"The baby?" Gabriel said.

Andrés made an irritable swatting gesture, as if he could knock Gabriel's idiot question from the air. "Not the baby. Just promise."

"Cross my heart."

"Nico?"

"Swear to God."

It took Andrés a moment to speak. When he did, his voice was so soft it almost vanished in the wind. "My dad's got to leave the country."

Gabriel jolted forward. "What?"

"Why?" Nico asked, sounding as stunned as Gabriel felt. Both scooted closer to Andrés, whose eyes were red and glazed, as if he were stoned. He hadn't cried in front of them since his dad first went underground.

"Marco's been hiding him. No ranch, nowhere to hide."

Branches rattled above them. Across the courtyard, the canteen staff hauled the wooden window shutter closed. Surely none of them could have heard. Gabriel had the thought, as he occasionally did at school, that if Catholics were right, privacy here was a joke. God was eavesdropping. All the classroom crucifixes and hallway saints were like divine bugs, relaying their words to the Holy Ear.

"How long?" Nico asked Andrés.

"Four months." He shook his head. "It's not good."

Gabriel assembled his courage. "What happened?"

"Don't know. Some mission at the Navy base in Talcahuano. It wasn't in the news. All my mom will say is that it went badly, and my dad's been hiding since then. It's ironic, really. Nobody supports land reform more than him, but now that the ranch is getting expropriated, he can't stay there. He has to go to Cuba, I guess."

Andrés covered his face with his hands. Gabriel's stomach tightened around the peanuts he'd eaten. Nico made a strangled sound beside him, but neither of them tried to offer comfort. What comfort could there be? If Dr. Lucas, who had already been in hiding since 1971, now had to go hide in Castro's Cuba, then he must have committed or attempted to commit a crime so serious that even Salvador Allende's Socialist Ministry of Justice, which had legalized and was on good terms with MIR, would be compelled to sentence him to an unbearable prison term. He must have done something undeniably treasonous: killed an officer, stolen state property, conducted sabotage.

Andrés dropped his hands. His face wasn't wet. He gave Gabriel a terrible rictus of a smile. "Better see if Caro's here," he said, twisting the words. "Don't want to keep your new girlfriend waiting."

Gabriel didn't move. "Andrés."

"Don't. And both of you"—he fixed his red eyes on Gabriel, then Nico—"forget I mentioned my dad. The ranch is getting redistributed, my mom wants to say goodbye, and she's dragging me on her nostalgia trip. That's it."

THE THOUGHT OF DR. LUCAS in Cuba clouded the May Day march for Gabriel. So did Andrés's foul mood, though he was walking ahead with Nico, letting Gabriel guide Caro through the packed streets. Andrés's blond head bobbed past flat wool caps and bright knit hats, glinting between a pair of toddlers waving red flags from their fathers' shoulders. Gabriel envied Andrés's height. Also Andrés's dad, Cuba or no Cuba. He'd rather have a father he could admire than one he saw every day.

Caro held his hand tightly as they waded deeper into Plaza Bulnes. Bodies surged around them, close and warm. Gabriel smelled body odor, unbrushed teeth, unwashed clothes, seared meat, the harsh chemical sweetness of gasoline. The presidential palace loomed at the square's far end, white marble glittering despite the lack of sun. The windows were all shuttered, and the center balcony had no speaker system set up for Allende to address the crowd. He must not be in La Moneda. Gabriel was disappointed for Caro—and, he supposed, for the workers that May Day was meant to celebrate—but he recognized that the president was extremely busy. Though he rejected his dad's idea that Allende had no more military support, it was true that the radio constantly reported Army unrest, discontent in the copper mines, union leaders declaring allegiance to the right wing. What kind of union rejected Socialism? It made no sense.

The demonstration was bigger than the plaza. Marchers spilled down side streets, forked around La Moneda, clambered onto statue plinths and streetlight poles and road barriers. Drums and tambourines jangled on all sides, and someone kept banging a gong. Its brassy echo hurt Gabriel's temples. His scalp buzzed with awareness of the bodies pressing behind him, moving him on. A woman in front of him twirled her plywood ARRIBA ALLENDE sign, nearly dropped it, then grabbed and raised it higher. Beside her, two construction workers shared a cigarette. Riot police bracketed the plaza. They stood like jetty posts in the ocean, face shields lowered, hands on their guns. Probably they hated protecting Unidad Popular marchers, but today's demonstration was an official one. It was the cops' job to make sure it went well.

Caro seemed not to notice the police. She was too absorbed in the crowd. She kept shouldering Gabriel, then pointing with her lips at a person of interest: a Benedictine monk dragging an armpit-height cross; a bearded man spinning a globe with all seven continents, including Antarctica, painted red; a dirty-cheeked little kid selling bright yellow packets of Ambrosoli Frugelé candies; a middle-aged woman leaning on a barricade, wool slacks sagging at her waist as she tried to flirt with a jack-booted, poker-faced cop.

Gabriel envied Caro's enthusiasm. Ordinarily he loved the people around him at demonstrations. Today, he could only notice them. He entertained himself, briefly and childishly, with the idea of a Communist Antarctica—would the penguins unionize? Were the sea lions, with their heavy mustaches and gruff, honking voices, the ice floes' industrialists?—but that was the furthest from himself he could get.

He nudged Caro, then pointed with his chin at the red globe. "You think there's a working class in Antarctica?"

She laughed. Before she could answer, a megaphoned woman shouted, "Jump if you're a worker!" and Caro bounded from the asphalt. Her mother and father were, respectively, a baker and a state-school teacher: she counted. Gabriel, who did not, kept his feet on the ground. Fighter jets buzzed overhead. Air Force exercises, he guessed, though it made no sense for the Air Force to be sending planes over La Moneda.

An amplifier shrieked, drowning out the jets. Guitar chords

rang over the crowd. The disjointed drums fell into time, then the gong and tambourines, but nobody sang. The guitarist kept riffing, letting the music spiral through Plaza Bulnes. A girl who looked Gabriel's age slipped into sight with a tray of golden empanadas, calling, "Corn-cheese-corn-cheese-corn-cheese." Her black hair was matted, her blue dress pristine beneath an open wool coat. Steam rose in plumes from the pastries, which were still visibly wet with oil. Gabriel wondered how that was possible. She—or her boss—must have a fry vat on wheels.

He turned to Caro, who was looking at the empanada girl too. "Hungry?"

She shook her head. "What's her story?"

He studied the girl. He could smell her empanadas' fresh crusts. Her skin was perfect, her gaze distant and level. She'd fit right in at an Ítalo party if she brushed her hair. "Rich girl," he said. "Or rich until recently."

Caro considered this. The empanada girl's skirt swung at her bare knees. She passed Nico and Andrés, elbowing Nico a bit, and Caro said, "I doubt it. Did you see her shoes?"

Gabriel shook his head.

"Totally worn out. Hard to walk in, I bet."

The girl vanished into a cluster of farmworkers, who soon settled between Gabriel and his friends, blocking even tall Andrés from sight. Pale dust rose from the street, kicked up by thousands of loafers and sneakers, Oxfords and boots. It caked in Gabriel's nose and congealed on his tongue.

"Having a good time so far?" he asked, swallowing dirt.

Caro nodded. "This is the most interesting date I've ever been on."

"Normally demonstrations are even better. Better energy."

"Better energy? You sound like a hippie."

"I could be a hippie," Gabriel said, not meaning it. He opposed the Vietnam War, which was now staggering to an end, but other than that, he didn't see himself fitting in well with the Jesus-curled backpackers who appeared periodically in Santiago's parks. He didn't like smoking pot enough; the thought of LSD terrified him. His aspirations were all wrong, besides. He didn't want to drop out. He wanted to live permanently in Chile, and blend in.

Caro was shaking her head. "You could not." Her braid, slung over her shoulder, wagged on her chest. "Hippies are relaxed."

"I can be relaxed."

"Can you?"

Gabriel felt himself reddening. He remembered perching on Ítalo's rug with Caro, telling her—he'd been drunk, but it was true—that he disbelieved in inner peace. "I have been," he said. "One time."

She pulled him close, then kissed him. "I don't want a relaxed boyfriend."

"What kind of boyfriend do you want?" He pressed his mouth to her cheek. The crowd rippled around them. Strangers' bodies brushed at his back. He felt at once conspicuous and invisible. The combination, to his slight alarm, turned him on.

"A medium-short Jewish one."

He laughed, then kissed Caro harder, bending her back as if they were in a movie. Men hooted behind him. One called, "All right, kid!"

Gabriel's chest swelled with pride. Caro broke away, scowling. "Asshole."

"I'm sorry."

"Him." She waved her arm in the heckler's direction. "Not you."

Tambourines rang through the plaza, and the guitarist, finally, began to sing. The amp garbled his words into nonsense, but slowly the crowd recognized the tune and launched into "La Batea." Caro tipped her head back and sang the first verse, the one about right-wing barbarity. Her voice, to Gabriel's delight, was raspy and off-key. An imperfection. He reached for her hand.

Slowly, the demonstration moved forward, lapping wavelike at La Moneda. Caro kept singing, and Gabriel, defying his self-consciousness, joined in. After the march, he decided, he would invite her to Trabajo Voluntario. She could take Andrés's spot. Maybe her parents would let her skip school; maybe she'd lie to them. She and Gabriel could have their first conspiracy together. It was an oddly romantic thought.

He surveyed the crowd once more for his friends, who had disappeared entirely. Instead, he saw the empanada girl moving against the crowd's current. Her tray was gone, as was her coat. A wide grease stain darkened the chest of her blue dress to black.

Gabriel's throat tightened as he watched her approach. Fat pastry flakes clung to her clothing, and yellow-white corn kernels shone, puckered with fat, from her hair. Tears ran down her face. Her nose was bleeding, and above her neckline, her skin flared a scalded red. Those empanadas couldn't have been out of the fryer more than a couple minutes. She was going to have grease burns for sure.

His first, shameful impulse was to hope Caro wouldn't notice. Even as the thought formed, Gabriel registered how selfish it was. He stepped into the empanada girl's path. "Are you all right?"

"Do I look all right?" Her accent was rough, rural. She smelled intensely of oil. Blisters were already rising above her collarbone.

"I meant—" He swallowed dust, acutely conscious of Caro at his side. "What happened?"

"I got mugged." She laughed harshly, showing crooked teeth. "Excuse me. Some comrades redistributed my empanadas to themselves. Also, my jacket and my money."

"I'm so sorry," Caro said.

The girl ignored her. She glanced at Gabriel's left hand, which was moving, as if independently, toward his wallet—which, if he remembered right, contained two hundred escudos. Not even the price of an empanada. A humiliating amount of money to offer. Instead, without giving himself time to consider, he let go of Caro's fingers and removed his coat.

"Here," he said. "You must be freezing."

The empanada girl looked at him with plain hatred. Her burn climbed the right side of her neck, mapping territory not unlike that of Caro's birthmark. Gabriel wanted, bizarrely, to kiss her, even as she snarled, "Put your clothes on." Then, before he could apologize, she shouldered her way into the crowd and was gone.

CARO DID NOT BREAK UP with Gabriel over the coat. She didn't break up with him for being silent with shame the whole bus ride home, or for bringing her to a party that weekend that turned out to be ten San Pedro Nolasco boys and a single bag of coke, or for possibly—he wasn't sure—failing to conceal his erection while sitting beside her on a park bench, trading complaints about school. She didn't even break up with him when he confessed, on a walk by the Mapocho, to having wanted to turn the taps on during their bathtub kiss.

"Is that weird?" he asked. Heat rose between his collarbones.

"Yes." Caro sounded highly amused. "Maybe you have a

water fetish." She waved at the steel-colored river behind her. Plastic bottles bobbed on its surface, mixed with yellowish scum. "Does that turn you on?"

Gabriel wrinkled his nose. "Too much trash."

"What about the ocean? The Pacific's kind of sexy, right?"

He gathered his courage. "It would be with you in it."

Caro rolled her eyes. Then she kissed him—a real kiss, not the in-public kind. When she was done, she said, "We can go to the beach in the summer. Take the bus to Reñaca or Concón."

Gabriel saw the trip instantly: a cramped, sweaty ride to the coast, books and towels jammed in their backpacks. Caro would wear a bikini. Her hair would shine like mica in the December sun. He'd buy them plastic cups of ceviche, icy fruit juice, a liter of beer to share. Maybe she'd fall asleep with her head in his lap, and he'd have a Caro-shaped tan line all summer.

He reached for her hand. "I'd like that."

"Good." She shook her braid free from the collar of her wool jacket. "It's not like I'll be going anywhere with my family."

"Even though your dad's a teacher?"

"What's that got to do with it?"

Gabriel shrugged. "Summers off?"

"He finds work."

She didn't elaborate. Gabriel bit the inside of his mouth. "What does your dad teach?" he asked. He knew that Señor Ravest worked at one of the public secondary schools downtown, but that was it.

"Literature."

"Is he good?"

Caro rolled her head to the side. After a moment, she said, "I doubt it, but I don't really know."

"He's never invited you to his class?"

"My dad? Invite me somewhere?" She snorted. "He barely

talks to me. I take his books off his shelves and read them in front of him, and he never even asks what I think."

"His loss," Gabriel said fervently. He had never met a person who had more ideas on more subjects than Caro. He suspected he'd never met a smarter person, except Raúl Colinao, who was a psychologically certified genius and therefore didn't count. Colinao seemed to absorb information by osmosis, not especially caring what he learned. Caro cared. She asked the nuns at her school about Catholic theology. She could explain what poems were about. In mid-May, she informed Gabriel that she'd begun reading *Capital* so she could talk about it with him, which meant he finally had to read it himself. On his best days, he could figure out every third sentence. He would have liked to blame his Spanish, but the problem, he knew, was his mind.

One problem, rather. Gabriel suspected he would have been able to absorb Marx better if he weren't in a constant state of arousal. Now he understood how Nico had gotten himself dumped. It took an astounding amount of self-control for Gabriel not to beg Caro to take her bra off. At night, he fell asleep with his hands cupped, wondering how her breasts might feel. In class, he wrote lists of distractions, which he then recited to himself from roughly 3:30 to 5:00 p.m., when Caro smuggled him into her empty apartment. He had to be vigilant, though: the lists lost their power fast. Colo-Colo stats lasted ten days; minor Chilean cities lasted a week. Lizards of the Atacama Desert had more traction, possibly because visualizing them was unsexy and a little disturbing. Gabriel relied on them heavily.

He kept the lizard situation to himself, but Caro he wanted to share. On weekends, he brought her to the banks of the Mapocho to drink and talk shit—two activities at which she excelled—with his friends. He got Father Recabarren, who taught literature, to lend him some of the many books she recommended; when the old priest praised Caro's taste, Gabriel found himself bragging about her until the lunch period ended and he had to hustle off to math.

When his Communist Youth group met in late May, Gabriel persuaded Caro to come see what it was like. She had already signed up for Trabajo Voluntario—with, enviably, parental permission. Her grades were good enough to be undamageable. Also, Allende's Ministry of Education wanted students to learn the inextricability of physical and mental labor, and although Caro's dad strenuously disliked Allende, he still saw professional opportunity in letting the administration of the public school where he taught hear he'd sent his daughter to do farmwork.

Gabriel knew that Claudio would leap at the chance to sign the child of conservatives up for the Communist Youth. He also imagined how much Claudio and Caro would impress each other: Claudio with his knowledge, Caro with her desire for it. He reminded himself often, in the days preceding the meeting, not to be jealous when they got along well.

But Claudio was in too grim a mood to pay attention to Caro. He paced the living room of the crumbling house where their group still met, chain-smoking and waving his arms like a prophet. Sweat stains blossomed on his denim shirt, though the air was unusually cold. Gabriel could see the frayed place where he'd ripped the Levi's pocket tab off. He'd never noticed that before. Nor had he noticed how ratty the furniture here was. Only fifteen of their group's two dozen members had shown, and the half-empty room was all tobacco smoke and creeping mold.

Gabriel tried not to care. Andrés didn't look as if he cared. He was on the ratty sofa, sharing a cigarette with an Universidad

Católica student named Lautaro, who kept nodding in fervent agreement as Claudio condemned the copper strike that had been going for a month. It might, he said, tank the economy. It was provoking violence. Bus hijackings. Bombings downtown. Gabriel saw Andrés wince: the hijackings were MIR's doing, part of its effort to push Chile into the true crisis its members thought would lead to revolution.

Claudio rolled on. The copper strike, he said, had emboldened Patria y Libertad to march more often and behave more violently: threatening bystanders, beating up Indigenous vendors downtown. Gabriel thought of the empanada girl at the May Day march. He didn't think it was the right wing who had hurt her.

"I don't want anyone downtown alone." Claudio ground out his cigarette on the heel of his boot, then flicked the butt into a corner. "Anyone who's been writing graffiti should stop. It's not worth getting jumped by Patria y Libertad."

Lautaro lifted his chin. "What about the mural project?"

"On hold," Claudio said, looking pained. For months, he'd been designing a mural for their group to paint outside a settlement youth center. "Until the cops quit doing weapons raids in the settlements. If we're painting and they show up, they'll arrest us without thinking twice."

Everyone nodded. The raids were common knowledge. According to Radio Magallanes, the police were not only beating up settlement inhabitants but also destroying their food supplies by raking through grain sacks in search of hidden guns. Gabriel's dad claimed these events were harbingers of civil war: the cops, like the Army, were distinctly right-wing and supported Allende less every day. Gabriel rejected the thought, just as he rejected MIR's push for violent revolution. Chile was a peaceful country. Under Salvador Allende, it was pioneering a new and democratic Socialist model, one that countries around the world would someday copy. Also, Gabriel might be American, but Chile was his home. In recent weeks, he'd instated a new policy. When his dad started predicting civil war, he left the room.

Gabriel had been telling himself Ray was just spouting CIA propaganda. Everyone knew that the United States was terrified of functional Socialist governments in the Americas, and everyone knew how much money U.S. industry had lost when Allende began nationalizing businesses in Chile. It was in the Nixon administration's interest for Chileans to get scared of civil war and vote out Allende and his government.

Now Gabriel felt a new stirring of unease. He wished he had a way to confirm that his dad was getting the civil war idea from the CIA. If he could, then he would know that Claudio's warnings—and his visible fear—were results of psychological manipulation, not actual portents of violence to come.

Beside him, Caro pressed her shoulder into his arm. Gabriel lifted his chin at Claudio, who broke off mid-sentence, visibly startled. Ordinarily, Gabriel spoke in meetings only when spoken to.

"Question or comment, Lazris?"

"Question." Gabriel's saliva tasted like cigarettes just from his sitting here. "What's all this pointing to? I mean, the right wing says civil war, but—"

"But that's garbage," Claudio interrupted. His expression was bright, but his voice had a manic edge. "A cover-up for their coup plots. We saw this in Brazil in '64. Civil war happens when conservatives and liberals come into conflict. Not our conditions here in Chile. We have no liberals in power. We have a Socialist-Communist coalition, we have some ultra-left agitators, and we have fascists fighting to take our coalition down."

Beside Gabriel, Nico said, "So?"

"So we have three possibilities. One, we remain on the Chilean road to Socialism and achieve a bloodless revolution. Two, the fascists, or our friends in MIR, provoke violent conflict, which turns into the kind of revolution that looks like war." Claudio flicked his glittering eyes toward Andrés. "And, three, the fascists pull off a coup."

Gabriel flinched. Caro curled closer—whether to comfort him or herself he couldn't tell. Why had he asked? He never asked Claudio questions! Now he had to drag the thought of bloodshed around, carry it within himself like undigested food. On the drive home, he told Caro to ignore Claudio, which he personally had never done. He wanted to say the same to Andrés, but he had no idea how his friend would react. It was not clear to Gabriel whether Andrés agreed with MIR or the Communist Party. His silence in the meeting indicated that Andrés himself wasn't sure.

At the moment, Andrés was in the front seat, discussing safety precautions with the cabdriver. After Claudio's doom-and-gloom lecture, it had seemed reasonable to take a taxi rather than a bus home, but now, jammed in the back seat, Gabriel was hot, a little motion-sick, and obscurely embarrassed. He shouldn't be afraid to ride the bus.

All evening, he sulked and fretted over Claudio's three possibilities. Allende had campaigned on the promise of a slow-motion Socialist revolution. Gabriel, at thirteen, had believed that promise so wholeheartedly it was life-changing. He remembered walking around Chicago on his last visit to the States, pitying everyone he saw for not having an Allende of their own on the horizon. Allende was possibility. He was peace and change wrapped into one man. For years, Gabriel had thought himself too cowardly to want to join MIR, but now, awake long past midnight, he saw the truth: the quick and violent revolution MIR wanted was no less antithetical to Allende's promise than a coup would be. If either thing happened, Gabriel's faith in Allende—maybe even his faith in Chile—would fall apart.

He barely slept, but he arrived at morning with a plan. It was Sunday, which meant his parents would be at the Polo Club from noon till evening, playing tennis and socializing with the embassy Americans who flocked to the club's courts and saunas. Gabriel very rarely accompanied them, though he had to admit that the dining room had extremely good food. He hated the expatriate social scene, and he disliked knowing how many of the club's employees lived in the tin-and-plywood settlement built against its back wall.

Usually, Gabriel devoted his Sundays to watching TV, masturbating, and communing with Sammy. He ate dinner with Luz, and sometimes sat beside her for the evening news, but otherwise, their tacit agreement was to give each other the privacy and quiet unavailable throughout the week. It occurred to him that his plan, which seemed to have arrived fully formed in his brain overnight, would get both of them scolded if he got caught, but how could that happen? His dad's study wasn't booby-trapped. Ray rarely even locked the door.

Half of Gabriel was ashamed of himself for snooping. The other half was ashamed it had taken him so long. He was perfectly free to walk into his dad's study, even if he wasn't technically allowed there. His dad kept the blinds partly open, which at midday meant Gabriel didn't even have to turn the lights on. He sat briefly in the carved wooden desk chair, surveying his surroundings: plush red carpet, white-shaded lamps, beige metal file cabinets, tannery ads framed on the walls. On the shelves, mixed in with dictionaries and biographies, were pictures of Gabriel's parents' wedding, his grandfather August as a young immigrant, Gabriel in early childhood.

Ray's desk was close to bare. His typewriter sat empty, releasing the faint smell of ink. Beside it sat an unclean tumbler, an enameled pen, and a small sea lion made of green stone. Gabriel had never noticed it before—though, granted, until today he had entered this room only to receive lectures and punishments, which meant he'd never been attentive to his dad's decor. He picked up the sea lion, which told no secrets. It had little whiskers engraved on the sides of its nose. Gabriel felt a strong urge to take it. Give it to Caro, or make it his friend.

He set the sea lion down. He was being childish. He was here to seek evidence, not steal paperweights. What that evidence might be he was unsure. Presumably the CIA wasn't writing down its instructions. Gabriel wasn't going to dig up a postcard from Kissinger or a cable from Richard Helms.

Gabriel slid his dad's top right desk drawer open. Paper clips, staples, stapler. The drawer beneath it creaked when it moved and held only stacks of empty yellow legal pads. The third down was empty; fourth down, old *Courier*s. Gabriel rifled through them, hoping his dad might use the papers as a hiding place, but all he found were three issues of *El Mercurio* mixed in with the English-language news.

He moved on to the left side of the desk. An emotion that could have been either disappointment or relief began to settle itself in his stomach. Possibly he was just hungry. Ordinarily he'd be eating cheese straight from the fridge around now. He considered the various snack options available to him as he examined the pay stubs—all from the *Courier*—in one drawer, tax paperwork in the next. It seemed that partial tannery ownership represented a higher percentage of Ray's income than Gabriel would have assumed.

The third drawer gave a promising rattle when opened. Secret booze stash. Too bad Gabriel couldn't swipe any for later without revealing that he'd been nosing around. He could, however, drink some now. Surely his dad wasn't checking the levels on his private scotch. He had three bottles: one full, one half-full, one empty. The empty one had a different label from the others. More expensive-looking, Gabriel thought. It also had a card tied to its neck with blue ribbon. *Appreciate all your help this year*, it read. *Cheers to a less red 1972. Winters.*

For a moment, Gabriel was baffled. Then, with only a heartbeat of warning, he was humiliated—not by his father, but, worse, for him. "Winters" was a signature. Donald Winters. Gabriel had met him at the Polo Club, talked soccer with him at the awful annual embassy Christmas party. He was a diplomat. Younger than Gabriel's parents, though evidently not by enough to keep Ray from prizing his approval. Why else would Gabriel's father hold on to an empty bottle of scotch Winters gave him a year and a half ago?

Gabriel plucked at the ribbon, which was fraying. Alcohol fumes rose from the drawer. *Appreciate all your help*, the card said. A journalist could not help a diplomat. Starting before Gabriel could remember, his father had told him with great pride that it was the journalist's mandate to help the reading public, and only by providing them the truth.

He replaced the empty bottle. His interest in the half-full one appeared to have vanished. Ditto his hunger. He felt clogged and heavy. He had never found his father truly pathetic before. Even shouting at Dr. Lucas in his catastrophic Spanish, Ray had retained, in Gabriel's eyes, a trace of dignity, if only through his anger. But clinging to the jocular praise of some stiff-suited lunk half his age? That was pitiful. It was the behavior of a man who knew he had fallen but hoped to convince himself he was still on the rise.

Although he still didn't want it, Gabriel uncapped the half-full scotch and took a long drink. His esophagus burned. He screwed the cap on, shoved the drawer shut, and went outside to sit in the dirt with Sammy, who wanted to have his belly scratched. His purplish lips curled into a canine grin as Gabriel drummed rhythmically on his rib cage, chanting, "Ap-*pre*-ci-*ate* all your help." It was the way he'd taught himself Chilean idioms years ago. Lately he did it with Communist language: repeated the proper phrase over and over, reciting it like poetry.

Now, though, he was just picking a scab. Worrying at a word he wanted gone. His father should not be *helping* Donald Winters. If he was, then Winters was not the aboveboard State Department official he claimed to be, and Ray Lazris had left his journalistic mandate behind.

Gabriel recalled, as faintly as if last night had happened years ago, that he had wanted proof his dad was a CIA collaborator. Worse: he'd wanted his dad to be one. It hadn't occurred to him how humiliated he would feel on Ray's behalf. A small voice inside him suggested that he force his father to confront his descent. Another voice offered that, really, what he should do was report his findings to Claudio, but Gabriel knew perfectly well he would not do that. It wasn't safe. In other countries, CIA agents and assets, suspected and real ones alike, had been stalked, beaten, kidnapped. In Uruguay, the far-left Tupamaros had murdered Dan Mitrione, a cop from Indiana who was teaching the Montevideo police American interrogation techniques, which was Kissinger-speak for teaching them how to torture prisoners. Gabriel had never been certain Mitrione deserved his fate. He did, however, feel sure that his father had not earned a similar one. Propaganda wasn't torture.

Gabriel twisted a tuft of Sammy's fur between his fingers. His eyes ached from suppressing tears. He reminded himself that informing on your own family was Stalinist. Also that he should be happy. He had wanted proof that his dad's doomy predictions were Kissingerian propaganda, and now he had it. He knew that Ray was in the service of fear, not fact.

But what he'd failed to consider in his sleepless night was a future that now appeared before him with brutal clarity. It was plausible that the idea of a civil war was fake, a psychological operation being carried out by the CIA. It was also plausible that the CIA wished to start a civil war in Chile. Anything could change. Anything was possible. Gabriel no longer had any excuse not to be afraid.

IN THE FINAL WEEKS OF FALL, San Pedro Nolasco imposed some unwelcome new rules. Guards appeared at the school gates and had to be respected. Calling one a pig, even under your breath, resulted in a week of detention. Students were officially encouraged to take private transportation; bus-related delays were no longer accepted as excuses for tardiness, even if you were less than a full minute late.

Nico and Andrés condemned the new policies but seemed untroubled by them. Andrés, like Gabriel, kept taking the bus to school. He never brought up his approaching trip to Bío-Bío or his dad's looming departure from Chile. Gabriel refrained from asking questions, if only because he was avoiding the subject of fathers. His current tactic toward his own was to repress all awareness that Ray existed. Not a sustainable strategy, but Gabriel couldn't come up with a better one.

Nor did he have a solution to the issue of Aldunante's rising social status. He was becoming king of the school. It was, to Gabriel, unfathomable. Aldunante was the same pasty, reed-necked degenerate he'd always been, but their classmates were acting as if he'd transformed into some kind of alpha male. Gabriel didn't understand how a sane person could stand talking to him, let alone listening to his fervent outpourings of racist bile. Aldunante hated Black and Indigenous Chileans. He wanted to ban immigration from Bolivia, Brazil, Ecuador, Paraguay, and Peru. On the last day before Gabriel and his friends took off for Trabajo Voluntario, Aldunante derailed their history class to inform everyone, with an entirely straight face, that historians in the United States had recently discovered compelling evidence that the Holocaust never occurred.

"Half my family died in the Holocaust," Gabriel fumed later. He, Nico, and Andrés were skipping Friday Mass to get high in the women's bathroom, a school-wide haven for smoking, jerking off, and secret tears. "He knows that. Everyone knows that. Have I not talked about it enough?"

"You've talked about it," Nico said from the windowsill, where he was constructing a joint. His weed smelled troublingly high-quality to Gabriel, whose drug tolerance was not good. "You had to do that speech."

Gabriel groaned. "Don't remind me." On the twenty-fifth anniversary of the liberation of Auschwitz, the priests had decided it would be a good idea to ask thirteen-year-old Gabriel to deliver a special chapel talk on concentration camps. He had tried to erase the memory, which involved copious sweat and his first-ever fear boner, but, so far, no success.

"Sorry," Nico said, still adding weed to the joint.

"Put some tobacco in," Gabriel requested. Andrés, who was sitting on the toilet tank, pulled a face. Gabriel imitated him, stretching his mouth wide, then said, "I just want to understand what the fuck Aldunante's problem is. You think he's got a psychological compulsion to be an asshole?"

Nico crumbled more weed into the rolling paper. "His problem," he said, "is that he's a little rat."

"That's an insult to the rodent kingdom."

"True." Nico dipped his head. "My apologies to rats."

Sun shot through the diamond-paned window, catching in Nico's gelled hair. It illuminated Andrés's pilled sweater, the stepped-on hems of his uniform slacks, the graffiti-etched wall behind him. In the sudden light, the room looked almost pleasant, even with its sickly green paint and domino-shaped holes in the floor where bored students had pried up tile. Gabriel felt a small wave of gratitude for this bathroom. It was an important sanctuary, even if it did smell like semen and bleach.

"I know why Aldunante's an asshole," Andrés said.

"Please." Gabriel scowled. "Enlighten me."

Nico waggled the finished joint. "You fight, you don't get to smoke."

They assembled themselves on the floor, Andrés tossing and catching a lighter. Nico scooped it from midair, lit the joint, and passed it to Gabriel, who took a long, irritated inhale as Andrés began: "Pretend you're Aldunante. Your dad's a lawyer, but from a family of—what is it? Carpenters?"

"Bricklayers," Nico said.

"Okay, bricklayers. So you have money, but not money like us." Andrés motioned between the three of them. Gabriel nodded unwillingly, which sent a crackling looseness up his neck. Andrés exhaled smoke, then continued, "Your parents are proud to have money now. They spoil the shit out of you." Dropping the "you" pretense, he added, "We know that part for a fact."

He was right. Gabriel had been to Aldunante's house in the primary-school years of whole-class birthday parties. He'd seen the crates of toys in his bedroom, the overflowing dresser drawers, the signed 1966 World Cup team poster on the wall. By now he probably had a first edition of *Mein Kampf* in there, and a nice little bedside stand for his brass knuckles.

"And spoiled equals entitled," Andrés said. "Right? He

thinks he should get what he wants. But at school, he gets nothing. He's lazy, so his grades are no good. His friends are all cavemen. Girls won't talk to him. No one interesting will. Like you." Andrés pointed at Gabriel with the smoldering joint.

"Give me that," Gabriel said. Only as he reached for it did he register Andrés's argument. "Me?"

His friend laughed. "You. Gabriel Lazris, the only foreigner at San Pedro Nolasco. You're a hot commodity."

"Bullshit."

"Nico, confirm?"

"Confirmed," Nico said. "You're American, and you never stop thinking." He rapped Gabriel's head gently, then confiscated the joint. "People want to know what's happening in there."

Gabriel burst into stoned, incredulous laughter. His thoughts weren't interesting. He wasn't a commodity. He was, if anything, an easy route to Nico and Andrés.

"Look," Andrés said coolly. "You can laugh, but you have to admit I have a point. Aldunante is jealous. Or he was. But he can stop envying you if he decides Jews are scum. If he tells himself Mapuches are biologically subordinate to white people, he can stop envying Colinao for being an official genius. See what I mean?"

Gabriel saw and did not give a shit. He refused to extend his empathy to Aldunante. He looked at Nico, hoping for backup, but Nico was slouched against the wall, killing the joint. He'd been right to take it. Gabriel, through his annoyance, noted that he was still laughing. His throat itched. His head felt as if it were hovering slightly left of his body. He'd overshot his weed-consumption mark.

"I don't care how Aldunante feels," he said.

Andrés shrugged. "Never said you should."

"Then what the fuck?"

"Hey," Nico said. "Easy."

"Sorry."

"Just relax." Nico tilted his head back. Two zits competed for real estate at his jawline. Gabriel shook his gaze from them before he could fixate. That was a risk when he was high: unmitigated staring. Also pacing, also babbling, also fear.

"My dad always says we should understand our enemies," Andrés said, in the soft tone he used for apologies. "Get in their minds. When I was little, he'd make me practice. If I got in a fight, I had to tell him about it from the other kid's perspective."

Gabriel felt cheated. He couldn't complain now that Andrés had invoked Dr. Lucas. Besides, he was no longer in shape to argue. He doubted he could formulate even a valid grievance, and he was no longer sure it was valid to object to a foray into the Nazi mind.

He slid backward until he could pillow his head on his arms. The floor moved gently beneath him, like a boat in shallow harbor. He was too high, but for the moment, it felt good. He imagined that he was in Zapallar watching pelicans, or in a canoe on the Bío-Bío ranch, whose streams and lakes he had long heard Andrés describe. The tile rocked peacefully. He was almost asleep when Andrés said, "Am I high, or is there an earthquake?"

Gabriel sat up. The floor was, in fact, visibly tilting. "Shit," he said. "My nap."

Nico was scrambling to his feet, looking alarmed. Of the three of them, he disliked earthquakes most. Gabriel, even in his first months in Chile, had never particularly feared them. He'd rather wait out an earthquake than get punished for skipping Mass.

"We should go to the patio," Nico said.

Gabriel sighed. "You really want to?"

"If the school collapses, I don't want to die in the girls' bathroom."

"You won't die," Gabriel said, pitching his voice low and soothing. "It's already over. Nothing's moving." If Nico got paranoid, he would too, and then their afternoon would be shot.

"There could be another one," Nico said. "And this is an old building."

"I know."

Andrés unfurled his legs. He rolled his eyes at Gabriel, then said, "Let's just leave."

Gabriel levered himself upright, then heaved the bathroom door open. The hinges' squeals skidded unpleasantly down his spine. Another problem with getting high: sensitivity to sound. Fresh air rolled toward him, filled with the chirps and shouts of primary schoolers gathered outdoors. He felt a sudden, piercing desire for something hot and fried: a cheese empanada, a ham croqueta, a sopaipilla still dripping oil.

Andrés and Nico were in the hall already, eyeing him. "Come on," Nico said. "You can blame me if we get busted."

"Don't worry." Gabriel slouched through the door. The sun sent wheels spinning through his vision. He wondered if Luz could be persuaded to make sopaipillas. "I will."

THERE WERE EARTHQUAKES ALL WEEKEND. Not major ones, but unpleasant enough to keep Gabriel home rather than drinking on the riverbank. After the coup, after he'd been dragged back to the United States, that weekend became a frequent stop on his mental tour of regrets. It was wasted time. Two precious nights he could have spent with Nico and Andrés, or with Caro. With all three. Why had he not taken every possible opportunity to be with them? He had been so clueless. So stupid. So unappreciative of his good luck.

In this case, the answer was partly the earthquakes, but also, he'd been pissed off. It wasn't always fun to be friends with the King of Empathy. Gabriel was ashamed of himself for not extending his imagination as far as Aldunante's inner life. He was also annoyed that, apparently, he had to. It would be much more satisfying just to declare Aldunante his enemy.

On Sunday morning, Gabriel pulled himself out of his sulk long enough to call Andrés. He meant to wish his friend luck, but he was too late. The phone rang without answer, which meant no Andrés for three weeks. Just Gabriel, Nico, and Caro harvesting produce in the fertile swath of land between Santiago and Viña del Mar.

His mother padded into the living room wearing socks and a tennis dress. The diamonds in her ears caught the light. "Your father and I are going to the Polo Club," she said as he hung up the phone.

Gabriel stretched his legs down the couch. Bare tree branches shook outside: wind, or a tremor too small to feel. "You think you can play tennis with the earthquakes?"

She glanced at the window. Sammy emerged from his doghouse and trotted across the lawn. "If the club lets us play, we'll play."

Gabriel knew that the Polo Club would let his parents onto a court. Its management was very much in the business of refusal, but only where nonmembers were concerned.

"You're welcome to come," his mom offered.

"Thanks, but no."

"You don't have to make that face."

"Didn't mean to," he said, which was true. He had his objections to the Polo Club, but he knew that his parents needed tennis court access. Racket sports were the main arena in which their relationship still seemed to thrive. Gabriel wouldn't criticize any place or habit that kept his parents from divorcing before he was a legal adult. If their marriage ended before he turned eighteen, he would, at best, be faced with a bleak decision: Chile with Ray or the United States with Vera. At worst, he wouldn't get to choose.

It occurred to him now that the Polo Club likely served dual purposes for Ray. Cheer his wife up with some competition, then meet Donald Winters in the steam room. Gabriel squashed the thought. Today was not a day to be angry. It was an important opportunity: the first Sunday of the month, which was both a Polo Club day and Luz's day off. Her brother-in-law picked her up early in the morning and drove her to Quilicura, where she would remain until late at night. When Gabriel went into the kitchen to make breakfast, he saw that she had left him a roast chicken to pick at all day.

His parents left before he finished his cereal. He waited six full minutes to call Caro. They had, so far, been alone only on park benches, in bathrooms at parties, and in her barely heated bedroom, where saints monitored their behavior from three walls. The first time Caro brought Gabriel to her apartment, she showed him the fire escape outside her fourth-floor window: if her mother came home early, she said, Gabriel would need to climb down.

Today, they ran no risk of discovery. Gabriel's parents always ate Sunday dinner at the Polo Club. "If you come over," he told Caro, wrestling his voice into a tone he hoped resembled calm, "we can be alone all afternoon."

He waited in the front yard with Sammy. Questions rolled through his brain. Could he ask to touch Caro's nipple today, or would that be pressure? Could he slide his fully clothed body between her fully clothed legs and not come? What if she strad-dled him, which she liked to do? Did he have powerful enough distractions for that?

Sammy showed no signs of noticing Gabriel's anxiety. He rolled on his back, collecting twigs and dirt clods in his red fur, and panted with delight as Gabriel tickled his bald armpits. "You," Gabriel informed him, "are good. You are a good boy."

"He is," Caro called. Gabriel snapped his head up to see his girlfriend beaming through the fence. She had on loose cordu-roys and her usual green wool coat; her hair, ordinarily pinned tight for school, fell halfway down her back. Sammy bounded at Gabriel's heels as he let her in.

Caro kissed Gabriel, then got right down on the lawn. Sammy panted in her face, waggled his furry ass, and released a yip of canine glee as she scratched his ruffled chest. "Okay, Sammy," she said. "Show me your tricks."

The dog grinned at her, snout quivering. A bead of drool rolled from his black lip. Gabriel commanded, "Sammy! Dead!"

Sammy panted. His ears fluttered. He looked profoundly alive. "Shit," Gabriel said. "He was supposed to fall over."

Caro laughed. "Maybe if he were calmer. Meeting a new person is exciting."

"Maybe if I practiced with him more." Gabriel stroked his dog's soft head. "Sammy," he said. "You were supposed to help me impress my girlfriend."

"Do I still need impressing?"

"Why not?"

Caro answered by kissing him. "Are you going to invite me inside?"

"Would you like to come inside?"

She kissed him again. "I would."

They left Sammy lounging in the brown grass. Caro let

herself in, slipping her shoes off without being told. Gabriel hung up her coat as she examined her reflection in the gilt-framed front hall mirror, or else examined the mirror itself. She skimmed a foot over the carpet, lifted her eyes to the ten-armed chandelier, lowered them to the marble-topped side-board with its spindly iron legs.

"Nice house."

"Want to see the rest?"

"I want to see your room."

Only as Gabriel opened the door to his bedroom did it occur to him that a different person, a cooler person, might have made some decor changes between the ages of eleven and sixteen. Gabriel had not. His room was a shrine to Colo-Colo. He had a black team scarf tacked over his mirror, a green away jersey hanging at the head of his bed, and posters of Carlos Caszely everywhere else. He silently requested guidance from a chubby, mustache-less 1969 Caszely. A bit of expert advice would be helpful right now.

But even in imagination, Caszely was not forthcoming. Gabriel nudged a pile of socks across the floor with his foot. He was responsible for cleaning his own bedroom, which generally meant it was not clean. Currently, it smelled like worn undershirts—not ideal, but a significant step above certain other frequent smells.

Caro seemed unconcerned about air quality. Her face was bright with intent. She closed the door and hooked two fingers into Gabriel's jeans. Then she undid the top button.

"Oh God," he said involuntarily.

She smiled. "I have an idea."

Standing in the center of his bedroom, Caro shucked off her clothes. Brown pants, white sweater, shell-pink bra. She unhooked the silver chain of her cross necklace and laid it on the floor. Her breasts bobbed as she stooped, and when she straightened, Gabriel saw a crease form and vanish at her waist. He wanted to touch it. Wanted to touch her. She stood in her blue cotton underwear, which sprouted elastic strings from its satin trim, and met his gaze.

"Nice not to be cold," she said. "Almost like it's not winter."

Gabriel gulped. "Never winter in here." He sounded like a stranger. He was amazed that he had enough blood left in the upper half of his body to speak.

"So you're warm too," Caro said. Her eyes glittered.

"Yes."

"Then why are you still dressed?"

Gabriel tugged at the hem of his sweater. The thought of lifting it—of interrupting the sight of Caro's body, even for an instant—was terrible, or terrifying. He wanted to freeze her, to capture forever the shifting reds of her birthmark, her snub-nosed breasts, the slight inward curve of her stomach, her long pinkish thighs and gravel-scarred knees. He wanted to kiss her knees. Could he do that? Would she mind?

She took a step closer. Gabriel let go of his sweater and put a tentative hand on her bare hip. It was rougher than he'd anticipated, which somehow reassured him. She was real. She had dry skin. A small jolt moved through him at the thought. She slid her fingers under his shirt, then tugged upward. Naked from the waist up, he maneuvered her onto the bed.

Caro undid his fly, and they rolled on the mattress together, Gabriel kicking his pants loose as Caro pulled her underwear off. They were laughing without reason or warning. They had been a couple for less than nine weeks. Caro scooped her hand beneath Gabriel's balls, investigating, and arousal ran up his spine to his scalp. She showed no sign of nerves. Possibly she'd never been nervous in her life. Possibly she'd done this before.

"Have you ever—" he started.

"No."

"Do you know what to do?"

"I think we can figure it out," she said, her breath warm in his mouth. "Just don't come inside me."

Gabriel promised not to. He wondered whether it was possible to die of good luck. Maybe that was how the rapture worked: the luckiest people alive got jetted into the clouds. If that was true, he was one of the chosen. How could he not be, when, even now, he was sliding his hand down his girlfriend's stomach? He brushed over hipbone and coarse hair, touched a slick fold of skin. When he pressed experimentally down, Caro sighed.

Desire fountained through Gabriel. He slipped a finger inside her. Her ribs heaved, and as he pushed upward, she lowered her hips to his hand. Fear rose in him, and he stopped moving to ask, "Was that good?"

She rolled her head so he could see her face, which glowed like stained glass in the sun. He had never in his life been more turned on. Later, he would remember the feeling as less erotic than pure: no rush, no regret, no looking at another girl and pretending she was Caro, no closing his eyes and pretending his own hand was hers. Maybe some fear, but fear was his constant companion. He would have been lost if it left.

"I don't know." She was smiling, her eyes alight with private pleasure. "I think you might have to do it again."

TRABAJO VOLUNTARIO BEGAN THE NEXT DAY. At dinner, Gabriel reminded his parents that he'd be going to school early to start installing a vegetable garden in the little kids' courtyard. In his humble opinion, it was a brilliant lie. It contained a sliver of truth, explained any and all dirt on his clothes, and would never be disproven, since his parents would never go to San Pedro Nolasco. He had trouble imagining that they'd bother even to see him graduate.

He woke before sunrise to catch a bus to the Estadio Español in Las Condes, where he met Caro, Nico, and a trio of extremely tall brothers who spoke only to one another, despite Nico's sleepy efforts to engage. Gabriel had imagined a bigger group—he wasn't quite sure three high schoolers and three storklike university students qualified as a brigade—but this, evidently, was it. At seven o'clock, a dented VW camper van arrived, driven by a man who looked old enough to be Chile's first Communist. He honked for them to board, announced that today's destination was a cabbage farm in Limache, and lurched into motion before the last of the antisocial brothers sat down.

Gabriel took Caro's hand, feeling warm and complicit. He liked having a secret with her. He also knew he'd tell Nico the second he could. If it were possible, he would beam the knowledge that he was no longer a virgin directly into his friend's head. He thought of a joke his dad liked: An ordinary man gets shipwrecked with Marilyn Monroe. The two fall in love, and after weeks of sexual bliss, Marilyn offers the man a favor. *Whatever you like*, she says, and he asks her to pretend to be a man named Tom. She plays along, and he puts his arm around her shoulders, pulls her close, and whispers, *Tom, you will not believe who I've been screwing.*

Nico wouldn't believe it. Nor would Andrés. Even Gabriel couldn't believe that he, the human idiot, had managed to lose his virginity. He watched the sun crest over the concrete highway barriers and assessed himself for internal change. He felt calmer, he thought. Less roiled by anxieties and shames. He squeezed Caro's fingers, and she nestled closer to his side. He wondered what she would do if he told her he loved her. Surely she already knew.

What Gabriel did not love, it turned out, was Trabajo Voluntario. By the end of the first week, he couldn't even pretend to himself that he liked it. He'd rather be in school. He did not enjoy all the car time: two hours to a new farm every morning, two more driving back to Santiago every night. He hated that they never harvested the same fruit or vegetable twice, which meant he never had a chance to master a technique. On the first day, they harvested green cabbage in an enormous and dusty field. Stooping to slice through the cabbages' fibrous roots made Gabriel's back ache, and his dull knife gave him a blister on his thumb. He prayed to pick fruit off trees the next day—which they did, and which was even worse.

He never should have expected to enjoy the work. It should have been apparent to him that joining a labor brigade would involve an unpleasant amount of physical challenge. He'd imagined long political conversations in the fields, maybe some folk singing, but all the farmers worked in silence. The sky was always oppressively gray. The air always smelled like dried cow shit, though there were rarely cows in sight. He got new blisters every day.

It made matters worse that Caro was having a great time. She beamed every morning as they boarded the van. On the drives home to Santiago, she glowed like they had the night they met. Gabriel told himself it was an aftereffect of what was, to him, the one good part of Trabajo Voluntario: it was easy to sneak away and have sex. In the first week, they did it behind a brush pile, in a bathroom, in a toolshed, and twice in thick stands of trees.

For the first time in Gabriel's life, he was too tired to sleep.

Every night, he lay awake, tormented by exhaustion. On the Friday of their first week, he finally fell asleep quickly, only to dream about fighter jets strafing a cabbage field while he picked frantically, unable to put his knife down and run. A megaphoned voice boomed from one of the jets, but after he woke up, he couldn't bring back its words. He hugged his knees to his chest, wet blue light seeping in through the blinds. It was his first coup nightmare. He would, later, have whole strings of them; he would dream about bombs and guns, ruined city blocks, his dog starving and bleeding, his friends caged and hurt. He would grow used to waking up screaming, desperate both to banish his dreams and return to them, but that night he was terrified. He'd never before had a nightmare that felt possible. Normally, his bad dreams were about Hitler or showing up at school without pants.

Trabajo Voluntario, like school, didn't include weekends, but the nightmare infected Gabriel's days off. It buzzed around his head while he drank with his friends by the river. It haunted him while he played with Sammy, watched dubbed TV movies, ate roast chicken in the kitchen alone. It made him jittery on his return to farming that Monday, though before long, he was too achy to be afraid.

He had thought farming would be romantic. Exciting, maybe. He'd assumed that it would wake some new bit of his brain up, like the Ministry of Education said. But so far, he wasn't having intellectual experiences. So far, he had a nightmare, a sore back, and palms that looked as if he'd taken a cheese grater to them. Once, on an avocado farm, he sweat so much his hair got soaked through, then froze solid during lunch.

At least he understood now why Caro loved it. To her, Trabajo Voluntario was a return. Her paternal grandparents grew squash and bred sheepdogs in the same bowl of land to which the camper van brought them each morning. She'd lean on the window, pointing out familiar landmarks: she'd climbed this hill, bought dulces de La Ligua at this roadside stand, swum in this murky green pond. At each farm, she examined the dogs—bony, matted mutts, for the most part, with brown teeth and visible ribs—to see if she'd known them as puppies. Gabriel loved dogs, but he didn't want to approach these ones. He had no desire to stroke the cart horses' noses or feed carrots to the mules. Exploring the farms held no appeal for him. He envied Caro's comfort, her ties to the land, but he couldn't share them. He was a city boy. A spoiled one, too.

Gabriel kept his feelings to himself, however. He pretended not to be sick of dirt, of poker-straight vegetable rows, of mud-crusted hand forks and the pervasive smells of fertilizer and damp earth. The farms all had the same peeling stables and filthy sheds to store tools in, the same dusty huts for eating lunch and, in Gabriel and Caro's case, sneaking off for mid-afternoon sex, at which he was fairly sure he was improving. His lists of distractions continued to be helpful: he could last longer if half his brain was on an imaginary Colo-Colo field. It helped, too, that he was constantly afraid of getting caught, though they had been lucky thus far. Gabriel wanted to take their sexual impunity as a good omen, though he recognized that it was more likely a testament to the work ethic the farmers had in abundance and he clearly lacked.

He found the farmers highly impressive. Also terrifying. Most looked old enough to have worked for decades pre-collectivization, contracting themselves to enormous farms like the Gibsons' Bío-Bío ranch, places where the average laborer had barely earned enough to eat. Their faces were lined and sunken, their hands hardened and cracked. Their fingernails were black with dirt; several workers were missing digits. Nearly all were male, mestizo-looking, frequent seed-spitters and cigarette-rollers with index fingers that were stained nicotine-yellow. They shared the habit of covering one nostril, then rocketing mucus from the other. None seemed to take breaks except to eat the lunches the VW van delivered: square, homemade whole-wheat buns stuffed with greasy, pink mortadella and pale cheese. Gabriel suspected that the farms participated in Trabajo Voluntario only to get the sandwiches that came with the useless urban volunteers.

He was ashamed of himself. He shouldn't be intimidated by his farm supervisors or flinch when he saw the dark rime beneath their nails. Nico seemed not to notice the farmers' hand hygiene, which meant the problem was less about class or upbringing than about Gabriel. He was, apparently, both prissy and lazy. Not a combination that made him proud.

Also, he was losing his political imagination. He had a block between himself and the news, which got worse every day. According to the increasingly anti-Allende *El Mercurio*, which prophesied doom constantly, MIR was gearing up for the violent revolt it had long promised. According to the Socialist and Communist weeklies, which laid the blame for all unrest at the military's door, the Armed Forces would illegally snatch power from Allende any day. Gabriel rejected both sets of predictions. Any news outlet, he now knew, could be subject to CIA manipulation, and what the CIA wanted was to convince Chileans that disaster was coming. No newspaper was worthy of trust.

He kept that opinion to himself until the second Friday of Trabajo Voluntario, when Radio Magallanes reported that, within days, the Communist Party would officially break with Allende's Unidad Popular in order to join MIR in preparing for armed revolution. If Gabriel had been listening at home, not in a rickety Party VW, he would have called Claudio to ask what had happened to nonviolence and the Chilean road to Socialism. Instead, he convinced himself—it wasn't hard—that the journalists involved were misinformed.

"What do you mean, misinformed?" Nico said when Gabriel brought his idea up. The two of them were crouched in a carrot patch; Caro had gone to pee in the woods. "Radio Magallanes is the Communist station. They report Communist Party policy."

Gabriel wiped his eyes, which were watering with cold. Carrot fronds waved around him. The sky was a layered, unwholesome white. He wanted to believe that Nico was wrong. He wanted Radio Magallanes to be more independent than *El Mercurio* or the *Courier*, to offer its listeners not a chosen Party story but genuine, propaganda-free news.

"They report *on* Party policy," he said. "Different."

Nico crossed his arms. "How do you know?"

"I don't."

Across the field, Caro emerged from the trees, small and ornament-bright in her red windbreaker. She waved at Gabriel, then headed for the lunch shed. He recognized his cue to follow, but Nico was saying, "So, what: you just want them to be independent?"

"I want them to be not like my dad."

Nico looked startled, which made Gabriel's stomach lurch. He shouldn't have said that. Hadn't meant to. The carrot fronds beside him rustled; a sparrow hopped between them, eager-eyed. Gabriel lowered his knees to the packed red dirt and waited for Nico to ask, but his friend only studied him, chewing his bottom lip.

Eventually, Nico said, "What's wrong with your dad?"

Gabriel shut his eyes. The light nudged itself through his lids. He wanted to tell Nico that his dad was a CIA propagandist. He was sick of carrying this knowledge around by himself. Sick, too, of protecting his father. He had little will to be a good son.

"He could be a lot worse," Nico suggested.

"No, he couldn't," Gabriel said, quickly and bitterly. "He couldn't."

Now Nico looked truly worried. "Why?"

"He works with the CIA."

Nico's mouth dropped open. Gabriel waited for relief, which did not arrive. He had overstated the situation. Made his dad sound like a spy.

"You're not fucking with me," Nico said.

Gabriel pinched a hard clump of dirt till it burst. "I wish."

"He's not a reporter?"

"He is, but a corrupt one. I think he lets them tell him what to write."

Nico tugged a carrot from the dirt. It swung from his fingers, lank roots dangling like unbrushed hair. "Like Claudio says."

"Pretty much."

"Fuck." Nico tossed the carrot into a waiting crate. "That's not good."

"Very bad," Gabriel agreed.

"I won't tell anyone."

"You can't."

"I won't even tell you."

Gabriel made himself laugh. "Wouldn't want me to find out."

"Exactly." Nico mimed zipping his mouth shut. "It'll be like I don't know."

Gabriel flopped on his back in the dirt. Streaky clouds swirled above him. He felt worse than before. His throat ached. His mind seemed as flat and dull as the winter sky. He wondered vacantly if Andrés had been comforted by telling the secret of Dr. Lucas's coming flight to Cuba. Gabriel doubted it. Besides, how could he compare the two situations? Andrés had to reckon with the fact that his dad was in danger. Gabriel had to keep his dad out of it.

"Hey," he said, not sitting up. "Nico."

"Gabriel."

"What would you do?"

"What would I do?"

"If it was your dad."

Nico barely hesitated. "I wouldn't report him, if that's what you're asking."

Gabriel levered himself from the ground. Nico had four carrots in his right fist. One was forked at the bottom; another appeared to have its legs crossed, like a little kid desperate to pee. "I hate carrots," Gabriel announced. "I hate Trabajo Voluntario."

His friend's mouth twitched. "No shit."

"You knew?"

"You should see yourself in the van." Nico slid his jaw out and collapsed his back into an imitation of Gabriel's slouch.

Despite himself, Gabriel laughed. He spotted Caro tramping back from the shed, hair whipping about her. In the next row, the three antisocial brothers who rounded out their brigade picked while standing, stooping at the waist like hinged telescopes. Gabriel lifted his chin at them. "That can't be comfortable."

"No," Nico agreed. "You'd hate picking vegetables even more if you did it like that."

Caro was coming closer. Gabriel tipped his head in her direction. "Don't tell her I hate manual labor."

"Better do some, then."

"Fine." Gabriel reached for his trowel. "Race you to the end of the row."

AFTER THE SECOND WEEK OF TRABAJO VOLUNTARIO, Gabriel and Caro subjected themselves to a twin ordeal: lunch with her parents Saturday, lunch with his Sunday. The idea was to gain their trust in order to exploit it, but within fifteen minutes of entering the Ravests' chilly apartment, Gabriel understood that it would be impossible for him to win Caro's mom over. She watched him with the measured suspicion of a downtown cop. Even as she refilled his Coke, passed him dishes of salted peanuts and green olives, and ushered him into the dining room, Gabriel felt thoroughly unwelcome.

He recognized that he could be projecting. Also, he had no idea how to charm adults. It had never occurred to him that he'd need to try. He did achieve some light bickering about Colo-Colo's Copa Libertadores performance with Caro's father, a man so quiet he seemed distant even when he was sitting directly beside Gabriel, but once that fizzled, everyone seemed at a loss. Caro kept twisting her hair. Her mother asked Gabriel a battery of questions, but none that lent themselves to answers longer than a sentence. It was tough to elaborate on not having siblings, or not liking his school, or not knowing what job he wanted someday.

The meal itself was not on his side. Caro's mom had made trout with lemon. It was delicious, but it was also very full of translucent bones. Gabriel kept failing to notice them, which meant he kept having to spit fish ribs into his napkin. He had the strong suspicion that the dish was a table-manners test. If it was, he knew he had failed.

After dessert, Caro went unbidden to the kitchen, returning with a thermal carafe of hot water and a brown jar of Nescafé. Her mother produced four floral china cups from the sideboard, asking, "Gabriel, how many scoops?"

"Two, please," he said, mindful of instant coffee's scarcity.

She narrowed her eyes. "Two?"

"Yes, please."

"So you like watery coffee?"

"Ma," Caro interceded. "Let him drink it how he wants."

"I'd like your boyfriend to drink his coffee how he wants it," her mother said, sinking a spoon into the coffee crystals. Pope Paul VI glared from a framed magazine cover behind her. His cassock fluttered; his crucifix reflected the sun, or the camera's flash. Señora Ravest went on: "Instead of asking me to make it weak because he thinks we can't afford more Nescafé."

Gabriel couldn't recover from that. No chance. He gulped his thin coffee, sick with shame, and fled the moment he could. On the riverbank that evening, he informed Nico that the lunch had been an unqualified and possibly unprecedented disaster and that he'd probably have to go into hiding, since there was no imaginable way he could live it down.

Nico thumped his back, then handed him a flask. "What'd you expect? To have fun?"

Gabriel drank, wincing at the alcohol's burn. The settlement across the Mapocho shone with lantern light. He picked burs from his socks with his free hand. "How'd it go when you met Alejandra's parents?" he asked.

Nico shrugged. "I knew them already."

"So it went well?"

"No."

They both laughed. Gabriel knew Alejandra's parents too. Her mother had a habit of popping her head out the window and asking Andrés, Nico, and Gabriel to play backyard soccer more quietly. Alejandra's father, Caro's uncle, captained a merchant marine ship, and, according to Caro, imposed maritime order during the months he spent at home. Knowing this made Gabriel feel sorry for both Alejandra and her mother, which he found disorienting. Alejandra wasn't a person who invited pity.

"Don't worry," Nico said, reclaiming his flask. "Doesn't matter how bad meeting her parents was. Introducing her to yours will be worse."

Nico was right. Ray and Vera insisted on taking Caro to the Polo Club, where she had never been. It took Gabriel ten minutes to explain to his mother that it was not, in fact, astonishing that Caro had lived most of her life in Vitacura without entering the club's dining room. It was completely normal, and could Vera please just not make a big deal?

Gabriel hoped Caro would enjoy the Polo Club more than he did. It seemed possible. She'd get a great meal and great people-watching, and she liked the challenge of easing herself into unfamiliar settings. He had seen her do it on farms, in Claudio's moldy house, at the May Day march. He told himself the Polo Club would be no different. She might even think it was fun.

He released that hope within a minute of walking Caro through the club's massive wood doors. She seemed to shrink beneath its vaulted ceiling. She bit her lips and held herself taut as the maître d' escorted them to a table. Seated, she unfanned her starched maroon napkin and sat on the edge of her gilt chair, glancing at the dining room's high brown beams and painted faux-heraldic shields. The walls were heavy with framed pictures of members past, a legion of black-and-white white men holding oars and rackets, mallets and clubs.

Gabriel had the brief, terrible thought that if Caro were mestiza—if she were even the slightest bit brown—this meal would be a crisis just by virtue of its location. As it was, the situation didn't look good. His father had ordered a double scotch before sitting down, which sent his mother into a fit of silent ring-spinning. Caro couldn't stop staring at the buffet, which meant Gabriel couldn't either. It no longer looked like a treat to him. It looked, now, like an impossibility. How could it be that in Chile, in June 1973, when the average bread line stretched two blocks and a sweet potato cost more than a pack of cigarettes, the Polo Club could have a buffet?

The chafing dishes were full and sparkled with Sterno and silver polish. Their domed hoods winked open, displaying sliced grayish roast beef, herb-crusted chicken breasts, scalloped potatoes, roasted potatoes, shoestring fries, cubed zucchini, and more little golden cups of individual quiche than any club members could eat. The excess was both unconscionable and confusing. How could an aboveboard, tax-paying business get this many eggs? This much beef? Did some club member fly it personally in from his not-yet-expropriated ranch in the south?

If Gabriel had been alone with his parents, he might have voiced his questions. As it was, he filled his plate. How could he not, given the hungry wonder on Caro's face? She seemed otherwise miserable. He refused to increase her discomfort. Instead, he trailed her down the buffet, taking exactly what she took. At the table's end, he looked up to see that somehow the afternoon had gotten worse: the maître d' was leading Carlos Aldunante and his parents into the room.

Gabriel tried closing his eyes. Aldunante was still there when he opened them. He tried praying, but God neglected to prove His existence by airlifting Aldunante from the room. Instead, Aldunante sat and shook out his napkin, looking delighted to be there.

"Can we sit back down?" Caro asked. "People are looking at us."

He pointed with his chin at Aldunante. "See that kid? The ferret-looking one? He goes to my school."

"So?"

"So, nobody at San Pedro Nolasco knows about Trabajo Voluntario. I told them I was going to the United States."

"Will he tell?"

Gabriel nodded. "He's a fascist. He hates me."

Caro balanced her plate in one hand and tucked her hair behind her ears with the other. "Aren't most people here fascists?"

"Yeah, but not like him. He's an actual Nazi. In Patria y Libertad and everything. A couple weeks ago he announced to our whole class that the Holocaust didn't happen."

Her eyes narrowed. "You didn't tell me that."

"I didn't want—" Gabriel sighed. He appreciated the horror in Caro's expression, but what could he say? I didn't want you to imagine me getting Jew-baited? It was humiliating enough to have to deal with Aldunante. Now that he'd told her, he knew his instinct had been right: Caro knowing about it made him feel worse.

She stepped closer. For the first time since their arrival, her shoulders dropped to their usual height. Behind her, the Polo Club gleamed the dull gleam of brass and mahogany, feather dusters and floor wax. "Didn't want what?"

"To make you think about him. He doesn't deserve it."

"What's his name?"

"Carlos Aldunante."

"Carlos Aldunante," Caro repeated. A new expression crossed her face, eclipsing the discomfort that had set in when they entered the club. Gabriel couldn't identify it. Only once she had led him back to his parents' table, set her plate down, and directed herself briskly across the dining room did Gabriel, trailing in her wake, realize that the look had been malice.

Aldunante was alone at his table; his parents had gone to the bar. His eyes lit up when he saw Gabriel and Caro approaching. "Lazris!" he called. "I didn't know you were in town. And I didn't know they let Jews in here."

Caro raked a hand through her hair. "You must be Carlos."

"I am."

"I go to Santa Úrsula. I've heard all about you." She lingered on the "all," spinning and stretching the word. Gabriel had never heard her use a tone this nakedly flirtatious. It was like listening to a different girl.

"You have?" Aldunante asked.

"Of course! You're famous." She paused. "For having the smallest dick in Vitacura."

Gabriel burst out laughing. His girlfriend was a genius. He wished he had Ítalo's camera. Aldunante's horrified face should be preserved in its full glory till the end of time.

"All the girls talk about it," Caro continued. Her voice was matter-of-fact now. "They say scientists are going to study it after you die. But, you know, better tiny than circumcised. Right?"

Aldunante didn't respond. Gabriel felt as if he were levitating. Victory glowed in his chest. "Don't tell anyone you saw me," he said. It was the toughest he had ever sounded in Spanish—or possibly in any language, including the private mix of his own mind. "And I won't tell anyone at school about this."

As he and Caro crossed the dining room, he told her, "I was wishing I hadn't let my parents drag us here. Not anymore."

She rewarded him with a kiss. "I enjoyed that."

"So did I."

At the Lazrises' table, Gabriel's father was eating already, which was a major violation of family etiquette. Gabriel had been trained to not even touch his fork until everyone was seated. His mother asked, in her awful Spanish, "Who was that?"

"A classmate of mine," Gabriel said in English.

His mom showed only marginal relief at switching languages. "Who you absolutely had to go see?"

He grinned; he couldn't help it. Beside him, Caro cut a careful square of roast beef, looking highly pleased with herself. "I'm sorry," Gabriel said, doing his best to sound, if not sincere, at least meek. "I promise, we're all yours now."

Gabriel's delight got him comfortably through the first half of the meal. His father, having wolfed two chicken paillards, slowed down and began asking Caro questions. He spoke Spanish but couldn't understand her replies. Caro, in turn, did her best with her Santa Úrsula English, but her vocabulary was too limited for her efforts to make much difference. Gabriel still had to relay to his parents that she was an only child; her mother was a baker, her father a high school teacher; she wasn't a fully subscribed Communist but was seriously contemplating joining the Party; she was worried about civil war, yes; no, she didn't—"Mom! Why would you ask that?"—want to move to the United States when she grew up, but she did want to leave Santiago.

"Really?" Gabriel said, aside. "I didn't know that."

Caro nodded. In her regular Spanish, she said, "Not necessarily for my whole life, but I like the idea of living in different parts of Chile. The mountains, the desert." She shrugged. "I know a lot of people want to live abroad, but I'd rather figure out what part of my own country I like best."

Ray cleared his throat. "What was that?"

"Caro was telling me she wants to live in other parts of Chile."

"Very admirable." Ray reached for his drink, which was his third. He had a green fleck of parsley in his teeth. "Tell her I like to see young people taking an interest in their native country."

Gabriel looked at his mother, who looked at the chicken bones on her plate. He was tempted to snatch and drain her full wineglass. Also to march his dad across the room to Aldunante, saying, You wish I were more patriotic? Ask Carlos here about patriotism. Ask him about Patria y Libertad. Maybe you'd like him to be your kid.

He glanced behind him to see Aldunante hunched over his plate, curled into himself like a snail. His parents visibly paid him no mind. Pity crept into Gabriel's chest, unpleasant and unwelcome. Aldunante deserved to be mocked and ignored. Deserved worse. He, Gabriel, wasn't going to wreck Caro's gift to him by feeling guilty about it.

"Gabriel," his dad snapped. "I told you to translate."

"Eat fast," Gabriel told Caro in Spanish. "My dad's going to start a fight."

"What was that?" Ray asked.

"Nothing."

"Don't lie."

Gabriel lifted his hands in fake surrender. "I was translating for you."

"I don't think so." His dad's face turned the high lilac of anger mixing with alcohol. He reached for his scotch glass, and Gabriel's mother, as if killing a fly, swatted his hand to his lap.

Ray twisted to face her. "Vera."

"Yes?"

"Am I a child?"

She squared her narrow shoulders. "Apparently."

Gabriel heard his own breath catch. Beside him, Caro set down her fork. He tried and failed to speak. What could he say? He was so accustomed to inserting himself into his parents' arguments, or starting new arguments to derail theirs. His mother had never, in his memory, performed the same service for him. Was this her backward way of making Caro feel comfortable? Or was he watching his mother's marital patience finally run out?

"Only children can't control their reactions," she said. "Children and drunks."

Nobody moved. The dining room clinked around them. Soft classical music washed between the tables. A tweed-jacketed woman to Gabriel's right released an absurd, trilling laugh, like a human xylophone. Gabriel glared at her; at the immoral buffet; at the over-washed windows and the useless, empty clay courts. For the past two weeks, the weather had been too cold and dreary for tennis. He should have anticipated conflict. In winter, fighting was his parents' only sport.

"Vera," Ray said again, enunciating hard. "I am under significant stress."

"I know."

"Of which you are a leading cause."

She coiled her shoulders back, rising in her seat like a charmed snake from its basket. Her various diamonds glittered. Alarmingly, so did her teeth. This was not like her. Her truthtelling was helpless and soft, not sharp-edged and frightening. "I refuse," she said, "to let you blame me for your paranoia."

"And I refuse to let you be willfully ignorant."

The back of Gabriel's throat swelled. His lunch congealed before him: overdone chicken drying white as sawdust, creamed corn solidifying in its pale gold fat. Though his stomach turned, he kept his gaze on his plate. If he looked at Caro, there would be a non-negligible risk of tears.

"Maybe," his mother said, "if you shared what you claim to know—"

"I know you and Gabriel need to leave."

Gabriel snapped his head up. His mother's face blazed with

fury. His father's cheeks were newsprint-colored, his eyes red and bulging. He looked like a street-corner crank. A soapbox preacher. He looked like Nixon on TV.

"Good parents want their children to be happy," Vera said. "And our son is happy here."

"He won't be happy once war breaks out."

Gabriel couldn't speak. Caro took his hand beneath the table. He was still frightened to look at her. He tried to concentrate on the tablecloth, which had faint fold lines running across it, a coffee ring half hidden by the salt shaker.

"The Chilean government," his father continued, "is weeks from collapse. A few months at best. Nobody—and I mean nobody—knows when the end will come. It could be September, or it could be next Sunday. And if it's next Sunday, Vera, how am I supposed to protect you? How can I keep you and Gabriel safe if you won't go?"

Gabriel dragged his chair forward, making its legs screech on the polished wood floor. "I live here," he said. "This is my home."

"I'm your father. My job is to shield you from danger."

"I don't want to be shielded."

"When the Air Force bombs Santiago, you will."

Rage coursed down Gabriel's spine. The victorious glow he'd felt earlier returned, harder and hotter. He hated his father. "Whose Air Force?"

"Chile's."

"On whose orders? With what money?"

Ray shook his head. For once, he was silent. Gabriel could not bear to meet his eyes. He stood, tugging Caro to her feet. Blood hissed in his ears. His vision glowed like it did before orgasm. He leaned over the table and spat, "You should get some new sources. Talk to somebody who tells the truth."

His father gave no sign of hearing. His mother was as impassive as a doll. Caro let him lead her across the dining room, past Aldunante, through the club's vaulted hall, and onto the abandoned patio. Stacked wicker furniture loomed at its edges. The winter sun stung his eyes. Icy air washed over him, shrinking his anger to fear.

"How much of that did you understand?" he asked Caro.

"None."

Gabriel glanced past her. Brown polo fields rippled into the distance. Beyond them, high wooden fences concealed the shanties—*settlements*—in which the ball boys and stable hands lived. If he were Caro, he would claim not to have understood even if he had. He would lie out of secondhand shame.

"Nothing at all?" he asked.

"I heard 'Air Force,'" she said. "Nothing else."

Gabriel dug his elbows into his sides. He remembered his fighter-jet nightmare, the real jets buzzing over the May Day protest. He had been working so hard not to be afraid. "My dad," he said, "is full of shit."

Caro nodded.

"He has no idea what this country is like. He isn't a real reporter."

"What is he?"

"A CIA mouthpiece."

Caro stepped back. "No."

"He helps them," Gabriel said, twisting the word "helps" as hard as he could. His fear receded a notch.

"He told you?"

Gabriel shook his head. "I figured it out."

"How?"

"Looked in his desk."

Caro opened her mouth but didn't speak. Gabriel attempted

a smile. He doubted that it worked, but effort counted. He imagined his parents watching through the dining-room windows. Aldunante, too. Donald Winters could be in there right now, wondering what the hell his pet writer's kid was doing out in the cold.

He took Caro's hands. She drew close enough that their noses touched. Softly, she said, "I'm happy you trust me."

"I do."

"You know," she said, "I bought a *Courier* a couple weeks ago. Some of the newsstands downtown sell them. I thought I'd practice my English by reading your dad's column."

His whole body warmed. "Did you?"

"I gave up after a paragraph." She laughed a little. "I would have tried harder if I had known it was propaganda." She paused. "Is anything he writes real?"

Gabriel hesitated. It was possible that not all of his dad's columns contained propaganda, but he had read enough to know that every single one was intellectually bankrupt.

"No," Gabriel said, looking squarely at his girlfriend. "Nothing at all."

CARO SKIPPED TRABAJO VOLUNTARIO the next day. In the morning, she called to tell Gabriel she was sick—"or else," she added, "my body forgot how to digest red meat." He made sympathetic sounds, doom already pulsing in his chest. He was prepared to bet she wasn't sick. She was probably bracing herself to break up with him. Who could blame her? Who would willingly subject herself to future episodes of the Ray and Vera Show?

He was so miserable he didn't even tell Nico about Caro decimating Aldunante's pride. Why bother? Caro would never come to his defense again. He spent the day harvesting greens in grim silence, imagining his bleak, girlfriend-less future. How had he lived nearly seventeen years without Caro's questions? Without her awful singing voice, or the particular glint in her eyes before sex? He'd been like a prisoner in Plato's cave—a favorite concept of Father Recabarren's, though in the priest's telling, the allegory was about discovering God, not girls.

Fucking priests. Plato had no Jesus. Plato was centuries before Jesus. Gabriel was sick of San Pedro Nolasco. He was sick of teachers and parents and being underage. He wished he could dig a hole in the dirt, curl up inside it, and not emerge until he was a legal adult. He wished he could start university tomorrow and never again talk to anyone from his present world—barring Andrés, Nico, and Caro, if by some miracle she didn't dump him.

On Tuesday, she returned. She seemed a bit pale, and didn't lead Gabriel to the lunch shed for afternoon sex, but that could mean either romantic disenchantment or lingering sickness. She skipped again on Wednesday; for the first time, one of the antisocial brothers in their brigade approached Gabriel, asking if Caro would be back.

"I have a friend who wants to join," he said.

Gabriel scowled. He was tempted to say, You have friends? Instead, he snapped, "She's coming. Tell your friend to sign up faster next time."

He hoped he wasn't lying. What if Caro vanished? What if she decided she never wanted to see him again? On Thursday, Caro boarded the old van as usual, but Gabriel was not reassured. His mind swarmed like an anthill. He knew better than to ask Caro if she wanted to break up with him, but he couldn't help it. He needed to know.

That day's farm grew potatoes, yams, and sunchokes, which

they were digging and collecting in crates. Gabriel tried to distract himself with the tactile sensations of farming: wet dirt stiffening his hands and massing under his nails; cold creeping through his jeans and long underwear; humidity swelling through his sinuses. Not helpful. He wondered if the intellectual side of farmwork was learning to catch and release these feelings, or to enjoy the muddy chill instead of resenting it.

It didn't matter. He appreciated nothing. He would appreciate knowing if he was going to get dumped. Caro wasn't behaving unusually, but what did that mean? She was, in general, a highly controlled person. She could hide her emotions. She could be suppressing a massive wave of preemptive relief.

Gabriel couldn't stand it. He managed to wait only the amount of time it took Nico to fill one crate of tubers. As soon as his friend trundled away with his box, Gabriel turned to Caro and asked, "Were you actually sick yesterday?"

Caro narrowed her eyes. Wisps of hair danced at her forehead. "Puking till noon. Why?"

Embarrassment needled at Gabriel. Also doubt. "I just want to know."

"I'd like a reason." She sat back on her heels. Her face was taut with annoyance. "Do you think I'm a faker?"

Icy wind raced between them, smelling vaguely of laundry starch. Gabriel stuck his finger into the sugar-brown dirt. "No."

"So?"

"So I was scared—" He swallowed. "I got scared that you want to break up with me. I'm still scared."

"Why would I do that?"

"My parents."

Her face softened, and she reached for him. Her gloveless hands were chapped and striated with earth. Clouds moved behind her, thin as pencil marks. "I don't want to break up with you."

Gabriel laced his fingers through hers. Pressure began to gather behind his eyes. "I would be sad if you did," he said. "Worse than sad. But I wouldn't blame you, or get angry, or anything. I would understand."

To his astonishment, Caro laughed. "You don't have to understand. I'm not dumping you." Then, for the first time, she added, "I love you."

Gabriel heard himself squeak. Completely involuntary. A mouse's sound. Caro smiled at him. She looked pleased with herself, not regretful. She wasn't blowing away like dandelion fluff, or sprouting a second head, or otherwise revealing herself to be a dream or hallucination. She was his real girlfriend; he was sitting in a real, cold potato field, with real wind wailing around him, real tears about to freeze on his lashes, real mucus threatening to drip from his nose.

He wiped his face on his sleeve. "I love you," he tried. "Too. I love you too."

Caro's mouth curled up. "You better."

"I promise." His heart was racing. "I do."

She leaned forward to kiss him. Her lips were chapped, her tongue mildly salty. He had never felt so fully as if someone else were in charge of his life. He could have been Caro's pet, or her puppet. It was a perfect sensation. He hoped it would continue till he died.

"You know," she said, ending the kiss, "I never met a guy who actually listens before."

"You're fun to listen to."

She shrugged. "You have to believe that in order to find it out."

"So at Ítalo's party, the whole time we were talking, were you testing me?"

"Maybe."

Happiness spread down Gabriel's limbs, accompanied by a

new confidence. He'd passed a hidden test and passed it by following his own instincts. From the moment he met Caro, he'd
wanted to listen to her. If that was why she liked—*loved*—
him, he was safe. She wasn't under illusions about him. She
saw him not as Andrés's American friend or her medium-short
Jewish boyfriend but—miraculously, improbably—as himself.

The thought bubbled through him all afternoon. It warmed
him through the dusk hour before the van came, when his
hands were stiff from digging and the light was too dim to tell
sunchokes from stones. During the drive home, it helped him
steel himself against the radio's predictions of military upris-
ing, and at dinner it distracted him from his father, to whom,
after Sunday's catastrophic lunch, he was speaking only when
unavoidably necessary. Rather than acknowledge Ray's ongoing political commentary, Gabriel looked quietly at the candelabra, imagining a life in which he and Caro ate their meals together in a small apartment, sitting at a card table or on the
couch. He pictured himself cooking for her, not that he knew
how to cook. He'd get Luz to teach him. Start with pebre and
scrambled eggs, then work his way up to full meals.

After dinner, he went into the kitchen to ask for a lesson,
but Luz was plainly not in the mood. Her hair, ordinarily immaculate, was in a net, through which he could see her silver
roots growing in. When she turned to greet him, her face was
sunken and tight.

"Worried?" he asked.

She handed him a dish towel. "Very."

"More than before?"

"More every day."

Gabriel did not like that answer. "What do you think is going to happen?"

Luz made a small, displeased sound. "How would I know?

Maybe this all blows over. Maybe the Party realizes it was a bad idea to break with Allende, or maybe my sister and I rot in prison for becoming Communists when we were sixteen. Who can say?"

Gabriel restrained the impulse to tell her she wouldn't rot in prison. Luz was right: no one knew. He could imagine a peaceful future all he wanted, but he needed to accept that his daydreams were no guarantee. He dried the saucepan Luz passed him, then a casserole dish that had contained pastel de choclo. He would have kept drying till she finished washing, but Andrés called, which was a surprise. It was nearly July. He'd be home soon. Andrés ordinarily went incommunicado on trips: no phone calls, no postcards, no souvenirs when he came back, but now here he was, voice tinny on the long-distance line.

"How's home?" Andrés asked.

"Shitty. Normal." Gabriel scooped his legs onto the couch. Across the room, the iron stove gusted window-fogging heat. "How's the ranch?"

"Same."

"Seriously?"

"My parents left," Andrés said gloomily. "And I'm trapped here with my fascist grandparents. Marco won't even talk about anything serious. He and Romina are baby crazy. I've been spending my time in the barn with the cats."

"Is your mom coming back?"

"Meeting me at home."

Andrés sounded hurt, which Gabriel understood. If he were Dr. Lucas's son, he, too, would resent time his parents spent together without him. He wondered if Andrés's mother was helping her husband escape. That seemed highly risky for her. Even getting Dr. Lucas off the ranch seemed borderline impossible, and after that, what could he do? Stow himself in a boxcar? Drive with false documents? Walk? How far could a person walk before he keeled over and died?

Years later, Gabriel would learn that Dr. Lucas had escaped via private jet. Hardly revolutionary, but highly effective. The pilot Andrés's mother hired flew Dr. Lucas from Bío-Bío to Caracas, where he boarded a commercial flight to Havana. Years later, in interviews on Cuban state TV, Dr. Lucas would describe fighting over the plan with his wife, fearing that the pilot would, under duress, report her role in his escape to state security forces. She had laughed his fears off. Our wedding, she said, was in the society pages. The cops already know exactly who I am.

"When are you back?" Gabriel asked. "Saturday?"

Andrés sighed. "Sunday. Taking an overnight train."

"We can pick you up," Gabriel offered. "Me and Nico. We can go to the river."

"Sure." Andrés's tone brightened a bit. "Have some actual fun before school starts."

"Exactly. What time does your train get in?"

"Right at 3:30. Bring me some cigarettes, okay?"

Gabriel laughed. No wonder Andrés sounded so cranky. No dad and no nicotine. His friend must truly be suffering. "Done," he said. Outside, Sammy gave a small yip. "Now tell me how big an asshole Marco's been."

GABRIEL WOKE THE NEXT MORNING to a state of emergency. The radio and TV—his father, despite not speaking Spanish, had cranked both to maximum, competing volume—agreed that General Carlos Prats, commander in chief of the Army and minister of the interior, had shot at a heckler's car downtown the previous afternoon. The heckler, a rich housewife named

Alejandrina Cox, was unhurt. On the radio, she apologized for her behavior, patrician voice looping and crackling as she admitted the inadvisability of cutting off a general as he drove. Still, Patria y Libertad had begun amassing downtown, eager to protest on her behalf. Gabriel watched dully as jackbooted fascists clumped before the TV cameras, ignoring the government's official declaration that, as of last night, public assembly in Santiago was suspended until further notice.

Gabriel had serious doubts about the emergency order. The heckling woman was unhurt. The minister of the interior had offered to resign. So what if Patria y Libertad marched about it? They were always marching. Their demonstrations were repellent and sometimes violent but not new or dangerous enough to merit partial lockdown. Allende had to be dealing with some graver issue: military unrest, Gabriel imagined, or some new industry privately threatening to strike.

"Or," his dad countered, "Salvador Allende is a tyrant, and this is how tyrants behave. One little insult to a cabinet member, and poof! Civil liberties vanish into the night."

Gabriel scowled across the kitchen table. His dad's coffee steamed in his mug. So did his bowlful of stewed prunes, which released a thick, sweet smell. At the stove, Luz stirred oatmeal, then adjusted the radio antenna and quickly spun the dial to Radio Magallanes. Gabriel's father showed no sign of noticing, and Gabriel stifled a smile. Luz was good at exploiting the flaws in his parents' Spanish. A necessary skill, he had to assume.

Cinnamon wafted through the room, mixed with the soft sugar of warming milk. "Gabriel, come get some oatmeal," Luz said. In English, she added, "Mr. Lazris, would you like?"

He groaned. "No, Luz. Thank you."

Gabriel had to acknowledge that his father looked miserable. His skin was smog-colored and swollen under his eyes. A broken blood vessel forked from one iris. The prunes, presumably, were not having their desired effect. Gabriel felt an unwilling surge of sympathy for his father. Someday, he decided, he'd train himself out of feeling sorry for everyone, but for today, he would speak to his dad.

"I still need to go to school," he said, sitting down with his breakfast.

"I'll drive you," his father said. "I can drop you on my way to the office."

Gabriel ate a spoonful of oatmeal. "You don't have to."

"I don't want you to walk."

Over her shoulder, Luz said, in Spanish, "If your father wants to do you a favor, you should accept."

He ducked his head. "I know." He hadn't told Luz about Trabajo Voluntario. It seemed unfair to make her keep his secret. Now he was trapped. San Pedro Nolasco wasn't on the bus route he needed. If he let his dad drive him there, he'd miss the van pickup. Besides, it would be apparent that no construction or garden projects were happening.

On the radio, General Prats apologized on the same broken audio loop as Alejandrina Cox had earlier. "Immature," he crackled. "Impulsive." Gabriel wished the general were describing the heckler, not himself.

In English, shooting for flatness but missing, Gabriel said, "I'm not actually going to school."

Ray lifted his head. "Is that right?"

Gabriel nodded.

"So you just lied to my face."

"I did."

"You aren't doing a construction project for extra credit."

"No. I'm doing volunteer farmwork with the Communist Party." He saw Luz's back stiffen. "Me, Caro, and Nico. We get picked up at the Estadio Español."

For a moment, Ray was motionless. When he stood, it was with the jerky movements of a marionette. "Finish your oatmeal," he said. "I'll still drive you. We can discuss this in the car."

But Ray was quiet for most of the drive. The sun was barely starting to rise, and Vitacura's high walls glimmered cleanly beneath the streetlamps. The radio was on too low to understand, but rather than turn the volume up, Gabriel tilted his face to the window, distracting himself from looming punishment by speculating about the real threat lurking beneath the emergency declaration. Military trouble seemed most likely. Prats was the commander in chief of the Army and the last general left in Allende's cabinet. If Allende lost his troops' support, the government could be in real trouble, though a new labor strike could be catastrophic too. The copper miners still weren't working. If another nationalized industry joined in, the Chilean economy, already strained over the past three years by inflation, sanctions, and the complete loss of U.S. aid after Allende got elected, might shut entirely down.

Ray turned right at the Los Leones Golf Club. His knuckles were pale with tension. He cleared his throat, then glanced over. "You know," he said. Gabriel could see his Adam's apple lurching. "I love you."

Gabriel's shoulders tightened. He hugged his elbows in. His second declaration of love in two days. This time, though, he felt no need to reciprocate. He did love his dad, more or less, but he wasn't inclined to say so.

A rust-bumpered sedan cut them off. "Jerk," Ray muttered,

leaning on the horn. Once the car was gone, he said, "I never want you to wonder."

Until this moment, Gabriel never had. Now he tried to remember the last time his dad had told him he loved him. It wasn't a good line of thought. "I don't wonder."

His dad seemed not to hear. "I worry."

"About?"

"Losing you."

Gabriel suppressed the urge to tell his dad it was too late. "We have different politics," he said. "It's normal."

His dad drove half a block before replying. The car smelled as if nobody had ever opened its windows. Gabriel had just begun to hope the conversation was over when Ray said, "Volunteer farmwork."

"Yeah."

"On Communist farms?"

"New farms. Ones that got redistributed. I guess they need help getting the winter harvest done."

Ray looked at him. "Good for you."

Gabriel tensed immediately. He was halfway to anger before he registered that his dad wasn't being sarcastic. "You mean that?"

"I do. Not a lot of kids your age would give up their time to help out." Ray turned back to the road. "Do you like it?"

"No."

Both of them laughed. Warmth moved between them. Before it could vanish, Ray said, "If we have to leave Chile, the reason isn't going to be politics. I want you to know that."

"What will it be?"

"Safety."

Gabriel slouched in his seat. He heard his laughter lingering in the car. Outside, the street looked two-dimensional in the shadowless dawn light. He imagined himself as an ornament wrapped in plastic, an heirloom on the highest shelf. Safe but useless. That wasn't who he wanted to be.

"I would rather be here than be safe," he said. His voice emerged louder than he had intended. It made the words sound less true.

Ray was silent. On the horizon, the Andes seemed almost violet. Gabriel could no longer remember what it was like to live someplace without mountains. When he tried to visualize the edges of the D.C. suburb of his early childhood, he filled in peaks and valleys, not the flat expanse he knew was there.

His dad pulled abruptly to the side of the road. He turned the hazards on, and a frightened degu scuttled from their sudden light. "Gabriel," he said. "Would you like to tell me what you found in my desk?"

Gabriel took a deep breath of stale air. He saw no point in lying. He knew he had only shoddily covered his tracks. "A scotch bottle," he said. "With a note."

"From?"

"From Donald Winters."

"Do you know who he is?"

Gabriel fixed his gaze on the lights in the Estadio Español parking lot. Even through the windshield, it hurt to look directly at their white bulbs. "I met him a couple times."

"I meant do you know what his role is."

"He's a diplomat."

"He has diplomatic cover." Ray was not speaking in his patient voice. He sounded neither angry nor righteous. His face, when Gabriel turned, was tight with grief. "Donald is the deputy CIA chief of station here. He's a friend. We work together often. He tells me—"

Something blazed in Gabriel's chest. "Dad." The word felt like a rock in his mouth. "Dad. Stop."

Before long, Gabriel would be ashamed of his childishness, but in this moment, he couldn't help himself. He put his hands over his ears and lowered his head to his knees. He wanted to shut out his father. Shut out all language. If he could, he'd silence his own thoughts.

It wasn't possible. It was barely possible to refuse to respond.

"Did you hear me?" Ray repeated. "Donald Winters says there's going to be a coup."

THE TRABAJO VOLUNTARIO VAN arrived on schedule. The antisocial brothers didn't show. The driver gave Caro, Nico, and Gabriel a horse-toothed smile as they boarded. "Kabocha squash today," he said, hauling at the van's hand brake. "Good, hard work."

Nico fell asleep within ten minutes. Caro curled against Gabriel and did the same. Gabriel sank into the scabbed vinyl seat and considered his mental state. He supposed he was relieved not to be in trouble. He'd thought his dad would ground him, not compliment him, but it seemed absurd to care about praise now. He tried to be happy his father had trusted him with the truth, but that was even more ludicrous. Ray's truth was too enormous and awful to enjoy.

Ray was never quite recruited. His predecessor as Santiago bureau chief had been a CIA officer installed at the *Courier* years earlier, and when he retired after Allende won the presidency, his old colleagues began floating around Ray. Ray's only salary—he'd emphasized the word "salary" in a way that now struck Gabriel as transparently fishy—came from the *Courier*. But when explicitly asked to help, he'd agreed.

Help, Gabriel had repeated. Meaning?

Meaning if there's a tough message to disseminate, it sometimes goes through me. If it's hard to publicly spread a claim without blowing a larger operation, I can feed it to a reporter. Or if there's a problem with public opinion about Socialism back home, I can write a few columns. Help get the voters on track.

And the *Courier* knows?

The *Courier*, Ray had said, is proud.

Gabriel now leaned his head on the van's cold-fogged window, which buzzed and rattled in its frame. He felt doomed. Chile was fucked. His dad had helped fuck it. His dad had helped sell the world a story about a violent, undemocratic, unstable Chile that was now about to come true.

The driver bumped off the highway and began snaking through the brown-grass hills between Pachacamita and Pocochay. Goats clambered over the pitted black rocks, kicking their sharp hooves in the air. The biggest boulders were grimy with graffiti, white lettering flaking to gray. Gabriel couldn't make out most of it, but he caught an ALLENDE HIJO DE PUTA, a COMUNISTAS AL PAREDÓN. The latter was a new threat. Until recently, fascists had limited themselves to crossing out Allende's name, or spray-painting the spider-legged Patria y Libertad symbol on walls. Now they called for firing squads.

Nico awoke as the van jounced down the squash farm's pocked road. He stretched and groaned. "Are we here?"

Gabriel pointed with his chin at the window. "Think so."

The farm had the usual sheds, one with a weather vane slowly spinning on its flat roof. It had chicken coops, rabbit hutches, a stable, and a green barn. Low, dark fields unfolded behind the coops. Gabriel flexed his palms in his lap, attempting to shift mentally from familial crisis to imminent work. His blisters from the first week of labor helped; they had healed incompletely, and the flesh around them pulled when he stretched his fingers. The sensation was equal parts painful and gratifying, like squeezing a zit.

Picking kabocha squash, in contrast, was torture. At first, that made it a perfect distraction, if not an enjoyable one. The vines and leaves were covered in thin, prickling hairs that sent a red rash marching down Gabriel's hands. The skin beneath his nails stung, as did the soft undersides of his wrists. By midday, he had pebbly whiteheads rising in the webs beneath his fingers. The backs of his hands were rough as basketballs.

Gabriel tried his best to keep his rash to himself. He picked steadily, scratching only when Caro and Nico weren't looking. Neither of them seemed affected. Nor did the actual farmers, whom he could see crouched down the rows, barehanding squash into crates. Maybe the rash was karmic punishment, but he wondered if he should get tested for a kabocha-squash allergy.

He managed to hide his suffering till Caro came over to kiss him. Gabriel tried to conceal his hands, but she caught one, then recoiled. "What happened?"

"I think I have a squash problem."

"That's an understatement." She wiped her hands on her jeans, then peered at his teeming palms, looking both fascinated and vaguely sick. "You should ask for gloves."

"Too late."

Caro flared her nostrils. "Nico," she called. "Come here. You have to see this."

Nico took one look and mimed puking. "Jesus Christ. You look like you have gonorrhea of the hands."

The proper response, Gabriel knew, was to say he got it from finger-fucking Nico's mom. Then, ideally, he should chase his friend through the fields, afflicted arms outstretched, fake-threatening to pass the rash on, but he had no energy for teasing. He resettled himself in the dirt, feeling as if termites were eating both his skin and his mind.

He sliced a squash from his vine, which set his hands burning anew. His bone marrow itched. Nico whistled tunelessly behind him. The sun was out in force today, warming Gabriel's jacketed shoulders and his dark hair. By the stables, two dogs wrestled in the dirt, snapping and wriggling with glee. He wished he could be a dog. Dogs had no family trouble. No moral dilemmas. Sammy never had to know that the CIA had helped pay for his kibble, his doghouse, his dried pigs' ears.

Caro was watching the dogs too. Her wheat-colored hair blew gently at her back. Gabriel tried to move his full attention to her, as if it were possible to pick his mind up and set it down elsewhere. Not a success. Still, he slid down the squash row to give his girlfriend a shame-laden, hands-free kiss.

"Sad this is our last day of farming?" he asked.

She nodded. "But I'm glad I got to do it." Sun glinted from her cross necklace. Gabriel hadn't noticed she wore it even in the fields. "If the country's doing better, I want to volunteer again for the spring harvest."

Gabriel liked the idea that a country, like a person, could do better. Be healthier. During their class's World War I unit, Father Camelio had described the declining Ottoman Empire as the sick man of Europe. Maybe now Chile was the sick man of the Americas. By that standard, Brazil, Paraguay, Uruguay, Peru, Bolivia, Ecuador, Guatemala, and Panama, all of which had right-wing dictators, would be not just suffering but dead; Argentina, which had expelled its junta in March, would be freshly risen, like the biblical Lazarus, from the tomb; and the United States, which claimed to be an exemplary democracy while oppressing both a significant minority of its own citizens and a decent quantity of everyone else's, would be, what, a zombie? An automaton? A wax figure approximating life?

Withered cornstalks rattled in the fields around them. A mouse scurried nearby, tail whispering in the yellow grass. Velvety pines ringed the farm, obscuring all but the peaks of the low local mountains. It was beautiful here. Gabriel hadn't seen it before.

He felt a profound sense of disorientation, or of clarity. How could he possibly be naive enough to think that Chile, alone among its neighbors, was invulnerable to both American pressure and its own militant right wing? Until March, every country Chile touched had been a dictatorship. Why was he so sure Chile was immune to civil war and fascist takeover when he had half a continent of evidence to the contrary? Because he, Gabriel Lazris, wanted to continue his political life in the downtown streets and fancy schools of Santiago? Did he think he was so truly fortunate, so beloved of the gods, that his luck extended over an entire nation? That Chile would be fine because he loved it here?

Terror moved through him. His bladder contracted. His rash throbbed. "Caro," he said.

"Gabriel."

"Is there going to be a civil war?"

"I don't think so," she said. Sun shone through her flyaway hair. She brushed it back from her forehead. Gabriel remembered how her prettiness had terrified him at Ítalo's party, how he'd misinterpreted it as light.

"Why not?"

She didn't answer right away. He remembered Claudio claiming civil war was only between conservatives and liberals. Did Caro believe that? It made no sense! War was war, Gabriel thought.

"No reason." She paused for a moment. "Just hope."

Gabriel's face heated with gratitude. He glanced down the rows of vines at Nico, who was cradling a squash like a child. The sight of his broad face was immensely reassuring. Nobody in Gabriel's life was as knowable as Nico. Nico was changeless. He was so kind it was probably a diagnosable condition. He'd do whichever drug was closest, but in his seventeen years of life had never tried a zucchini or a nonhallucinogenic mushroom. He was frightened of earthquakes, bats, and Colo-Colo losses. Once, he'd had a nightmare about Andrés and Gabriel renouncing soccer fandom, and he'd held it against them for a month.

"Hey," Caro said softly. "Gabriel. Worry less."

"What else is there to do?"

"Pick squash." She grinned. "Even though you hate picking vegetables."

He groaned. "You know too?"

"You're a terrible actor."

He pushed out a laugh. "I guess so."

Leaves crackled behind them. Gabriel turned to see two farmers tramping through the fields. He recognized one as Domingo, the farm's Party liaison, who had greeted them on arrival. He had stooped, square shoulders and an exceptional mustache, ruler-straight and bristling with health. His companion looked younger than he was, though not young. Over her shoulder swung a steel-colored braid, its end sharp and ragged as an old paintbrush. She looked profoundly annoyed.

"Ofelia," she said, presumably as an introduction. "You three are our only volunteers today?"

Gabriel nodded.

"Usually our brigade is six people," Nico said, approaching. "But the other three bailed."

"Smart of them," Ofelia said. She had a clipped, clean voice, like a librarian. It was easy to imagine her behind a high wooden desk, surveying her enclosed terrain. Domingo rearranged himself beside her, and Gabriel tried to gauge their relationship: rival coworkers? Relatives? Husband and disillusioned wife?

Domingo lipped his mustache. "We have a little bit of a situation."

Ofelia jerked her head, taking over. "The fascists staged a coup in Santiago," she said. "And it failed."

A gap opened in Gabriel. Then a void. Blood raced in his veins, boiling beneath his rash-covered skin. The muscles in his legs twitched and tensed, as if preparing to sprint through the squash fields, but his thoughts went slack and stagnant, a mixed pool of panic and thick relief.

"It was a total fiasco," Ofelia continued, her face completely impassive. "It could never have succeeded. One tank regiment against half of the Armed Forces? Impossible." She gave a harsh laugh, which reverberated in Gabriel's head. A laugh was good. She wouldn't laugh if the president remained in danger. If she was laughing, the threat must be gone.

The sun burned his eyes. He felt strangely collapsed, as if his rib cage were shrinking inside him. Beside him, Nico made a small, bitten-off sound. Caro locked her hands over her stomach. Ofelia narrated the coup as it had unfolded, her voice bright with disdain for its would-be architect, a colonel named Roberto Souper, who had intended to take over Chile on behalf of Patria y Libertad. Apparently, his plot had been uncovered a week ago; last night, he'd learned he had been discovered and was about to get dishonorably discharged, so he'd hurried his few followers into motion. At La Moneda, he'd issued his demands—give us the country, or else—and then let his troops shoot seemingly at random, wounding civilians and killing a helpless Argentine cameraman, but not harming even one loyal soldier, of whom there had been legions. Prats had sped to Allende's defense. Souper was on the run in under an hour. Half of Patria y Libertad's leadership was already sheltering in the Ecuadorian embassy, seeking asylum.

The idea of fascists in retreat narrowed the gulf inside Gabriel. The word "coup" bounced in his head like a frantic bird's call. He told himself it was too late to be frightened. It was pointless. The coup was over. The worst moment had already passed. Now the fascists were in retreat. Their Nazi leaders would skulk off to Ecuador, and the country would say a unified good riddance. Who could side with Patria y Libertad now? Bullies didn't align themselves with losers, and weaklings like Aldunante sheltered behind the strong.

Gabriel wished with all his might that Aldunante were here. He'd rub his face in the crumbling dirt. He'd kneel on his sunken little chest and not let him up till he apologized in itemized lists for his slurs and swastikas, his nasal outpourings of poison, his very presence on earth.

"The problem," Domingo said, cracking through Gabriel's rage, "is that Souper hasn't been captured. As long as he's at large, Santiago is sealed. Nobody in, nobody out."

Gabriel's first thought was of Andrés, trapped in Bío-Bío with his fascist family. Not until Caro said, "Including us," did he realize that he, too, was stuck.

"Including you," Ofelia agreed. "Which means you'd better call home."

The five of them crossed the fields together, passing stables and a row of abandoned vines. Light caught like water on their thick, horrible leaves. Three weeks Gabriel had spent in this swath of farmland, appreciating it not at all. Three weeks without caring how red the loose dirt was, how the sun carved crevasses into the parched hills. Now the farm's details anchored him in himself. The dried squash stems and dead, bony trees insisted that time was progressing. The day was already retreating. Soon it would be history he'd lived through, a story he couldn't imagine wanting to tell.

Calling his mom rooted Gabriel further in normalcy. She was angry at him for lying but relieved he was all right. She and Luz were safe at home, shades drawn and doors bolted. Sammy was shivering under the couch, terrified of the military helicopters biting through the sky. Ray was—"Where else?"— at the newsroom, planning to spend the night.

Gabriel dug his nails into his free palm. He was in Ofelia's living room, a concrete cube warmed by a wild array of bright, woven blankets and rugs. Her house smelled like bleach and quebracho smoke, though he saw neither fireplace nor stove. The only furniture was a hard-looking love seat on which Caro and Nico sat uncomfortably, waiting their turns on the phone. Gabriel imagined his mother on the brocade sofa, clicking her rings, smelling the acrid gusts of Sammy's frightened breath. His mother, the unwitting CIA wife. Did she know? Was she complicit or willfully blind? Which was worse?

"Where's Luz?" he asked. Luz, who was kind to him; who cooked for him; who, when he was freshly arrived in Chile and panicked by his utter lack of Spanish, planted him daily at the kitchen table, his feet swinging from the too-high metal chair, and spoke to him in an unbroken stream until the day he laughed, startling them both, at a joke she told about a talking hippo.

"In the other room."

"Can I talk to her?"

"Gabriel. She's working."

"Fine." He let his disappointment ring clearly. "Then I should get off the phone."

When he hung up, Ofelia beckoned him into the kitchen. A scratched green gas tank hulked over the white stove, and a disk of unbaked dough sat on the rough wooden table. Ofelia pressed a knuckle into the floury mass, then asked, "American?"

Gabriel rocked onto his heels. Sunlight moved through the room, catching dust. He opened his mouth to deny it, then remembered the phone call. Christ. He'd completely forgotten that she'd heard him speaking English. What did he think? That switching languages made him disappear?

She stepped closer. "Or Canadian?"

"American."

"Interesting."

Gabriel balled his blistered hands, waiting for Ofelia to say more. She looked him over, then poked the dough a second time, looking dissatisfied. Beside it was a fruit bowl overflowing with winter harvest: cherimoyas, clementines, fat chartreuse pomelos. Gabriel loved pomelos' clash of bitter and sweet. He imagined peeling one and letting the acidic juice trickle down his lesioned hands, which Ofelia was now eyeing.

"From the squash," he said.

She nodded once, briskly. "Contact dermatitis."

Gabriel had never heard of dermatitis. Under other circumstances he'd ask what it was, but he was too embarrassed to admit to not knowing a word when Ofelia would already be probing his Spanish for holes and failures.

"I'm sorry," he said. "I shouldn't have touched your phone."

Ofelia waved the apology away. "It's not contagious. Sit down."

She produced a pink calamine-lotion bottle and a bag of cotton balls from a cabinet, and Gabriel held still while she wiped the lotion between his fingers, though it stung so badly he felt possessed. Itches scuttled around his body: his gums, his nostrils, his back. He tried to move his focus to the soft smell of ripening bananas, the cold chair beneath him, the sound of Caro reassuring her parents on the phone.

"Palms up," Ofelia said. "How did you get here?"

He blinked. "The van."

"To Chile. To a Communist work brigade."

Gabriel shrugged as best he could. His fingers were beginning to cool, but he felt no relief. He missed Luz. He missed his house and his dog. He would kill to spend the rest of the day in the cold yard with Sammy, wrestling and practicing tricks.

"You don't want to answer my question?" Ofelia said. Her tone told Gabriel that he had no choice.

"We moved here for my dad's work."

"What year?"

"1966. I was eight."

She looked him over. "Your parents are Communists?"

Gabriel suppressed a laugh. "No."

Ofelia let the answer sit. She finished Gabriel's left palm and moved to his right. He bit his cheeks, neutralizing pain with pain. In the living room, Caro was now arguing about whether it was inappropriate for her to spend the night in the same house as Gabriel.

"Your girlfriend?" Ofelia asked. "Or the other boy's?"

"Mine."

"Also American?"

Gabriel shook his head. "Only me."

Ofelia released his hands. "Shake," she said, rotating her wrists to demonstrate. Gabriel obeyed, and a wild, sparkling pain raced from his knuckles to his elbow bones. Tears welled in his eyes. Once they subsided, she asked, "What's your father's job?"

Convincing the American voting public that Chile is a dysfunctional mess and Socialist leadership is a predictor—a guarantor—of crisis. Aiding and abetting Henry Kissinger in his far-right mania for killing Communists. "He's a journalist."

"Where?"

"The *Washington Courier*."

Ofelia gave no sign of recognition. She capped the calamine bottle and stood. The red weave of her sweater glistened with wear. At the sink, she washed her hands, then rubbed what looked like solid tallow into her palms.

"Tomato vines can provoke dermatitis too," she said. "So be careful in summer."

He nodded.

"But don't sign up for more work brigades." Ofelia struck a match and stooped to light the oven. The sulfurous smell of gas rolled from its mouth. Once the flame caught, she straightened to face Gabriel. "You really shouldn't be here."

OFELIA RETURNED CARO AND NICO to squash-picking but kept Gabriel in the kitchen for the rest of the afternoon. Protected by rubber dish gloves that made his hands smart with sweat, he wilted panfuls of spinach, stirred onions till they collapsed into brown heaps, tried clumsily to grate cheese. Ofelia stirred his ingredients together and stuffed them into pie crust for pascualina, a dish Gabriel chose not to mention he hated. At least she seemed to be omitting the hard-boiled eggs, which were the worst part: their yolks went chalky in the oven, then crumbled and corrupted everything else.

The radio was on but offered no updates. Patria y Libertad hadn't issued an official statement of either animosity or remorse. Souper remained at large; Santiago, locked down. They would not be going home tonight.

He tried not to sulk at his exclusion from the harvest. It was logical not to send a person with dermatitis back into the fields. Besides, hadn't he wanted cooking lessons? He should appreciate learning to make pascualina, even if, first, he didn't like it and, second, his teacher was not Luz, whom he loved, but Ofelia, whom he was working very hard not to resent. He disliked her plain desire to keep an eye on him. His American passport didn't mean he was a little kid in need of supervision. He had chosen freely to be here.

He wished he were in Luz's kitchen. He wanted her thoughts on the failed coup. What he very badly did not want to know was whether it had been the one Donald Winters had told Ray was coming. In other countries—Guatemala, Laos, the Congo—the CIA arranged coups. What about in Chile? Gabriel found it unlikely that a United States–backed effort would be so easily defeated, but he wasn't exactly an expert. He was just a propagandist's kid.

Gabriel caught himself clenching his teeth. His head ached, and his eyes felt dried solid. His hands hurt so much that even holding a wooden spoon made him feel as if he'd shoved his fist into a wasp's nest. He wondered if it would make him seem weak to ask Ofelia how long dermatitis tended to last.

The sun began sinking outside the window, casting an orange glow on the gas tank. Ofelia gave Gabriel baking instructions, then, finally, left him alone, though he heard her lock him inside the house. He watched sullenly as she tramped past her denim-heavy clothesline and into the sunset-scorched distance, braid flapping against her bulky coat. He wished he had the personality to snoop in her house, wreak a little spiteful havoc, find liquor or some unimaginable evidence of sex. Instead, he put the pascualina in the oven and sat breathing its hot-butter smell, waiting for the radio to tell him something new.

It told him nothing. Maybe there would never be news again. Maybe Souper would vanish, Patria y Libertad would disband, Allende would successfully nationalize every industry in Chile, Ray would quit the *Courier*, and Gabriel would grow wings like his namesake angel and fly away. He needed to quit being hopeful. Replace his optimism with some willingness to confront the world as it was.

Caro, Nico, and Ofelia returned before the pascualina was done. Nico came into the kitchen alone, glowing with some combination of cold, exertion, and anxiety. "Smells good," he said. "How's the leprosy?"

"Improved." Gabriel flexed a red hand.

Nico knotted his mouth to the side. "Is it?"

"Maybe."

"Any news?"

Gabriel shook his head. In the living room, Caro and Ofelia arranged blankets into beds, Caro asking a steady stream of questions: Where had Ofelia lived before coming to Pachacamita? Did she like it here? Did she like farming? What did she like best about it? Through his layers of distress, Gabriel felt a flicker of admiration for his girlfriend's bottomless curiosity. Irritation, also, that he'd spend his first-ever night with Caro on a concrete floor with Nico sleeping beside them, Gabriel's hands blotchy and swollen with pus.

Once the beds were done, Ofelia summoned Gabriel and Nico to the living room. "No word on Souper," she said. "Which means no word on sending you home. But Osbaldo is planning, as of now, to come tomorrow."

"Osbaldo?" Nico said, echoing Gabriel's thought.

"The van driver." Ofelia stood, brushing her thighs as if she'd dropped crumbs in her lap. "You never asked his name?"

Gabriel's face heated. Both Nico and Caro looked mortified.

Ofelia gave a small, satisfied nod, the physical equivalent of checking a box. "Come help in the kitchen," she said. "Pascualina smells done."

Dinner passed mostly without conversation. Ofelia left the oven on, door open, to warm the room. She set the table with rough linens and battered metal plates, put out candles but didn't light them. Gabriel imagined his mother eating alone with her candelabra. Maybe, for once, she would invite Luz to join.

The radio crackled as they ate their slices of spinach pie—better than Gabriel had anticipated; leaving the eggs out helped a lot—and drank their farm-brewed wine, which left streaky sediment in its bottle and residue on Gabriel's tongue. It was bitter and metallic-tasting, but he didn't care. He drank his share, then drank Caro's when she nudged it aside. He wanted all the mind-blurring he could get.

He was emptying Caro's glass when Radio Magallanes announced that Souper had been caught and imprisoned to await charges of—the reporter sounded gleeful—sedition, insubordination, theft of military property, and the murder of Leonardo Henrichsen, the poor Argentine cameraman.

"Good," Ofelia said, letting her fork clatter on her plate. "You can go home."

"Good Souper got caught," Gabriel added. It sounded more like a correction than he'd meant it to.

Ofelia shook her head. "Not good. Irrelevant."

Caro shifted forward. She'd eaten only half her food. "Why irrelevant?"

"If he's convicted, Patria y Libertad gets a martyr. If not, they get permission to try again."

Half of Gabriel—the half fueled by two glasses of home-brewed wine—wanted to argue, at least with the latter claim.

A failure was a failure, no? But he kept his mouth shut. Ofelia was teaching him a lesson in pessimism, or at least in separating hope from prediction. He wanted Souper's capture to be a victory. That was no guarantee it would be. In the coming months, Gabriel would both envy and condemn Ofelia's capacity to acknowledge that Chile was no longer on the road to Socialism. For now, he just wanted her to shut up. Her lack of hope seemed to manifest not so much as sorrow as an inclination to lecture. She was like a female Claudio, if Claudio had practical skills. Gabriel couldn't make himself listen. He picked flecks of pie crust from his plate and watched Caro toy with her food.

Eventually, Ofelia noticed too. She shifted into a gentler tone. "You worked all day," she told Caro. "You should eat more."

"I know." Caro touched her stomach. "But when I'm anxious—" She broke the thought off, and Gabriel, wanting to take her hand, nudged his shoulder against hers. He felt guilty she was trapped here. She wasn't even a Communist. She should get to be safe at home.

Ofelia ate the rest of Caro's pascualina herself, then rose to turn the oven off. The house cooled fast without its heat. The kitchen was icy before the dishes were done, and the living room was so cold it was impossible to sit on the love seat and talk, or even think. Ofelia filled a hot water bottle and took herself to bed, first warning that she was a light sleeper. After fifteen minutes of quiet misery, Gabriel, Nico, and Caro, still fully dressed, followed her lead, though Gabriel didn't anticipate actual sleep. His head ached; his hands burned; the cold seemed to have moved into his organs. His stomach grumbled faintly, though he'd eaten plenty. No part of his body was content.

The night here was darker than in Santiago. The air looked

like black leather. It felt animate, enveloping. Perfect for Gabriel to go creeping around like the spy Ofelia thought he was. He could wriggle out the kitchen window and skulk around the barns, or peer into houses. Find out how Pachacamita's squash farmers lived.

Not that he would. He was too cowardly. Too afraid of how embarrassed he'd be if he got caught. He rolled onto his right side and tucked himself behind Caro, who reached back and tugged at the blankets to combine their beds. Gabriel kissed the nape of her neck, burying his face in her loose hair. The closeness both comforted him and woke him further. Soon he had half an erection, which would have been a whole one if Nico weren't snoring behind him. Gabriel wasn't sure whether to be grateful or annoyed.

The generator hummed beneath the window. A pair of cows lowed in the nearest barn. Caro's body heat soaked slowly into Gabriel's chest, but his back still prickled with cold. His skin felt too loose to protect him. Still, for the first time all day, he felt something other than sad.

In the car with his father, he had asked no questions. He had only wanted the conversation to end. From now on, he would proceed differently. He would learn to be brave at home first. He would start by asking whether the CIA had been involved in today's events. From there, he'd collect the full truth from his father, and then he would use it to guide the rest of his life. He'd make a moral compass out of his dad's ethical failures, which meant he had to know their scope and scale.

He nodded to himself, resolved. The movement seemed to rouse Caro, who turned over and whispered, "Gabriel? You're awake?"

"Too cold to sleep."

She wriggled closer. "Same."

Gabriel kissed her forehead. A new softness moved through

him. He felt equal parts protective and vulnerable. Caro rolled onto her back, moving his hand from her hip to the hard fall of her stomach. "Gabriel," she said again.

"Caro."

"Can I tell you something?"

"Of course."

Nico groaned in his sleep. The bedroom door creaked open. Ofelia padded to the bathroom and pissed eternally. The pipes sang like crickets as she washed her hands. Gabriel kissed Caro's ear, then her jaw. He breathed in the sweet smell of her hair, mixed with lanolin from the wool blankets, onion from the pascualina, the damp funk of winter cold.

Ofelia returned to her room, but Caro waited a moment to resume talking. When she did, her voice was even smaller than before. "It could be nothing," she said.

"But?"

"But I was supposed to get my period last week."

Gabriel's whole body tightened. His half erection vanished. Salt sprang to his tongue. The dark rose around him. The soft, unified burr of Nico and the generator rattled in his head.

"Last Monday," Caro continued. "So, twelve days ago." She made a choked little sound. "I keep track."

"Twelve days," Gabriel echoed. His whole body was buzzing with alarm now. He felt as if a second self were breaking its way from inside him, like Athena bursting through Zeus's skull. His new self wasn't wise, though. Wasn't powerful. This new Gabriel was head-to-toe animal fear.

He had to concentrate. Not on terror. Not on Greek myths. Not on his chattering teeth or cold sweat. Not on his erection, which had roared back for Christ knew what reason. On Caro.

"How bad"—he tried and had to pause for air—"how bad is twelve days?"

"Bad."

Gabriel screwed his eyes against the darkness. The place behind his balls ached. His many lists of distractions flocked into
his head. Carlos Caszely's best goals. Patagonian snake species.
Sunken Chilean warships. Andean birds. He couldn't have a
baby. It was impossible. If, faced with the prospect, he went to
thoughts of outdated gods and headers across the Huachipato
goal box, then clearly he was unprepared.

Again he dragged his focus back to Caro. No soccer. No
birds. Pregnancy. How could Caro be pregnant? He had always
pulled out in time. Hadn't he soaked up the results with hay
behind barns, with already-stiff cleaning rags, with a San Pedro Nolasco scarf he'd then had to abandon? Once—behind
the brush pile the first day of Trabajo Voluntario—he'd cut it
close. Too close, apparently.

Gabriel tightened his hold on his girlfriend. He wanted so
badly to see her, but he saw only black air. "If it's real," she
said, and hope spiked in him, "I have to keep it." Her voice
twisted and dipped. "For God."

There was no possible reply. The alternative hadn't entered
Gabriel's head. It would be—would have been—so easy. He
was certain his parents could arrange an abortion in hours.
Pay for it without blinking. Get the first Chilean Lazris sliced
or scooped or hosed from Caro's womb.

A small and fervent gladness bubbled in him. If he had a
child here, he'd have roots. A valid claim. He could propose to
Caro. They could move to Patagonia, raise their baby in some
mountain town. Let the country collapse around them if it had
to, let their old futures pass them by.

He knew better than to propose now. He knew that he had
to apologize and that his apology would be worthless. What
words were the size of a baby? What would he ever be able
to say?

Gabriel shucked the heavy blankets off and stood, shivering, as his collected heat fled. He guided Caro across the icy floor, hands stinging with newly mobile blood, Nico somehow still gurgling peacefully at their backs. Panic fluttered at the top of Gabriel's head. The heavy darkness—how had his eyes not adjusted?—made it worse.

But the kitchen's concrete walls glowed faintly. A bitten hunk of moon shone in the window. Black-coffee light fell on the floor. Not much, but enough to show him the blond wood table, the gas tank, the tear tracks on Caro's face.

She sat, and he knelt before her. The moon glanced from her wet cheeks. It caught the zip of her outermost sweater, the button of her fly. Gabriel undid it, guided more by light than thought, and tugged at her waistband till she shoved her pants to her calves. Then she pushed him back.

"No hands. I don't want your rash."

Clumsily, Gabriel pressed his mouth to her cotton underwear. She had never let him lick her before. The fabric—should he remove it? Or would taking her underwear off count as hands?—was wet already. Caro angled her hips closer as he tried kissing, tried sucking, tried pressing the flat of his tongue to bone. Caro tightened her legs, and he licked harder, imagining talking to a baby who might yet not be real. He saw himself from above, hunched shoulders and curved back, a ball of a person on a moonlit floor in the middle of fields, of vines, of packed red dirt to which his child would belong.

Caro sighed and shivered. Her thighs tensed. She dropped herself to the chair's edge. Gabriel told himself that of all the omens he had sought and found, this was the truest. If he made Caro come, it meant that their future was possible. It meant that their life and the emerging life inside her were not only real but fated, that his destiny had always been here.

She dug her nails into his shoulders. He felt her buck, then go limp. He promised himself, this time correctly, that he would never forget this sensation, this combined feeling of arousal, terror, gratitude, and good luck. He remained in place for a moment. Only when he stood, wet-chinned and giddy, did he see the long shadow on the linoleum. Ofelia cleared her throat from the kitchen door.

"I think I mentioned I was a light sleeper," she said.

Caro buried her head in her hands. Gabriel resisted the urge to seal his eyes shut. He straightened his back and looked at Ofelia. Someone had to take responsibility. Face reality. Accept the consequences. He had skated through life long enough. No more, he swore silently to Caro. From now on, he'd assume the weight of their actions. He would shelter her. He was, after all, American. He could offer her all the protection in the world.

INTERPRETATION

\\\

Buenos Aires, Argentina, February 2015

Nina Lazris met her husband in the week between arriving in Buenos Aires and discovering the book that punched holes in her personal history. Besides that, she did little of note. She unpacked her bags, set up a writing space in her newly rented apartment, took long walks in the summer heat. She worked, though less than she should have, on the dissertation she had flown halfway across the globe to save. She spent too much money on fancy prepared foods before realizing she'd miscalculated the exchange rate. It didn't matter—Nina had resources to fall back on—but she tried to live within her grad-student means. It was part of being a serious person, which she worked hard at. Before she stumbled on *Guerra Eterna*, it was arguably the project of her adult life.

Nina wasn't positive her presence in Argentina qualified as serious. It was neither fully stipend-funded nor fully planned. In fairness to herself, she could only have planned so much. She'd come to Buenos Aires to study the protest movement arising from the suspicious death of special prosecutor Alberto Nisman, and he'd barely been dead three weeks. Hard to blame herself for not organizing her trip while he was still alive.

If somebody had told Nina a month earlier that she'd be spending her spring semester here, she would have laughed in their face. She had never been to Latin America before. Never traveled alone. Never imagined that, four and a half years into her doctorate, she'd wrench the scope of her dissertation open, shifting from social-media-driven dissent in the United States to social-media-driven dissent in the Americas. Of course, if that same clairvoyant person had added that she'd be making a chaotic last-ditch effort to rescue her dissertation—and with it her poor, shredded belief that she belonged in academia—she would have retracted her laughter. Fine, she would have said. Great. Cross your fingers it works.

She crossed her fingers at her sides now, waiting at the light on Avenida Santa Fe, the main commercial strip in her new neighborhood. Chic girls buzzed past in their giant earrings, hip-length hair flickering in the breeze. Sun bounced off the polished hoods of taxis, glared from bus windows, turned the street itself into a lake of glossy tar. The air smelled like hot asphalt mixed with warm fruit, dog shit, and the pleasant burnt-wood scent that wafted constantly from the pizzeria across Santa Fe. Nina had tried it two nights ago: not awful, but also not good.

She was en route to coffee with Ilán Radzietsky, a graduate of her program who now taught at the Universidad de Buenos Aires. Nina was working on a PhD in communications, but instead of getting funding from her department, she got it from her university's Center for Media and Social Impact, which adopted a doctoral student every few years. Ilán had been its first. Now he was a rising academic star who researched multilingual online identity formation.

Nina wished she knew what type of coffee this would be: semiprofessional? Full professional? Casual but platonic? Or would it be one of those first dates recognizable only in retrospect? She had no reason to even imagine the latter. Her stubborn hope that it would be a pre-date pointed, probably, to her fundamental unseriousness. She'd never met Ilán in person. One of her bosses had introduced them, which led to a flurry of emails, and then Ilán invited her to a welcome-to-the-country coffee. All very ordinary. Nina was thinking in date-or-not-date terms only because (1) she hadn't had a nontransactional conversation, barring phone calls with her dad, since she landed in Buenos Aires five days ago, (2) she hadn't had sex since Thanksgiving, and (3) Ilán was hot. In the headshot on his departmental profile page, he glowed like some kind of Modern Orthodox sex prince in his yarmulke and open collar. His mussed curls practically lifted from her laptop screen. His smile was crooked, his skin perfect. Since Google Imaging him, Nina had devoted far too much time to sexual and marital fantasies in which he was the star.

A block from the Facultad de Ciencias Sociales, Nina paused to lift her hair from her sweating neck. She checked her reflection in the plate-glass window of a store that seemed to sell only compressive underwear: girdles, control panties, distressing Velcro-sided bras. She reminded herself that, even if she was not a serious person, she was gifted at small talk, proficient in Spanish, and neither as dumb nor as ill-prepared as she felt. She had read every scrap of Nisman news since he died on

January 18. She had educated herself on his eleven-year inves-
tigation into the 1994 car bombing of the Asociación Mutual
Israelita Argentina, or AMIA, Buenos Aires's biggest Jewish
community center; she'd read his allegations that the sitting
president, Cristina Fernández de Kirchner, had concealed Iran's
involvement in the attack. Not even a week after he levied his
accusations, he was discovered dead in his bathroom. Online,
it had seemed to Nina that all of Argentina was in an uproar.
Now that she was here, she couldn't gauge how many people
cared.

She could ask Ilán. In a normal way, not a help-me-my-
dissertation-is-dying way. She did not plan to tell him that if
her research failed here like it had been failing in D.C., she
would quit academia. She would be confident. Not socially
starved. Not a freak. She would not ask insensitive or ignorant
questions. If she flirted, she would do it subtly. She smoothed
her hair, tugged her skirt straight, and texted Ilán that she was
close.

In her two weeks of feverish predeparture planning, Nina
had imagined herself working in the facultad library. Looking at the building, she had doubts. It was old and mildly
crumbling, with a tiny brown garden, a drooping Argentine
flag, and air conditioners dripping from every third window.
An engraved stone over the door confirmed that it really was
part of the Universidad de Buenos Aires, not a run-down office block. Neon-green flyers wheat-pasted to its walls declared
TODOS SOMOS NISMAN; matching hot-pink ones demanded
¡JUSTICIA YA! Beneath them, long black streaks of spray paint
declared the pope a fascist and Cristina Kirchner a traitor and
suggested that both go suck dicks. Nina was idly considering
Cristina's facial flexibility—she'd plainly had both Botox and
a face-lift; could she open her mouth wide enough to admit a

penis?—when the facultad's iron-barred door swung open and Ilán appeared.

He was, unfortunately, even hotter in person. Significantly hotter. Nina wished she hadn't just been contemplating oral sex. His shoulders were broad, his prayer-fringed hips narrow. The fringes themselves were somehow seductive—flickering little banners of religiousness, reminding Nina that he was almost certainly off limits. His sleeves were rolled to the elbows, revealing hairy forearms and delicate hands.

"Nina?" he called.

She waved and banished all sexual thoughts, though she did permit herself to appreciate how good he smelled when he kissed her cheek hello. A standard greeting here, but she'd assumed—ignorantly, she guessed—that an Orthodox Jew would skip it. She hadn't been prepared.

In English, he said, "I have a very serious question to ask."

"Already?"

He grinned. "You said your apartment is on Azcuénaga, right?"

"Right."

"Have you been to Rapanui?"

Rapanui was the ice cream place on Nina's corner. Every time she walked by, cold, sugary air rolled over her, heavy with the smell of caramel or baking sugar cones. She'd vaguely planned to take herself there for academic rewards: first set of research aims written, first interview completed, first real idea.

"Not yet," she said.

Ilán looked extremely pleased. "Would you like to fix that?"

"Fix?"

"You'll see."

He led her down Azcuénaga, past the frightening underwear store, two parking garages, a Subway, a delicious-smelling Lebanese restaurant. Drum-machine cumbia poured from car windows. Persimmons, at the fruit stand, were DE OFERTA; Nina would have to remember to come back. She hadn't had a persimmon since her best friend, Hazel, moved from California, where they were abundant, to New York.

"Are you liking the neighborhood?" Ilán asked.

"I like it a lot. The buildings are pretty, there's great people-watching, it's easy to get groceries, I'm near public transit. What else do I need?"

Ilán shrugged. "There's not much nightlife. A couple good bars, but no clubs."

"I can handle that," Nina said, with a spike of self-consciousness. "Not so much of a club girl." She'd read online that Buenos Aires was a major clubbing city, but she liked drinking and talking, not drugs and dancing. Besides, who would she go clubbing with? Her seventy-five-year-old landlady? Herself?

"Same," Ilán said. "I live a couple blocks over there." He waved his arm loosely toward the facultad. "Which means I should be ashamed that I had to meet you at work to bully myself into going there."

Nina laughed. "It's summer."

"Exactly. Time to write."

She wondered if he was performing laziness—a favorite pastime of grad students; presumably young professors did it too—or if he legitimately had a slacker streak. She hoped it was the second. It seemed consistent with the ice cream excitement, somehow. "Writing is overrated," she said lightly.

"My daughter tells me that every day."

Disappointment shot down Nina's spine. She willed herself to ignore it. Ilán carried himself like a younger man, but, per her Googling, he was thirty-nine to her twenty-eight. She should have predicted that he'd have a kid. "How old is she?"

"She turned five last month. She's very proud of it." Ilán had almost no accent in English, but, Nina noticed now, he hissed the *f* in "of," holding the letter a second too long. Nina knew she had equivalent tells in Spanish: letters she stretched, diphthongs she shortened. Her *r*-rolling was unreliable, though her dad had drilled her throughout her childhood, rewarding her with Klondike bars when she cleared the great hurdle of "ferrocarril."

She tried to conjure up a good question to ask about five-year-olds. People liked talking about their kids, she knew, but what did they like to say? The only parent in Nina's life was her dad. She had no siblings, no cousins on either side, so her family was baby-free. Her friends were all childless. None of them even had dogs.

"Did she have a birthday party?" she tried.

"She wanted to have a fancy dinner instead. We called it Restaurant Party."

Nina smiled. "I like that."

"She's a likeable kid. An odd one." Ilán's tone told Nina he was prouder of the second trait than the first, which she found charming. Before she could ask, he launched into a description of his daughter's ideas and habits: she was obsessed with dolphins and all dolphin-related content, which manifested, in part, as avid Miami Dolphins fandom; she'd struck up an imaginary friendship with Lady Gaga; she thought monsters lived in her closet, but she welcomed them and loaned them toys; she had only recently learned to separate English, Spanish, and Hebrew, all of which Ilán spoke to her at home, and was delighted with herself when she successfully communicated in one unmixed tongue.

Nina whistled. "Trilingual parenting. I knew you did research in a lot of languages, but still, that's hardcore."

"Or crazy."

She waved his self-deprecation off. A small corner of her mind suggested she ask why Hebrew: religion or Zionism? But if he was a Zionist, she didn't want to know. "Impressive," she said. "My dad raised me bilingual, and that was tricky enough."

Down the block, two silky women slipped into a building that Nina had realized yesterday was a plastic surgery clinic. A taxi honked at a jaywalking girl in palm-sized shorts. She swanned serenely onward, as if the noise were tribute, not rebuke. Over the horn's ongoing blare, Ilán asked, "English and what other language?"

"Spanish. I didn't tell you I speak it?"

"You did." His mouth spread into a smile. "But when I lived in D.C., I met a lot of Americans who"—he clawed his fingers into scare quotes—"'spoke Spanish.'"

Nina laughed. "I know the type. Memorized every verb in AP Spanish but can't carry on a conversation."

"Exactly."

"I'm terrified of people thinking that's me," she admitted. "Sometimes I pretend not to know Spanish to avoid giving the wrong impression. But I do speak it, I swear. I wouldn't call myself fluent, but I'm probably as close as a nonnative speaker can get."

"Is your dad a native speaker?"

Nina hesitated. She half-regretted bringing her dad up. On the one hand, she and her father were extremely close, and she missed him. Talking about him at length would be nice. On the other, parent talk was unsexy. If she wanted to begin flirting with Ilán, she should steer the conversation swiftly elsewhere.

She felt she had grounds for flirting. Ilán's elbow was extremely close to her bare arm, and his energy was not what she'd call professional. It was too bad he had a child. He was ringless and hadn't mentioned a wife, but she still had to accept the high odds he was married. Also, he wore fringes and a yar-mulke, which indicated a sincere belief that God could see the top of his head. God would not like to glance down and spot a married Orthodox man, or even a single one, flirting with an ultra-Reform agnostic.

Nina looked briefly upward, checking in. A window air conditioner chose that moment to drip directly onto her fore-head. She took the oily water as a sign that God was indeed watching and would like Nina to desexualize herself to Their servant. "He's not," she said, wiping her face, "but he lived in Chile till he was sixteen, so he went to school mainly in Span-ish. He always spoke English at home, but he claims he couldn't read or write it well till college." She shrugged. "Anyway, he believes in bilingualism. He says Americans only speaking En-glish is rude."

Ilán made no comment on her dad's language politics. In-stead, he asked, "Have you been?"

"To Chile?"

He nodded.

"I haven't."

"It's an easy trip from here. An hour flight, maybe." He left the suggestion unspoken, but Nina could fill in the blank. She knew she should go. She also knew she wouldn't. She wanted to—she'd wanted to visit Chile since she was old enough to know it was real—but it would be cruel to her dad. Bad enough, for him, that she'd come to the country next door.

Rapanui gleamed at the corner. Its windows were wide open, and Nina could hear pop reggaeton streaming from in-side. She pointed down the block before Ilán could ask follow-up questions. "See the building with the iron balconies?" she said. "That's mine."

Ilán squinted at it. "Who are you living with?"

"Myself."

She'd gotten exceptionally lucky with her rental. For $200 a month less than she was getting from her subletter in D.C., she'd landed a gorgeous, fully furnished apartment whose owner, a sculptor named Paula Valenzuela, had temporarily moved to a suburb called San Isidro to keep her daughter company through her divorce. Nina had Googled Paula's work: her sculptures looked like Henry Moore's, but smaller and sexier. She was very, very good. Nina wondered if she was famous enough that mentioning her would qualify as name-dropping. Always hard to tell with art.

Ilán refused to let Nina pay for her ice cream, which was unspeakably delicious. It was artisanal and somehow Patagonian and stretched like taffy between bowl and spoon. Nina took four Lactaid pills to eat her single scoop of dulce de leche. The caramel was rich and faintly bitter, as if it had been cooked to the edge of burnt. She forced herself to savor each bite, though what she wanted to do was shove her head into her paper dish like a horse eating oats from its trough.

Their table was inside the shop, but adjacent to a wide-open window. Warm air blew in from the street, tempering the air conditioning's chill. Behind them, a long display counter sold handmade chocolates. Blown-up photos of wild berry bushes hung by the register. Nina considered breaking her lease and moving in here, or quitting her PhD and apprenticing herself to these ice cream makers, who were clearly geniuses.

"This ice cream," she informed Ilán, "deserves the Nobel Prize."

"Good, right?" He licked chocolate from his spoon. "When they opened, Rebeca was a baby. My ex and I brought her so often, we thought her first word would be 'helado.'"

Nina took a too-big bite of dulce de leche, willing it to glue her mouth shut. She could not visibly or audibly react to the news that Ilán had—she presumed—an ex-wife. She wondered if he'd mentioned the ex on purpose, to alert her to his singleness. She hoped so. She hoped, too, that the ex was no longer relevant. With luck, she'd swiftly remarried and exited the scene like Nina's mom, who'd waited six months post-divorce, then moved to Napa and married a winemaker named Todd. He exploited migrant labor and never wore socks, but, after a full quarter century, she still seemed to love him enough.

Once Nina had swallowed and settled, she asked, "What was her actual first word?"

"'Gaga.'"

"I think that's baby talk."

"So did I. But her second word was 'lady.'"

Maybe he was gay. A divorced Orthodox Jew whose child had been fixated on Lady Gaga since birth? It would make sense. Nina sat back in her clear plastic chair and considered Ilán's disheveled curls, his movie-star eyelashes, his kempt stubble. He didn't seem gay, but the whole idea of seeming gay was bullshit, and why else would a woman divorce a man this hot?

Nina gouged a clot of frozen caramel from her ice cream. She hadn't mentioned her dissertation. In no way had she demonstrated that she was a serious person. She didn't especially want to start now. Ilán was easy to talk to, easy to relax around. Nina wasn't sure she could motivate herself to work at seriousness, or expose her academic insecurities. She wanted to have a nice time.

She and Ilán sat at their little table long after their ice creams, and the espressos that followed, were gone. He was full of ideas for leisure-time activities: museums to visit, neighborhoods to wander, restaurants to eat in, books to read. Nina tried, and failed, to resist being charmed by the associative depth of his suggestions. An indie film set in Montevideo reminded him of a book called *Guerra Eterna*, written by a Uruguayan Jew who was, basically, Elena Ferrante before Ferrante herself was, that Nina had to read: it was a classic, and, speaking of, if she wanted to read classic Uruguayan writers, she should seek out the Eduardo Galeano books published by Siglo XXI Editores, which had a gorgeous office-bookstore in Palermo Soho—not, incidentally, his favorite neighborhood (too trendy), but it did have terrific bookstores, and if she wanted to shop for clothes or find a good yoga studio, it was, without a doubt, the place to go.

After recommendations, they moved on to academic gossip. Ilán was extremely willing to make fun of Thijs Kuiper, Nina's adviser, whom she'd gotten stuck with after her first adviser went to teach at NYU. Kuiper was not affiliated with the Center for Media and Social Impact, nor was he interested in either of those things. He was Nina's enemy. He rejected her core belief in connection. Nina, influenced by the French philosopher Simone Weil, felt that the true purpose of studying was to learn to pay real, sustained attention to others. Kuiper felt that it was to win tenure and publish in prestigious journals. He thought scholars should be aloof and dispassionate and not have Twitter accounts. Nina thought he was a Luddite, a misogynist, and a Grinch. One of her major reasons for continuing in her program was that quitting would please him too much. She fully intended to spite-graduate, she said, which was true and also made Ilán laugh.

To stem aggravating thoughts of Kuiper, she asked how Ilán had liked D.C. He and Nina, it turned out, shared a favorite bar: the Red Derby, which was two doors down from her apartment. While discussing the District's restaurants, he pried from her the knowledge that she couldn't cook beyond eggs and pasta and demanded that she come over for dinner before she got scurvy. She couldn't quite gauge the nature of the invite, but the mere thought of entering his apartment sent a prickle of heat down her spine.

On her half-block walk home, she told herself to hope Ilán was gay. She felt in her bones that he was not, but also that, if he was straight, she could get herself into big trouble. Heartbreak trouble or, worse, step-maternal trouble. Already, she was imagining ways she might charm Rebeca. Contrary to parental stereotype, Ilán hadn't shown Nina a single photo. She wondered if they looked alike.

In her building's echoing staircase, Nina tried to remember herself at five. She remembered loving, in descending order, her dad, Scottie Pippen, and God, who she thought lived in trees. In playgrounds and parks, she'd shove her face into knotholes and root balls, braced to stare the God of her ancestors down. Eventually, she got poison oak on her forehead and renounced her search and, with it, her theological interests. She never lost interest in either her father or Scottie, though.

She wondered if her religious sureness had been a kid thing, or if it was her personality. Until her PhD, she had always been highly confident. She still felt that confidence operating below the surface of her mind, but her three failed case studies, combined with Kuiper's scorn for her project, had done major damage. Once, Nina had been positive that studying social media's political potential was her calling. Her purpose. She'd had all kinds of lofty ideals about the public benefits of researching internet dissent. Now she worried that her entire academic life was an excuse to dick around on Twitter instead of doing real nine-to-five work.

On the plane here, plunging through the dark sky over Brazil, Nina had promised herself that this was it. She was in the fifth year of her PhD, and now she was on her fifth possible dissertation subject. Already she had tried and failed to study Occupy Wall Street, which proved too diffuse; the opposition to the Keystone XL pipeline, which wasn't sufficiently online; Black Lives Matter, which she'd decided it was not her place to research; and a newly formed Jewish anti-Zionist group headquartered in D.C. and on Twitter, which had been perfect until it abruptly unformed. Not Nina's fault, but she took it as a bad sign. A cosmic alert that her work was misguided. If the Nisman protests failed to cohere into the movement she predicted and hoped for, she would take the universe's advice. She'd admit that she was not a serious scholar, that her whole research agenda was baseless bullshit. She'd pack up and go home—and not home to D.C. either, but to Chicago. She'd admit defeat. She'd get a job.

NINA HAD BEEN CONSIDERING moving back to Chicago for months. She had no real desire to live there, but she was worried about her dad. In April, he'd downsized from Nina's suburban childhood home to a sunny, narrow townhouse in Lincoln Park. In the spring, his choice had struck Nina as a good sign, an indicator of renewed interest in the city and its social and cultural life. But eight months after moving, he hadn't unpacked. His books, ordinarily his main companions, were still in their disintegrating cardboard boxes. His art leaned on the living-room walls, swaddled in Bubble Wrap and brown paper. One pot and one pan sat on the stove, but his beloved Dutch ovens were nowhere in sight. His dresser was empty: he was living out of suitcases. The only complete room was Nina's, and when she helped him move, she'd unpacked it and set it up herself.

Nina knew the patterns of her father's depression. She understood that disruptions to routine often triggered dark times. Her departure for college had been an especially rough one; Nina had needed to not only badger him back into therapy but find a therapist herself to deal with the guilt and terror of having left him alone. She should have been warier of the Lincoln Park move. Shouldn't have let herself be fooled by his supposed desire to get out more, or by his cheeriness when he came to D.C. in October. He always seemed happy when he visited her.

On the bright side, when she expressed concern, he told the truth. He was, he said, not in great shape, but he was handling the situation: seeing Dr. Wollheim; taking his meds; talking to his friend Nico every weekend; eating three meals a day, two of which were not cereal. He didn't protest when Nina rebooked her return ticket for the Saturday before her semester started, canceled her plan to spend New Year's in Brooklyn with Hazel, and started filling her dad's cabinets and shelves. Her college shrink would have said she was choosing more responsibility than was healthy, but what else could she do?

It was, still, a nice visit. She and her dad went to the Art Institute and, as was their inexplicable Hanukkah tradition, visited the turtles at the Shedd Aquarium. On Christmas Eve, her dad made Bolognese in his freshly unpacked kitchen, and on Christmas itself, they constructed a lasagna that, once baked and cut, had zero structural integrity but was delicious nonetheless. They watched movies, Skyped Nico, drank fancy scotch. Nina even persuaded her dad to let her take him shopping right before New Year's. Some of his khakis seemed to be growing moss.

On the way home from Brooks Brothers, Nina caught her dad quietly singing along with the Bob Dylan CD in his car.

When she joined in, he sang louder. At home, he suggested, for the first time, that they bundle up and take an afternoon walk. Lincoln Park was quiet in the pre–New Year's haze. Christmas lights still blinked from bushes, and flyers in bar windows advertised coat drives, turkey donations, Santa projects for homeless elementary-school kids. Nina had always liked Lincoln Park's neat brownstones, its farmers' market, its view of the lake. It was fancier—much fancier—than her neighborhood in D.C., but the rental market here was saner by far. She'd bet she could find an apartment here for three-quarters times price of her current one. It would probably be bigger too.

She could finish her PhD from Chicago. Before the anti-Zionists disbanded, Nina's work had briefly been promising enough to earn her a dissertation-writing fellowship, which meant she no longer had to work twenty hours a week at the Center for Media and Social Impact. Without a campus job to show up for, she could move back. See her dad daily. Find some Chicago activists to study. One morning, she woke to hear her father whistling in the kitchen, and, before she even got out of bed, she started drafting an email telling Kuiper she wanted to experiment with remote studentship.

If she had sent the email, or mentioned her plan to her dad, she would have ignored the Nisman news, which broke a week before Nina was meant to fly back to D.C. She had yet to decide whether she was returning to pack and sublet her apartment or to resume the normal flow of her days. She hadn't opened her dissertation document in weeks. She had been evading the question of who or what she was going to study now that her anti-Zionists were gone. As she scanned the *New York Times* account of Nisman's work, research questions flooded into her head. Methodology unfurled before her. She consulted Twitter: solidarity everywhere; plans for action; hashtags begetting communities. Her hands warmed with excitement. An entirely new protest movement demanding transparency about not only his death but also the government's role in hiding Iran's responsibility for the AMIA bombing. It was a potentially perfect case study and one that she, with her proficient Spanish, her bachelor's degree in Latin American history, and her total lack of on-campus commitments, was extremely well positioned to take advantage of.

Hazel thought Nina's idea was brilliant. Her second dissertation reader, a kind if ineffectual media theorist cursed with the name Brian Ryan, thought it was risky but had enormous potential. Even Kuiper conceded that it could, as he put it in his Flemish baritone, *vork*. Nina herself felt a level of purposeful enthusiasm she had nearly forgotten she could muster. It was like academic cocaine. She couldn't type fast enough to keep up with herself. She dug up the Argentine history and political theory she'd read in undergrad, tapped her feet as she took screenshots of tweets to use as primary sources, bounced up at night to record new background questions she needed to investigate. She slowed down only when she thought about telling her dad.

Nina had never traveled where her father would not go. She knew how ashamed he was that he couldn't bring himself to return to Chile, or even to the Southern Hemisphere. Before she was born, he had been heavily involved in the domestic anti-Pinochet solidarity movement. In 1990, when Pinochet finally slithered from the presidential palace, Nina's dad skipped his fellow activists' victorious return to Santiago. To this day, he'd never visited Nico. Never seen his friend Andrés's hollow-cheeked portrait—Nina looked at it online regularly—in the Museo de la Memoria. When his family's old housekeeper, Luz, died of pancreatic cancer in 2010, he booked a ticket, called

Nico, swore up and down he'd be at the funeral. Nina, home for the summer, drove him to O'Hare herself. An hour later, she looked out the window to see him hauling his suitcase from a taxi's trunk.

On her last night in Chicago, she volunteered to make dinner. Her dad, knowing her limited skill set, guided and supervised. It was snowing, and the kitchen windows fogged with the oven's heat. Nina wilted greens, poured wine, and waited for her dad to tell her the chicken was finished, feeling the whole time close to tears. She loved her father. She didn't want to hurt him.

She tried to keep her voice calm while she described her plan. It was a unique opportunity. It could transform her career. Kuiper hadn't shat on it. She felt as if she needed to pounce. She would be in Buenos Aires only through July. She'd miss her dad, but she knew—she totally understood—that he wasn't going to visit. She wouldn't ask him to. Nor was she asking him to like the prospect of his daughter living, even temporarily, next door to the country of his wrecked childhood.

"Nina." Her dad's face softened. He set his fork and knife down. "It's all right."

She swallowed. "I know."

"Then why are you apologizing?"

"I don't want to upset you."

Her dad looked directly at her. Behind him, the freshly unpacked kitchen gleamed. Nina had hung and filled a three-tiered copper fruit basket, lined the marble counters with crocks and gadgets, reconditioned the poor rusting cast-iron pan. Her dad's favorite painting, an early Claudio Aristeguieta, occupied the room's back wall. To Nina, it looked like wet sand, but she knew that it reminded her father of the happier years of his adolescence, the fervent Communist stage he still saw, more than forty years later, as the life he should have kept living. She wished she could give him a tour of the life he had now. Show him, as if he were an outsider, how good it was, how enjoyable his existence could be.

"You know what would upset me?" he said. "If you skipped your big chance—or *a* big chance—because of me. I'd feel terrible. Like I'd failed as a parent."

"I don't want that."

"I assumed." He reached for the half-empty wine bottle, refilling first Nina's glass, then his own. "And I also would have been a little insulted if you hadn't told me what you've been working so hard on all week."

She laughed. "You noticed?"

Her dad hunched himself into Nina's laptop pose, imitating her frenetic typing, her wide-eyed, excited face. He was a great mimic. When she was little, he could keep her giggling for hours by impersonating their neighbors, his parents, her babysitters. He uncurled his shoulders, looking pleased with himself. "I did."

"It's a good idea," she said. "Don't you think?"

"I do. And I'm proud of you for jumping on it."

"I had to. Kuiper said it could vork." Bafflement crossed her dad's face. She had not, sadly, inherited the mimicry gift. "Work," she corrected. "He said it could work. Nicest feedback he's ever given me. He could take it back any day."

Her dad shook his head. "What an asshole."

"I know."

"What did Brian Ryan say?"

"He said either I'll come back with a unique, groundbreaking case study that could potentially turn into a major publication and excellent odds on the job market, or nothing will happen, and I'll set my graduation back at least a year."

"Sounds like him."

"Poor guy," Nina said. "It must be awful to live in his head. No solid opinions." She'd made the same comment dozens of times, she knew, but she was distracted. Half of her was still braced for the conversation to turn fraught or difficult, for her dad to begin shutting down. The other half was getting excited again. It would be such a relief to be a continent away from Kuiper. Maybe his sour presence had been jinxing her work.

"I really am proud," her dad said. She could hear the effort in his voice, but she heard, too, that he was telling the truth. "You're taking your career into your own hands. And you're going to have a great time doing it. Buenos Aires is a wonderful city. One of your grandmother's favorites, actually."

"Good shopping?"

"Correct." He lifted his drink. "To your semester. And your dissertation."

"To showing Kuiper I can write one."

"To telling Kuiper to go fuck himself." Her dad touched his glass to hers so carefully she couldn't hear the clink. "Short war."

"Short war." Nina stood to be hugged. "I love you."

"Oh, Nina." Her dad wrapped his arms around her. He smelled like chicken and garlic; beneath, like cedar and Dove soap. "I love you too."

NINA WOKE, ON HER FIRST FRIDAY in Buenos Aires, to a text from Ilán. He'd enjoyed spending the afternoon with her, and he'd meant that dinner invitation. Would she like to come over Tuesday? And if so, did she eat meat?

I eat everything, she replied. Briefly, she considered a winking emoji, but thought better. Instead, playing it safe, she asked,

What can I bring? Dessert? Wine? Then she screenshotted the exchange, texted it to Hazel—*Date or not date??*—and pried herself from bed, leaving her phone behind. She would, she decided, do one full hour of work before checking for Ilán's response.

Ilán proved to be a slow but consistent texter, which meant that Nina, adhering to her one-hour rule all day, was highly productive. She parked herself at her desk and devoted the morning to indexing internet theories surrounding Nisman's death. In the afternoon, she messaged demonstration organizers to request interviews, then created a list of relevant slogans and hashtags. She tweeted several Nisman-related news stories to prove baseline engagement. She had yet to recapture the whole-body research enthusiasm that had brought her here, but she did feel good.

In the early evening, she quit working and took a beer onto the balcony. The sky was silky and blue, filled with crisscrossing wires and moonlike satellite dishes. Ash trees shook their green branches, stirred by pigeons and passing cars. It occurred to her that, except for her frantic week of work in Chicago, today was the closest she had come in years to the life she'd imagined for herself when she set out to be an academic. Ordinarily, her work-at-home days revolved around guilt, chores, and her vibrator; library days, guilt, Google, and snacks. She had fallen into a bad rut. Maybe coming here had snapped her free.

The next day, she worked till lunchtime, then walked to the used-book market on Avenida Corrientes. The selection was dizzying: art books, plastic-wrapped Penguin paperbacks, spooky biblical tracts, spooky sex manuals, medical sex manuals, woo-woo sex manuals, tarot guides, academic journals, encyclopedias, fancy Nobel-winning fiction, weird small-press fiction, the works. She bought a Henry Moore exhibition catalog as a hostess gift for Paula, who'd invited her to lunch in San Isidro the next day; a first-edition Spanish *Valley of the Dolls* for Hazel, who worked in the art department at Simon & Schuster and would love the Creamsicle-orange cover; and half the books Ilán had recommended at Rapanui, all of which she'd noted on her phone. She had to take a snack break halfway down the street, which led to a major discovery: in addition to containing the world's best ice cream, the city of Buenos Aires was home to the perfect grilled ham-and-cheese. Her sandwich was impossibly thin and crispy, with perfectly salty ham and the exact right amount of mozzarella to pull between bread and teeth without making a mess. She wanted to eat seven more. She hoped Argentine pharmacies sold Lactaid. At this rate, she was going to run out by March.

Nina left Avenida Corrientes content, dehydrated, and weighed down by books. Within days, she would see her walk home as a time of hilarious innocence. She'd had no idea that *Guerra Eterna* would be any more important to her than the six other books jammed in her *New Yorker* tote bag. As far as she was concerned, *Guerra Eterna* was relevant to her life because Ilán had told her it was good; relevant, in other words, because discussing it with him could help demonstrate she was a serious and intellectually engaged person worthy to audition for the role of his temporary girlfriend.

Nina understood that, to a thirty-nine-year-old tenure-track professor with a kindergartner, a six-month relationship might be too trivial to appeal. She understood, too, that it was unfair to hope for. It was not good—was probably objectifying, or tokenizing, or some other bad *-ing*—to want Ilán to be her tour guide and short-term boyfriend. It was an immature hope, a study-abroad hope. Nina disliked herself for it, and yet.

Months later, she'd admit to Ilán that she had initially wanted to date him for practice. She hadn't had a real boyfriend since college. She'd thought she could learn adult romance, then take her new expertise back to the U.S., where, presumably, some childless, American, age-appropriate version of Ilán would await. She'd thought her fantasies about marrying him, compelling though they might have been, were just manifestations of a crush.

Walking home, books swinging at her sides, she permitted herself one such fantasy. Beach ceremony, barefoot, very small. Maybe she'd even be pregnant. Nina would love to be pregnant at her wedding. She'd always wanted kids. A whole pack of them, ideally. Her whole life, she'd wished for a bigger family than her little Lazris unit. Growing up, she'd begged for a sister, though she would have gladly accepted a brother had one been offered. Even now, she occasionally imagined her dad falling in love with some younger woman and having a late-in-life baby. Her dad, who hadn't been on a date since he met her mother in 1983.

Nina wished she could somehow spy on her parents' courtship. Her mom, Wendy, was perfectly fine——Nina had no bad feelings toward her; she visited her in Napa before the start of every academic year——but strenuously boring. She had the inner and outer smoothness of a morning-show host. It was impossible to picture her attending an anti-Pinochet rally or caring who Pinochet was. Maybe Nina's dad had found it calming to be with a woman whose concerns didn't extend past herself. All he ever said about his brief marriage was that it had been ill-advised on both his part and Wendy's but, because it led to Nina, he was grateful for it every day.

She needed to check on her father. Make sure he wasn't too lonely. Really, she should email Nico, both to let him know her dad needed some extra support and to invite him to visit Buenos Aires. She'd love to see him. It had been—four years? Five? Too long.

When Nina was a kid, Nico came to Chicago every summer. He brought gifts, planned day trips, hauled them across the city to eat Indian dinners on Devon Avenue, pancake breakfasts at Ann Sather's, pierogi in the Polish Triangle. He was Nina's namesake, fake uncle, and role model. He was the only person alive who could reliably make her dad laugh.

Nina often asked Nico for help taking care of her dad. In high school, when she decided she needed to know Andrés's full story, she bypassed her father completely. She feared asking him to remember. Instead, she called Nico, who explained how Andrés had died, then described him when he was alive. He helped Nina imagine Andrés not as a martyr but as her dad's wiseass friend. Most importantly, he showed Nina that her dad felt as if he'd been living the wrong life since Andrés had gotten disappeared in 1973, and that she, Nina, did not have to feel the same way. She could love her dad without imitating him. She could know her family's, and her country's, past without beating herself up for what she had not personally done.

Only once, in college, had Nina deviated from Nico's no-self-flagellation doctrine. In her guilt over leaving her dad alone at home, she'd launched herself into researching Cold War–era dictatorships in the Southern Cone, with a special focus on Pinochet. She took every available Latin American history class, did two independent studies, then proposed an honors thesis. Her adviser, a sweet, bearded man named Doug Cope, supported the idea but wanted her to do original research in Chile. He was happy to help set it up, even to wrangle departmental funding. Nina balked. Later, she mocked herself for the whole plan. Studying Chilean history could not possibly have given her more access to her dad's grief than twenty years as his only child had.

She was approaching the Palacio de Aguas Corrientes, which she'd seen on travel blogs but not yet in real life. It had been, at one time, the world's most ornate waterworks. Now it was, if she remembered correctly, an archive, and a gorgeous one, all turrets and arabesques, high golden windows and rosy, power-washed bricks. Jacarandás shed purple blossoms on the lawn. A lone balloon bobbed from the fence. The building's beauty returned Nina to herself. She should have been concentrating on her very lovely and completely unfamiliar surroundings, not rehashing her lifelong worries about her dad. He was, after all, a grown man. Shielding him from his emotions was not Nina's job.

She admired the water palace a moment longer, reminding herself how lucky she was. Lucky to be here; lucky to love her dad so much, even if it brought complication; lucky to have Nico to help sort that complication out. Luckier than she knew to have met Ilán and to have *Guerra Eterna* biding its time at her side. No book would ever be more important to her. In the decades of their marriage, she'd often tell Ilán that no person would ever be more important than him, but she always hoped she was lying. She never gave up believing that her sister could someday matter most.

ON SUNDAY, NINA DISCOVERED that she was nervous for her lunch in San Isidro. She wanted her landlady to like her. Paula had been so kind in their email exchanges. She'd trusted Nina with her art, her carved-wood furniture, her weathered quilts and lushly soft rugs. Nina wanted her to feel confident that her belongings were in capable, tasteful, appreciative hands. To that end, she blow-dried her hair and applied minor makeup, wore a bra that had both hooks and wires, bought a bouquet of irises to accompany the Henry Moore catalog, and hoped neither she nor the flowers would wilt on the train.

She had *Guerra Eterna* in her bag but didn't touch it. Her ride to San Isidro was entertainment enough. First, the train cut through the gleaming business district, desolate except for a clutch of lost-looking middle-aged tourists in sun hats. Then it snaked beside the Río de la Plata before entering a series of residential neighborhoods in which glass-balconied condo towers and restaurant franchises—El Club de la Milanesa, Las Medialunas del Abuelo, Burger King—gave way to cream-colored houses with undulating red roof tile and small, browning lawns. Fat hibiscus flowers pushed through fences, and palm trees waggled their fronds at the train as it passed.

Her train car was nearly empty. Across the aisle, a chubby mother and child shared headphones; a college kid nursed a visible—and, unfortunately, smellable—hangover; a man in concrete-crusted jeans and boots read *La Nación*, rustling the paper as he proceeded through it. Nina could see Alberto Nisman on the front page, looking suave and lawyerly in a charcoal suit. He'd been handsome, Nisman. Was it creepy to think that? Since when did she like older men?

Nina tipped her head onto the window frame, feeling the floating presence of her crush. It had been a long time since she'd had one. Her grad-student social circle offered primarily suits-in-training, data freaks, and dudes who could name all 435 members of the House of Representatives. Not types that got Nina's heart racing. Neither did the arts-and-letters boys she met visiting Hazel in New York. She didn't want to spend her nights and weekends listening to a man talk about his Hill internship, or his *n+1* essay, or his band. She wanted a man with broad interests; a man who didn't think the world started at the Senate and stopped at the Beltway, or started and stopped inside his own head. She recognized that she had no reason to assume that that was true of Ilán. Academics did tend to be narrow thinkers. Still, didn't trilingual parenting point to some measure of intellectual breadth?

She sighed and slouched lower. Crushes were terrible. Dating was terrible. Wanting a boyfriend was terrible. For years, she'd been content to be patient. To fuck around. She'd made it a joke with her favorite bartender at the Red Derby, who gave her a free shot every time she showed up with a new loser. She had assumed that her true counterpart would—what? Descend from the sky someday? Show up at her door bearing flowers? Hazel had met her fiancé, Jake, on the subway her first week in New York. Like magic. But Hazel was six feet tall and built like a sex droid in a movie. Nina was normal-looking. If a man approached her on public transit, he was, without fail, either a drunk or a creep.

She wondered now if waiting for her ideal partner was a sign that she was spoiled or naive. Maybe a truly serious person would have spent her twenties testing out real relationships, not having sex with whoever turned up. In the fall, Nina had spent three months sleeping with a guy who, when she told him she had an IUD, asked if it was going to explode. Depressing in retrospect, but in the moment, she'd laughed so hard she cried. Imagine legitimately believing that an IED was a birth-control device, she said to Hazel later. How would that even work? It blows up if a sperm comes too close?

Nina grinned at the memory. She might be emotionally unprepared for her crush on Ilán, but at least she had good anecdotes. And she would deal with the Ilán situation. Rise to it, hopefully. For the moment, she put her romantic worries far from her mind. She could address them on Tuesday. Right now the train was pulling into San Isidro, and she had a good impression to make.

Paula was waiting on the platform, visible even before Nina disembarked. She wore voluminous culottes, a gigantic metal necklace, and two layered pairs of glasses. Her hair was hennaed and white at the roots, like Agnès Varda's, and when she spotted Nina approaching, she waved her arms and called, "Nina! Nina!" as if welcoming a prodigal child. She pulled her into a close, cinnamon-scented hug, accepted the exhibition catalog and the not-yet-wilted irises with delight, and praised, in turn, Nina's sandals, her hair, and her Spanish. Nina—reciprocating but also sincere—complimented Paula's necklace, which, up close, proved to be made of cast-bronze vertebrae, detailed and elegant.

"I made it," Paula said, leading her from the station. "In my bone period."

They emerged onto a wide, cobbled street. Fat-hipped trees flowered above the sidewalk. Blue umbrellas fluttered from plastic tables outside a corner bar, and sleek cars idled at the curb. A cathedral spire towered above them. No graffiti, Nina noticed; no trash. The air smelled wet and clean.

"Welcome to San Isidro." Paula spread her arms, presenting the town. "Not bad for a suburb, right?"

Nina took a deep, appreciative breath. "Not bad at all." She liked San Isidro more with every block they walked. The residential streets overflowed with vines and flowers, and the architecture was both beautiful and varied: crumbling old mansions beside neat little ranches, sleek minimalist facades mixed with brightly painted stucco that reminded Nina of row houses in D.C. She permitted herself, momentarily, to imagine moving here with Rebeca and Ilán, settling in, planting her first-ever garden.

Paula and her daughter Fabiana lived a ten-minute walk from the train station, in an architectural outlier. Their house was blocky, with stark white walls and cerulean shutters that made it look as if it had been scooped from the rocky coast of some Greek island and dropped unceremoniously onto its green lot. Paula led Nina directly to the garden, where her long-limbed daughter presided elegantly over a smoking grill, metal tongs in one hand and a Quilmes beer in the other. Alarmingly, she had a lit cigarette tucked behind her ear, burning amid the wild tendrils of her hair. When she saw Nina, she beamed.

"My savior!" Fabiana said in Spanish. She dropped her tongs and hurried over for a hug. "You have no idea how happy you made me by renting my mom's apartment. I can't even tell you. You're my hero. Did you know I put the listing up behind her back?"

"She did," Paula agreed. "Snuck around my apartment taking pictures while I was in the bathroom."

Fabiana looked pleased with herself. "Strategic, no?"

"I was so mad," Paula went on. "But then, Nina, you sent me such a lovely email, I thought maybe this was kismet. You needed a nice comfortable apartment, my daughter needed her mother, and I needed a break from climbing so many stairs." She settled in a red plastic lawn chair, stretching her legs before her. She looked undeniably pleased.

"Exactly." Fabiana took the cigarette from her hair and dragged on it. "We all win. Nina, sit." She waved at the lawn chairs. A bushy tangerine tomcat skulked between them, snaking his tail through the bright grass. Fabiana blew him a kiss, then lifted her Quilmes. "Want one?"

Before Nina had drunk half her first beer, she was convinced

Fabiana was an only child and Paula a single mother. Their intimacy was at once alien—Wendy had never been this animated in Nina's presence—and familiar. She missed her dad as she watched them tease and spar. Fabiana fixed Paula's hair without asking; Paula bragged about Fabiana's textile art, though Fabiana took pains to point out that she was early in her career and not necessarily optimistic about its future.

"She has gallery representation." Fabiana gestured at her mother. "She shows all over the world. I show inside my house."

Paula poked a silver-ringed finger into the air. "And at the Museo Lucy Mattos."

"Okay. Yes. And at the Museo Lucy Mattos, which, Nina, is in San Isidro. I teach kids' craft classes there."

"Still," Paula said. "A sale is a sale."

"Yes, yes, a sale is a sale, but I want Nina to like me," Fabiana said, which sent an instant, wild blush from Nina's scalp to her throat. "And she won't like me if I pretend to be the face of textile art in the Americas, when, if she Googles me, she'll get three hits."

Nina knew that her hosts were bickering for her, performing their mother-daughter friendship. She loved it. She wanted to crawl into the warmth of their relationship and never leave. Maybe she could move into Fabiana's luminous cube house and become an artist. Learn to grill and smoke simultaneously, or at least how to grill; let her hair snake into an untended fall of waving frizz; give her laptop to some underserved Argentine high schooler, abandon her so-called purpose, and trade the pretenses and hoop-jumping of academia for a calm, peaceful, bullshit-free life.

Nina recognized that she was projecting. The art world was famously full of bullshit and hoop-jumping, and surely both Fabiana and Paula had robust senses of purpose driving them to make tapestries and bone necklaces and sleek abstract bronzes.

Presumably, also, Fabiana was less relaxed than she seemed, given that she'd begged her mom to move in here. Maybe their relationship was the inverse of Nina's with her dad: parent, not child, serving as emotional stabilizer. Or maybe Nina was projecting again.

She had always been prone to overimagining other people's lives and to idealizing other women's ways of moving through the world. As a college student, she'd mistaken the latter habit for actual attraction to women, which caused significant embarrassment when she found that she was wrong. Supposedly, her ex-girlfriend Carlie still referred to her exclusively as "that bitch Nina Lazris," which was fair, but Nina couldn't help it. She had wanted so badly to be like Carlie, and she was only nineteen. Who besides Carlie could blame her for getting confused?

Now, at least, she was clear on her desires in romance, if not in much else. She didn't want to date Fabiana. She wanted to look like her, and grill like her, and have a garden like hers: cacti glistening in the sunlight, hot-pink hibiscus all but frothing with vitality. Fabiana's house was as clean as snow. The air smelled like pollen, charring red meat, pine sap mixed with honey. Her cat stalked by, hunting bugs, and Fabiana swung him from the ground one-handed, kissed his pink nose, and released him to continue his work.

"Nina," she said. "You like peppers?"

"I like everything."

"My kind of girl." Fabiana dumped a mixing bowl's worth of oiled red bell peppers onto the grate. Their skins hissed and sizzled, releasing puffs of sweet smoke as Fabiana lit a new cigarette, pulled up a chair, and said, "If you ever get divorced, Nina, make sure you end up with a house like this. Best consolation prize of my life."

"You moved here after?" Nina asked.

"No, I bought it with my ex. Or, rather, my ex bought it when we were married."

"He never appreciated it, though," Paula said.

Fabiana shook her head. "Not a visually inclined man."

"Same as Vicente." Paula glanced at Nina. "Vicente is my son. He introduced Fabiana to her ex-husband."

"I didn't realize you had a son," Nina said. She could hear her own disappointment. She'd wanted for Fabiana to be a fellow only child.

"Two," Paula said. "Vicente and Ignacio. Fabiana's mistake was marrying a friend of Vicente's, not Ignacio's. I told her it was the wrong way to go."

Fabiana nodded, unruffled. "She was right. Nacho's friends are sweethearts, and Vicente's friends are sharks."

"Sharks?"

"Power freaks. Bankers, lobbyists, politicians." She drew her heels onto her chair. "Sebastián, my ex, works on the trading desk at Banco Macro, and it was like he thought our entire marriage should be one trade after the next. He always had to be closing a deal, except I was the deal. You know?"

Nina knew the social type, but she could not imagine the dynamics involved in marrying one—or, to be fair, in marrying anyone. She said so, which made both her hostesses laugh. "Nobody can imagine marriage," Paula informed her. "Not till it happens to you."

"Even when it happens to you," Fabiana corrected.

"I wouldn't say I'm in much danger of that," Nina said dryly. "I'd just like a boyfriend to happen to me sometime soon."

Paula leaned closer. "How soon?"

Nina thought of Ilán, which made her cheeks heat. Before she could answer, though, Fabiana rose to return to the grill, saying, "Nina, let me give you one piece of advice about Argentine men."

"Yes?"

A wolfish grin spread over her face. "Date more than one."

Their conversation drifted and spiraled as they ate their peppers, followed by orange links of chorizo. Fabiana complimented Nina's emergent freckles; Nina complimented her untamed curls. They compared favorite movies, favorite foods, favorite food shows—Nina, despite her inability to cook, was addicted to *Top Chef*; Fabiana was a Nigella devotee—zodiac signs, nonastrological superstitions, dating histories. Fabiana was thirty-one but had been single for precisely three months of her twenties, so in romance years, she said, Nina was older.

"Or you grew up," Nina countered, "and I'm still functionally twenty-two."

Fabiana waved a long hand, dismissing the argument. "Maybe if my husband had been an actual grown-up," she said, which, once again, made Nina think irresistibly of Ilán. What could be more grown up, and less sharky, than raising a child alone? If Nina dated him, even as practice, would she ascend to a new stage of adulthood? Would she officially become a serious person? Or would she keep floundering, mired in doubt?

Paula rose to go inside then, and Fabiana gave Nina a conspiratorial wink. Once her mother was safely indoors, she said, "You knew we were getting friend-matchmade, right?"

Joy spilled through Nina, blotting out all other thought. "We are?"

"One hundred percent. The minute she read your first email, she was all, 'Oh, Fabiana, this woman sounds so smart, so fun, perfect to be your friend.' And," Fabiana added, lifting her beer in a loose toast, "I agreed."

Nina could not imagine wanting to be friends with a person Wendy picked out for her. Nor could she imagine Wendy caring enough to try. "I'm so glad," she said, clinking her bottle against Fabiana's. "I feel very lucky."

Paula returned bearing a jade-green camping thermos and

what Nina recognized from travel blogs as a mate gourd. She'd had yerba mate in its American forms: iced tea from Yes! Organic, dusty loose-leaf at coffee shops. When she said as much, both Paula and Fabiana laughed. "Not the same," Paula told her kindly, trickling hot water into the gourd. She examined it, then planted a metal straw deep in the packed leaves, added more water, and drank, looking content.

"You want to drink till you hear gurgling," Fabiana explained. "But be careful not to burn your mouth."

The warning was no joke. The straw was scorching hot. Nina flinched when it touched her lower lip. The mate itself, once she managed to get some, had a deep, roasted bitterness she'd never encountered. It was like green tea distilled to its essence, then mixed with mustard greens or citrus peels. While she was drinking, she thought she hated it, but as soon as she heard the sucking sound of empty leaves, she wanted more.

"So," Paula said, taking the gourd back, "tell us. What have you done here so far?"

"Nothing exciting. A lot of work." Nina considered her week. Research, wandering, Ilán—"Oh my God, the ice cream place on your block."

"*Our* block," Paula corrected, to Nina's delight. "I gained a kilo when that place opened."

"Same," Fabiana said. A hibiscus bush rustled behind her. A fat little finch pecked from its leaves, then, spotting the cat, retreated. "I used to go in and beg them to open a location in San Isidro. Best ice cream in Buenos Aires, hands down."

"The guy I went with said so too."

Fabiana wriggled her eyebrows. "The guy?"

Nina, to her great alarm, broke into an uncontrollable smile. In the months to come, Fabiana would tease her frequently and lovingly about that grin, which Nina felt broadening as she said, "Just a friend. Not even." She took a gulp of beer. "An acquaintance."

"Sure."

"He teaches at UBA. He went to the same PhD program as me, and one of the professors in my department introduced us in case I needed research help."

Fabiana smirked. "And did he help you?"

Nina bit the insides of her cheeks, which had no effect on the smile. "He suggested some books."

"Work books?"

"Some." Nina sighed. "I'd *like* to date him."

"No shit." Fabiana leaned forward. "What's he look like? Can I see?"

"You can," Nina said, fishing in her tote bag. She produced her book, then her water bottle, then her phone. Ilán had texted, which sent a brief little thrill through her, but rather than read his message, she navigated to his Ciencias Sociales department profile, then passed Fabiana the phone. She whistled, then showed her mother.

"That," Paula declared, squinting through her doubled glasses, "is a handsome man."

"Too handsome," Nina said.

"For you?" Paula leaned closer, necklace clicking softly on her sternum. She examined Nina with comic seriousness, frowning and humming to herself. Nina, ordinarily self-conscious under scrutiny, found herself playing along, posing like a pageant queen as Paula delivered her verdict. "Not quite handsome enough. But close."

Fabiana returned Nina's phone. Spotting the book in her lap, she asked, "Did he tell you to read that?"

"He did."

"What did he say about it?"

"Not much," Nina said. Her legs were starting to stick to her plastic chair. She ruffled the paperback's pages, fingers leaving faint prints on its glossy black cover. In her memory, the book would shine like a beacon. In the moment, she wondered if something was wrong with it. Was *Guerra Eterna* a bad recommendation? A reason to question Ilán's taste?

"No context?" Fabiana asked.

Before Nina could reply, Paula interjected, "*Guerra Eterna* is a great book. An important book."

Fabiana lifted a hand. "I never said it wasn't. It's an underground classic. But—"

"No 'but.' You're not old enough to remember. Nina, when *Guerra Eterna* was released in 1982, it got banned in five countries." Paula ticked them off on her gnarled fingers. "Argentina, Chile, Uruguay, Paraguay, Bolivia. My ex-husband smuggled a copy from Guatemala. We circulated it in secret, like samizdat."

"Okay, okay," Fabiana said, "no 'but.' *Guerra Eterna* is a crucial work of Latin American literature, except that it never gets taught or translated because nobody knows if it's true."

Paula didn't argue. Quebracho smoke leaked from the guttering grill. The cat batted his paw at a thinly spined cactus, which made a noise like soft rain.

"Ilán compared the author to Elena Ferrante," Nina offered. She'd assumed that this meant the book was a novel, presumably about female friends navigating socially turbulent times. She hadn't checked: she bought it without so much as reading the jacket copy.

"It's a common comparison since *My Brilliant Friend* got big here," Fabiana said. "In reverse, of course. People say Ferrante is an Italian Graciela Brechner because nobody knows who either of them really is."

Nina glanced at the book's cover. The writer's name was printed in much smaller font than the title. Suspiciously small, maybe. "I didn't realize it was a pseudonym."

Fabiana lifted an eyebrow. "Your hot friend didn't even tell you that?"

"He was recommending a lot of things at once. He's enthusiastic that way."

"A good trait in a future boyfriend," Paula said. She no longer seemed annoyed. "I remember how tremendous *Guerra Eterna* felt when it came out. It was one of the first books to show not just the political consequences of living under repression, but the personal, emotional ones. And it was so *female*. Its subject is a woman, and no matter what anybody says, I'll always believe the author is a woman."

"People claim she's a man?" Nina asked.

In unison, Paula and Fabiana said, "Of course they do." All three laughed, and Paula went on: "I feel solidarity with her for that reason. When I was starting out as a sculptor, people used to say my male teachers must have made my work. One critic said my pieces were too big for a woman to have thought of."

"That's so stupid," Nina said. "I mean, it's awful, but it's just so dumb."

"Isn't it?" Fabiana agreed. "And Nina, I don't question *Guerra Eterna* from a political standpoint. Not at all. I completely disagree with the idiots who try to discredit it as a way of claiming that the dictatorships here and in Uruguay and Chile weren't that bad, or didn't kidnap pregnant women, didn't steal babies—all that bullshit. But still, the book claims to be nonfiction, and yet nobody has ever identified either the writer or Manuela, the girl it's about."

"Have a lot of people tried?"

Fabiana nodded. "Tons. Journalists, human rights organizations, creeps on Reddit, you name it. Right-wingers are always trying to prove the book's a lie in order to discredit the left, and left-wingers are always trying to defend themselves by proving that it's real."

Nina made a mental note to investigate the Reddit creeps. In general, she needed to spend more research time on Argentine Reddit. She flattened her palm on the cover of *Guerra Eterna*. Part of her was disappointed: she'd been looking forward to reading a book like *My Brilliant Friend*, which she loved. The rest of her was fascinated. A mysterious work of nonfiction that had been sucked into the aftershocks of political schism? Sign her up.

She was intrigued enough by *Guerra Eterna* to forgo a final beer predeparture, though her buzz was already weakening under the mate's jittery force. She had planned to nap on the train back, but now she'd rather read.

Fabiana walked her to the station, where she and Nina hugged—like hugging a heron, if herons smelled of grill smoke and what Nina, having snooped in the bathroom, now knew was Chanel Chance—and agreed to get drinks on Wednesday. On the train, Nina tried to remember the last time she'd felt so certain she had found a friend. She and Hazel spent a full year of college circling each other before their true friendship began. In retrospect, it seemed impossible she hadn't known immediately that Hazel was meant to be the witness to her life, or that Hazel hadn't recognized Nina as the listener she'd sought since childhood, but the fact remained: until their sophomore fall, they socialized only in drunk, giggling groups.

Once she'd shown the conductor her ticket, Nina texted Hazel, *Made a friend! Skype soon?* She sent a Beyoncé video to Ilán, who was *suffering horribly. Rebeca discovered Katy Perry. Help?* She checked the Nisman hashtags on Twitter, then replied to a direct message from a woman helping to organize a pro-Nisman demonstration on February 18. In her avatar photo, the woman looked furious. Her face was pink and twisted, her fists balled at her chest. In her brief conversation with Nina, though, she'd been unfailingly chirpy and positive, adding kisses and exclamation points to every exchange. Nina anticipated either an extremely useful interview or a completely useless one. No middle ground.

She tucked her phone away, stretched till her spine popped, and dug out her book. Aside from the author's shrunken name, it was a good-looking edition, the kind Hazel would like: deckle edges, French flaps, a small sketch of an upside-down South America below the title. Nina settled into her seat to read the introduction, in which the writer calling herself Graciela Brechner explained that *Guerra Eterna* told pieces of two true and intertwined stories, one of which was her own.

I recognize, she wrote, *that some readers will object to the idea that I can tell the truth under a pseudonym, or while explicitly leaving certain elements out. These readers will be further distressed to learn that I have altered certain details, especially those of my own life. I should not need to explain these choices, but I will explain them regardless. I am Uruguayan. My country is struggling to survive a military dictatorship. Our jails overflow with political prisoners, one of whom is my husband. I may be safe in exile, but I refuse to risk his life by angering his captors. I will say, also, that no truth is total and no history is complete. All factual accounts have holes. This should not come as news.*

Nina laughed to herself. She liked this woman: her precise diction, her bitchy tone. She'd never encountered an author who made her contempt for the reader so plain, or who drew so much attention to her fake name or the fake parts of her supposedly true story. Wondering what was real did amplify the slight brain-glitch effect of reading in Spanish, which, for Nina, had much more often been a spoken language than a written one, but that was fine. Enjoyable, even. It was nice, having a challenge to rise to.

Graciela Brechner had grown up in Montevideo, the middle child of Milanese Jews who fled Italy just before World War II. Her family's politics were rooted primarily in gratitude to the state of Uruguay for giving them refuge. Not until university did Graciela begin to see the country's troubles: landowners all but enslaving sugarcane workers, wanton devaluation of the peso, abandonment of social services, disregard for union contracts. She moved sharply left, as did her brother, who went underground with the Tupamaros. Graciela considered following him, but her husband, a Trotskyist magazine editor, persuaded her that life as a guerrilla was a waste of her writerly vocation. She needed to argue for transformational change, even as the government cracked down on the Tupamaros, then began rolling back constitutional rights. In 1973, when the president officially handed power to the military, Graciela was publishing at least one essay a month on the need for a Socialist revolution. It was clear she was no longer safe.

She and her husband agreed to leave the country separately so that if one were detected, the other would still have a chance. Graciela disliked the idea, but her husband, who was the one arranging their escapes, insisted. He would leave through Argentina; Graciela, through Brazil. Marxists of various stripes would smuggle them up the continent to be reunited in Mexico. She made it. He did not. While she was waiting for her second fake passport in the tiny town of Feijó, Brazil, her husband was in custody at the Argentine border. When she got on a plane from São Paulo to Caracas, he was bound and blindfolded in a military transport van. By the time she reached Mexico

City, her husband was incarcerated—*no trial, no charges*—in Montevideo's Libertad Prison. Graciela found out only because her brother, also a political prisoner, *saw him and sent word through a network that I can neither name nor describe.*

Nina paused, briefly, over that last phrase. Why mention an indescribable network when you'd already said your brother was a Tupamaro and when you were already inventing details at will? Was Graciela-the-narrator reminding the reader that Graciela-the-writer was working under constraint? Was it habit? Slippage? Did it matter? Or was Nina overinterpreting, like the career student she was?

In Mexico City, which was, by 1973, filling quickly with exiles, Graciela discovered that *although I was now physically safe, I had become a combatant in an ideological war.* Her asylum lawyer introduced her to other left-wing Uruguayans, who, in turn, led her to left-wing Chileans, anti-Franco Spaniards, draft-dodging white Americans, and Black Americans attempting to escape their country's racism with, at best, mixed results. Quickly, Graciela got sucked into an exhausting whirl of demonstrations, letter-writing campaigns, visits to legislators, and benefit parties at which she was asked to speak on behalf of her husband and brother, *who I was meant to offer as symbols of political imprisonment and torture in Uruguay. Instead, I talked about their habits, their preferences, their strange little traits. I once delivered a whole speech about my brother's first heartbreak. I found it satisfying, even cathartic, but after that, my benefit invitations diminished significantly.*

She didn't mind. She found advocacy demoralizing. She tried removing herself from the political scene completely but felt guilty and went back. She started Freudian analysis, then ditched it. She burned through her savings and got a job at a Socialist bookstore in Colonia Roma. Her only coworker was a Chilean girl, Manuela, who flinched at sudden noises and slipped into the back room when certain customers walked through the door. She often had violet bags beneath her eyes; asked if she was getting enough sleep, she just stared. After a month, she informed Graciela that she had a toddler and that both she and her daughter had frequent, shrieking nightmares.

For Manuela, life in exile was less an ideological war than an eternal, personal one. Waking up in the morning was arduous, falling asleep infinitely more so. Leaving her rented room involved a protracted psychological battle. She had been disappeared and then returned to the world, but her defenses against it—against even the most innocent parts of life—were in shreds. Graciela tried to defend her, to take care of her, *but she loathed me for it. When I offered to cook her dinner, she sneered. She seemed to trust me less each time I suggested she nap in the back while I minded the store. For months, she wouldn't let me hold her little girl, which was an accidental kindness: my longing for motherhood grew worse daily. I understood her refusals. Still, I was hurt. I couldn't help my husband or my brother. I wanted to help someone. I will let readers decide whether this book is itself a form of help. I will say only that it was Manuela's idea, not mine.*

She set three conditions for me. The first was that I could not use her daughter's name. Her daughter, in fact, was off-limits beyond what I have already written, which is that she exists. The second was that I could not describe her flight from Chile, even if what I wrote was not true. The third was that I could not describe her physically—again, even if my description was invented. She preferred, and still prefers, not to be seen.

The terms intrigued Nina, and saddened her. It was hard not to assume that the second concealed sex work or sexual exploitation; the third, scars or other markers of abuse. Fleetingly, she wondered what else the conditions might hide, and whether it was ethical to include them. More broadly, she wondered about the ethics of the writer's sometimes-fake truth. She still found it admirable, but increasingly she also found it unsettling. She would need to read some criticism on the subject before she talked to Ilán. Maybe she would ask Nico's opinion too. He had been a human-rights activist, in various ways, since 1973. He'd almost certainly have thoughts about it. Nico, like Nina, always had thoughts.

The train was approaching the Río de la Plata, over which gulls and pelicans drifted like kites. As a little girl, Nina had loved a Roald Dahl book called *The Giraffe and the Pelly and Me*, whose protagonist, a kid named Billy, joins a window-washing crew staffed otherwise by a giraffe, a pelican, and a monkey. Rebeca would be the right age to read it. Maybe Nina could track down a copy, though she should check how Ilán felt about Dahl first, given the writer's well-known loathing of Jews.

She returned to *Guerra Eterna*, which shifted tone somewhat—less formal, less grouchy—as it began to describe Manuela's past life. She was the middle child of a devoutly Catholic Valparaíso family. Her two sisters were religious, like their parents, but she was never quite a believer. Nor could she persuade herself to fall in Socialist line behind Allende, though she admired him deeply. She never joined the Chilean Communist Party, even after she started going out with a dedicated member. She was never a militant or an activist. She got detained not for political reasons but because, after the coup, the morning Pinochet's new and illegal junta lifted its round-the-clock curfew, she walked up one of Valparaíso's craggy hills to her Communist boyfriend's house and found it abandoned. *She wasn't afraid that he'd been disappeared. His family was Amer-*

ican. Their government must have spirited them home. Manuela understood that but couldn't accept it. She was in love. She was three months pregnant. She was only sixteen years old.

At this point in her story, Manuela paused. She raised her eyes from my Dictaphone to my face. "I made a huge mistake," she said. "The worst mistake of my life. I persuaded myself that he wouldn't have left me. He hated his parents. His dad was in freight and shipping. Total capitalist. I decided my boyfriend would have refused to return to the U.S. with him. He'd probably moved in with a friend. One of his best friends lived next door to my cousin. I went straight there. I didn't even consider the fact that the friend's dad was a high-profile militant. A guerrilla commander. I should have known the cops would be watching their house. When I rang the doorbell, two undercover officers grabbed me. That was it."

Nina shut the book. A sick emptiness moved through her limbs. The train was passing low roofs sprouting satellites and TV aerials, stucco walls covered in dirty murals, pro-Nisman graffiti, and concert posters advertising FITO PÁEZ EN VIVO EN EL LUNA PARK. She stared at them dully, reminding herself that her father had not grown up in Valparaíso and was not the child of a shipping magnate. Granted, the writer could have switched the city of Manuela's childhood, but it didn't matter. In 1973, Chile was overflowing with both guerrilla commanders and Americans, plenty of whom presumably had leftist sons. Her dad could not have been the only teenage American Communist in Salvador Allende's Chile. More importantly, her dad could not have hidden this story from her. It was not possible that he had concealed a pregnant high-school girlfriend who was tortured in Pinochet's secret dungeons, then became the subject of a controversial, underground-famous book. It was unthinkable.

Nina resettled herself in her seat and summoned a memory

of her dad's most recent weekend in D.C. She'd released herself from dissertation drudgery to spend three days taking him to art museums and bookstores, strip-mall Vietnamese restaurants in the Virginia suburbs and Ethiopian ones in Maryland. She scrolled through her iPhone photos till she found her dad pinching up a bite of doro alicha at Lucy Ethiopian Restaurant, looking embarrassed to have his picture taken. Nina missed eating at Lucy. She missed eating with her dad. She reminded herself that in *Guerra Eterna*, the facts were explicitly scrambled. No detail was reliable. Possibly none of this was real.

With effort, Nina returned her attention to Manuela, who, after a year in a clandestine prison and three weeks in a Santiago hospital, made her way to Mexico, where she knew no one. She lived first in a shelter, then a hotel, nursing her baby and watching daytime TV. She felt raw and exposed, even with the door locked and blinds down. In the hotel lobby, she believed herself to be unbearably conspicuous. To be seen less frequently, or for less time, she began taking long walks through the city, bundling her daughter into a shawl she bought from a street vendor. She'd sit on park benches, observing ordinary lives. It was *difficult to believe that she, too, had been ordinary. She had been no different from the high school girls she saw hiking their skirts up to flaunt their legs. Manuela had shown off her body once. She'd kissed boys on beaches and in backyards. She'd gone to a pay-by-the-hour motel. Now the idea of sex was awful to her. It had been ruined. If she could have banned public displays of desire, she would have done so immediately.*

Slowly, the walks started helping. She learned to chat with the hotel clerks. She remembered that her daughter needed a pediatrician, and she herself needed a doctor. Her lawyer helped her find a room to rent—not quite an apartment, but it had a sink and hot plate, which was enough. To supplement her asylum support, and to train herself to live, she began working at the bookstore. She started taking her daughter on little excursions: playground, market, synagogue, park. After eighteen months, she acquired semipermanent legal status in Mexico but made no changes to her way of life. No bigger apartment; no impulses toward friendship; no calls or letters home. She was frightened that her parents and sisters were under surveillance. Contacting them might be safe for her, but not them.

"What about your baby's father?" I asked once. "He's not in danger."

She shook her head. "He'd offer me money."

"You wouldn't have to take it."

Manuela ignored me. I knew by then she hated charity. I didn't ask a second time.

Nina paused. She flipped back a page. She reread the short catalog of Manuela's preferred outings. Playground, market, synagogue, park. Synagogue. Manuela was Catholic. Graciela Brechner had devoted half a chapter to discussing Manuela's parents' religious devotion, their financial sacrifices made in order to send their daughters to Catholic school, their obedience to the Church over any political party. Nina could invent no reason for Manuela to take her daughter to synagogue, or for Graciela to claim that she did, except the one now ringing cleanly through her mind: the daughter was Jewish. The boyfriend was Jewish. The American Communist boyfriend whose close friend was a guerrilla commander's son, who got scooped out of Chile the second the coup came, who was rich enough that his first reaction to contact from Manuela could be to offer her money, was Jewish.

NINA STILL REMEMBERED THE FIRST TIME she read a book written for adults. She was eight, and it had led to a dramatic incident. She liked joking that the most Jewish thing about her was Philip Roth's impact on her childhood—or, rather, she said it as if she were joking, but she privately thought that it was true. In the spring of her third-grade year, her dad went on a major Roth kick. He also went on antidepressants, which Nina didn't know at the time. All she saw was her dad cracking up on the sofa, then refusing to read the funny parts of his books out loud.

Nina was pissed. Happy, too—she'd never heard her dad laugh this much—but she wanted to know what the books said. Her dad's secrecy was infuriating. It was both an insult and a breach of contract. For as long as Nina could remember, she and her father had lived under an official sharing-and-disclosure pact, which she took very seriously. She had a right to know what her dad was laughing at, and if he wouldn't tell her, then she had no choice but to take matters into her own hands.

She and her dad lived in Evanston, in a tall, narrow Victorian ten minutes from Lake Michigan and fifteen from the Northwestern campus. The house had back passages for long-ago servants, walk-in closets on all three floors, and, best of all, a laundry chute that Nina's dad let her throw anything down but eggs, glass, and herself. It was an ideal house for sneaking and secrecy. When her dad finished reading *The Counterlife*, Nina barely had to exert herself to swipe it and drop it down the chute. After school the next day, she left her babysitter, a math major from Omaha, engrossed in algebraic topology in the kitchen, then slunk through stairs and passageways to retrieve her contraband book. She smuggled it into the enormous linen closet, got a flashlight, and nestled herself into the corner where all the deflated reject pillows lived. One effect of living in a too-big house filled with giant closets was that Nina's dad never gave or threw anything away, though after the Roth incident, he did start purging his books.

Over the course of three baffled weeks among the flat pillows, Nina trudged through the wordy lives and multiple deaths of Nathan and Henry Zuckerman. She did not understand their concerns with erections and dental hygienists. Nothing they said or did made her laugh. She couldn't figure out why the plot kept restarting. Was it a choose-your-own-adventure? A terrible printing mistake? Did *The Counterlife* have one Henry and one Nathan, or five and five? Nina didn't get it. She was annoyed. This book clarified nothing. If she wanted to understand her father, she'd have to laundry-chute a second one.

She was thoughtful in her selection. After school, she slipped into her dad's study, where she wasn't allowed, and assessed the available options before choosing *My Life as a Man*. It seemed like the most promising, based on the title. Her dad had a life as a man. She, Nina, did not and never would. She would have liked to know what Philip Roth had to say on the matter, though after *The Counterlife*, she wasn't sure he was a reliable source.

But she never opened the novel. Her dad came home early that day. While she was browsing his off-limits shelves, he was pulling into the driveway. Out of earshot on the first floor, he chatted with the babysitter, then descended to the basement, where, that morning, he'd left a load of wet clothes in the washing machine. He'd just started the dryer when *My Life as a Man* flew down the chute. He waited a moment, but no other books or objects followed. Even a less engaged parent would have guessed his daughter's intent.

Nina remembered hearing the telltale clack of his leather-soled work shoes on the wooden stairs. She remembered racing to her bedroom, sprawling on the floor with her three-ring school binder, hiding behind its stickers and stars. She braced herself to pretend she'd been doing science homework for hours, but her dad didn't give her an opportunity to lie. He marched into her room, incriminating book in hand, and lowered himself, white-lipped with rage, to the floor.

Nina was no stranger to paternal emotion. She knew the sound of her dad's weeping. She had seen him disappointed, defeated, submissive, sunken completely inside his own mind. She had pushed the limits of all his moods and rules, tried to cheer him up when he was uncheerable, taken advantage of his many forms of distraction, learned when she had no choice but to ask for pizza and eat it alone, but she had never seen her father truly angry. Not at work, not at politics, not at Nina's mom, and certainly not at Nina herself. The moment she saw the look on his face, she started to cry with confusion and fear.

He didn't punish her. Didn't shout. Coldly, he informed Nina there was a reason his books were off-limits. There was a reason his study was off-limits, and if she couldn't understand or respect that, he would be forced to get a lock. Nina wept and apologized. She promised she understood. She respected. She'd never do it again.

Later, he apologized. He had overreacted. In high school, she made good use of the incident, flinging it in his face whenever she wanted more privacy. In college, she went on a Roth kick of her own, which swiftly explained her dad's anger. He was a single father who didn't date, whose ex-wife had checked out, and whose own mother was about as cozy and approachable as a python. He was working hard to be a good, feminist parent to a daughter with no available female role models. The idea of little Nina discovering male sexuality via Philip Roth must have terrified him to no end.

Until the day she opened *Guerra Eterna*, Nina had never wondered if there was some darker explanation. It hadn't occurred to her that her dad's bookshelves could have held a secret. Who would think that? What delusional person would have looked at her father's post-move stacks of still-unboxed books last month and suspected he'd left them sitting in a corner because hidden in one of those cartons was a deckle-edged, black-jacketed reminder that he had a long-lost daughter? And what would Nina do—the thought filled her with panic—if he didn't? If she was wrong? It was completely plausible that Manuela was fictional, or her daughter was, in which case Nina would be marshaling her hopes and furies for no one.

NINA WADED HOME THROUGH THE HEAT. Every street sloped uphill. Her dress clung to her. In her bag, the book swung and shifted, digging its sharp corners into her hip. In a cartoon, it would glow poison green or wobble at its edges. In a horror movie, it would ooze blood. Avenida Santa Fe was nearly empty, everyone home with their families, and Nina imagined crawling up the sidewalk on her hands and knees.

In her apartment, she drank water as if she'd just crossed a desert. She reached blindly into the fruit basket and, moments later, discovered herself on the balcony, holding a cucumber. She ate it like a banana, crunching through the waxy, bitter skin. The seeds were slick and faintly sour. Across the street, lights flickered in kitchen windows, though the sky was bright as noon. White-feathered pigeons bobbed along railings. Nina tossed her cucumber butt at one. She nearly hit it, which made her feel even worse.

Faults and flaws boiled around her. Not the book's or her father's: her own. She was self-obsessed. Overreactive. A drama queen. A story leech sucking up other people's pain. In college, she'd tried to wear her dad's grief like hand-me-down clothes. Now she was—what? Nina dropped herself into the hammock stretched across the balcony. If she was wrong, she knew, her dad would forgive her. If she called home making wild false allegations of treachery, cowardice, snakehood, and sister-hiding, her dad would barely take offense. Within weeks, he would turn it into a sad joke. Nina's Conspiracy Theory. He'd give it to Nico to tease her about.

The thought of Nico set off a new and useful flare of anger. If Nina was right, then Nico, too, had kept a colossal secret from her. Nico, who had always been her ally and friend. She sat up, setting the hammock rocking. Before she could lose energy, she reached for her phone.

Her dad answered before the second ring. "Nina! I hoped it would be you."

His audible happiness made her teeth hurt. The back of her throat was spacious and arid. Her tongue tasted like cucumber skin. Maybe she could hang up. Pretend the call was a mistake. Pretend the book was a mistake. Pretend this whole semester was a mistake and tell her dad she was flying home tomorrow to start her adulthood anew.

"Nina? You there?"

"Sorry," she croaked. "I'm here." She reached for her water. Her blood seemed to have slowed down. Her hair stuck to her neck. She felt sullied. The thought that she'd been discussing Scorpio personality traits with Fabiana three hours earlier struck her as unfathomable.

"Are you all right?"

"Are you in a book?"

The question emerged alongside an ugly, alien-sounding giggle. Fear laughter. It made Nina feel completely deranged. Maybe she was suffering from Victorian-type hysteria. Maybe having a crush on a single dad was inducing a full Freudian meltdown.

Her dad waited until the laugh petered out. Gently, he asked, "What book?"

"The fucking—" Nina flailed for the title. The Book, she wanted to call it. "*Guerra Eterna.*"

The line hissed like running water. Nina saw her life fork in two. Down one road, her sister—her mysterious, never-located, years-older half sister—was waiting. Down the other, Nina was still the only female Lazris on earth. ·

She heard her dad cough. "*Guerra Eterna,*" he said. "Yes."

The world seemed to speed up instantly. Taxis shot down Azcuénaga. Sparrows hurtled through the sky. Nina wrapped her fingers tightly through the hammock's weave, imagining her dad in the maroon reading chair in his study. He'd have the lamps on, the *Tribune* and *Times* creased beside him. He'd be wearing a horrifying decades-old sweater and an equally heinous pair of khakis from the pile Nina had designated house-only. Behind his reading glasses, his lashes would already be spiking with tears.

"Yes," she echoed, checking.

"Yes."

She considered parroting him once more. Their conversation could be built entirely of yeses. When she was very little, she and her grandfather had had a routine derived from a Winnie the Pooh cartoon in which she climbed onto his lap, pressed her nose to his, and inquired, Yes?, to which, always, he replied, Yes?, and so on, till she collapsed inevitably into laughter. But she had already tried helpless laughter on this phone call, and she wouldn't say that it had improved her emotional state.

"I was afraid this would happen," he said.

Nina didn't respond. Afternoon light fractured in her eyes. She rubbed them and glowered at the small cast-iron table before her, the three unwatered ficuses in their terra-cotta pots, the shriveling pink geraniums in her neighbor's window boxes.

Who planted geraniums? Junk flowers. Terrible flowers. Bodega-bouquet rot-petaled pieces of Barbie-doll shit.

She took a deep, yogic breath, which had no more of a calming effect than tossing cucumbers at pigeons had. Hatred and excitement seethed equally through her. She felt like a Medusa, except instead of snakes, she had emotions writhing and snapping in all directions. It seemed possible she would never again feel settled within herself; that when she asked her dad why he'd lied to her, why he'd denied her a sister, her psyche would splinter in some catastrophic and irreparable way.

Her dad cleared his throat. "I should have told you."

"Why didn't you?"

"I was scared."

"Of?" Nina asked, sitting up. The hammock bounced beneath her. Somebody's window air conditioner rattled and groaned against the heat. A Don Omar song, the one with the hands-in-the-air dance, floated to her on the breeze, nearly setting her laughing again. It was ridiculous to hear music now. Ridiculous to notice her body, or the weather, or the birds flirting on the phone lines. Ridiculous to think any single, fleeting thought that was not about her family.

"She was my responsibility. She and Caro were. I promised to protect them, and I didn't. American passport, tannery money—didn't matter. I couldn't keep them safe. I was afraid of you knowing that."

He sounded as if he wanted to continue, but Nina cut him off. "Who's Caro?"

"In the book, she has some made-up name. Her real name's Caro."

Nina felt a pang of absurd loss. "Not Manuela."

"No."

"Caro," Nina said experimentally. "Short for Carolina?"

"Carolina Ravest Giaconda." It was awful to hear the warmth with which her father spoke.

"She's not from Valparaíso."

"No."

"And you didn't tell me about her because you couldn't protect her?"

Her father hesitated. "No parent wants their child to think of them as a failure."

"You think you're a failure?"

"I *know*."

Nina screwed her eyes shut. Sorrow flooded through her. She heard the list her dad wasn't reciting: failed Communist, failed activist, failed lover, failed protector, failed parent, failed friend. Nico always said her dad believed he should have been able to save Andrés somehow. Maybe he'd never actually—or never only—been talking about Andrés.

"I wanted to give you a real sister," her dad said. "Not a missing one."

"She can be both."

"I know." After a moment, he added, "Your whole life, I've been hoping you would never read that book."

"Then why'd you teach me Spanish?"

"In case I found your sister. I wanted the two of you to be able to talk. I thought that way you could have a relationship, even if she didn't want one with me."

Nina screwed her eyes shut. Sorrow washed over her. She imagined her little self—six, seven years old, mystified by adult women but already longing to be one—barraging her sister with relentless, worshipful questions: How old are you? Where do you live? Can I sleep over? Can I spend two nights? After I go, will you miss me? Were you lonely before you knew me? Are you happy you met me? Do you know how to French-braid my hair?

Her dad's voice cut through her thoughts. "How did you find it?"

"The book?"

"Yes."

"Recommendation," Nina said, feeling sicker at the thought of Ilán. The fantasizing corner of her mind suggested, with inappropriate cheer, that his role in her life-changing discovery would someday become key to their marital origin story. Her long-lost sister would mention it in her wedding toast. It would be difficult to find a bridesmaid dress that flattered both six-foot Hazel and Nina's sister, who was presumably closer to Nina's five foot five, but surely it could be done.

Nina told the fantasizing corner to shut the fuck up. "Do you have a copy?"

"In my safe."

"It used to be in your office."

"Yes. Till you started sneaking my books."

"Who else knows about it?"

"In your life? Only Nico. And he always wanted to tell you. Fought me on it every time he visited. He still lobbies me all the time." Her dad slipped into Spanish, into his imitation of Nico's warm growl. "'Come on, Gabriel. Don't be an asshole. Nina deserves to know.'"

Relief rolled through Nina. It was her first unmixed emotion since the train, and it depleted her will to be angry. She loved Nico. It would have been horrible to be mad at him too. "Who else?"

"No one else knows about the book. Your grandparents knew Caro."

Her grandparents. Christ. Nina would be willing to bet that her grandmother, who in her final decade was constructed entirely of spite and SlimFast, had relished keeping secrets from her only granddaughter, but she'd have thought her grandfather would refuse to withhold. He always said that after Chile he swore off three things: drinking, lying, and irritating his son. He succeeded, too. When Ray died, Nina's dad said in his eulogy that his father was proof the human animal was capable of real and lasting change.

Ray must have kept Caro a secret to keep his son happy. Nina could think of no other explanation—unless her grandfather, too, had been ashamed. He was an adult in 1973. He was rich, influential, politically connected through both the *Courier* and the CIA. He was the one who would have been responsible, ultimately, for protecting his son's pregnant girlfriend. If he didn't shield her, or if he tried but didn't succeed, then he'd failed Caro—failed the whole family—infinitely more than Gabriel had.

Nina willed her dad to keep talking. She counted half a minute of silence before asking, "How well?"

"I told them she was pregnant." He laughed unhappily. "I had to. Her family's food rations weren't enough, and if I had stolen from our kitchen, your grandmother would have blamed Luz."

Nina swallowed more cucumber-tasting spit. Her palate was painfully tight, her throat hard and sore. She had loved her grandfather very much. She kept as treasures the little objects she'd collected from his apartment after he died: the soapstone sea lion, the baseball mitt made from the tannery's leather, the silver-framed wedding photograph that stood on his nightstand decades after his marriage fell apart. She had never held his historical crimes, for which she knew he was sorry, too much against him, never even resented his lingering right-wing politics. Suddenly she wished she had. It would have been good practice for blaming him now.

Before she could speak, her dad said, "He tried to evacuate Caro with us. Tried to get her out after too. Nobody would help him: no one in the CIA, no one in the embassy." His voice turned acrid. "None of them gave a shit. Not a single one."

"Was that why he quit the CIA?"

Her dad gave another rough laugh. "The CIA cut him loose. Didn't need him. His old contacts stopped taking his calls."

Nina couldn't imagine a person refusing her grandfather. She had known him as a tiny, bullish old man, a leather magnate with a shameless Chicago honk. He was charming like bright weather is charming: overt, undeniable, liable to change. He claimed that he had acquired charisma only in old age, but in 1973, charismatic or not, he had been as connected as a person could get. He was an industrial heir, an influential newspaper editor, a spoke in the CIA's vast wheel. All that was, apparently, enough for him to protect himself and his son, but not his half-Chilean granddaughter. His country sheltered only its own.

"Remember, he was just an asset," her dad said. "Not an officer."

"I know."

The hammock swung beneath her. She could almost feel the earth turning. To become a sister at twenty-eight was, she told herself, a transformation and a gift. "How long was Caro your girlfriend?" she asked.

"Five months."

"You knocked her up in five months?"

"Less than three."

The hammock's rope bit into Nina's thighs. She remembered how conscientiously her dad had described birth-control options when she entered high school. He'd explained the pill, the patch, the pros and cons of Depo-Provera shots, the necessity of condoms but never condoms alone, even the last-minute exigency of the morning-after pill, then offered to either take her to a gynecologist now or drop the conversation until she was prepared to reintroduce it. But, he'd added, always good to be prepared.

"Why did she keep the baby?"

"Catholicism. And curiosity. Caro was always curious. I loved that about her."

"You loved her."

It wasn't a question. Still, her dad said, "I did."

Nina could hear him holding back tears. She pictured him hunched and sagging, like an old vulture come home to roost. How could she stop herself from pitying her father? How could she harden her heart against his? She had never in her life tried to hurt him. Never rebelled. She had always, always tried to protect him from sadness. It had been her job since she was three years old.

"Tell me what happened." She fixed her gaze on a hot blue patch of sky. "When you left her behind."

"It was the morning after the coup." His voice was toneless. Who could Nina call tonight to check on him? She hadn't met his new neighbors. She had no one to ask to drop by. "A man came to our house, American military of some sort. He said we had seats on a Red Cross flight. I tried to run, and he caught me and dragged me to the car. He wouldn't listen to a word your grandfather said. Neither would his superiors when we got to the airport. While my father tried to persuade them to send someone for Caro, I ran again, and a soldier—could have been Chilean or American; both were there—decked me."

"And?"

"And I woke up at cruising altitude with a broken nose."

Nina instinctively touched her own face. Her hand was burning hot. "Then what?"

"Then I was a Sidwell Friends senior, even though I could barely read English."

"Not what I meant." She tried hard not to conjure her father slumped and bleeding in an airplane seat; her father skulking through high-school hallways, nose crooked as a bat wing, friendless and uncomprehending. She told herself again not to pity him. She wanted to rip the pity from her chest like an organ, hold it over the balcony's wrought iron edge, and drop it to splatter onto the sidewalk below.

"Then Pinochet was in power. I couldn't go back. I hadn't found the solidarity movement yet—not till college—so I had no lines of communication. I'd call Nico and hear the wiretap buzz. He was agitating night and day. This was before he had to leave the country. His dad was bleeding cash, bribing half the military to keep Nico out of prison and working with the Association of Families of the Detained-Disappeared. Nico was looking for Caro and Andrés. He identified Andrés's body. You know that."

Nina knew. She'd talked to Nico. She'd seen YouTube clips of him on RTV Española at the start of his exile, weeping as he told a permed Spanish anchor that when he was summoned to Santiago's Hospital Militar, he convinced himself that he would be bringing his friend home from some awful, secret incarceration—sick, injured, mutilated in body and soul, but home. He believed that he'd gotten Andrés back even as a stone-faced soldier led him down the hospital stairs to the morgue, where he found Andrés's body in a condition so awful, so impossible to describe, that before even identifying him, Nico asked that his friend be cremated. No one, he told the anchor, should have to be buried like that.

"When he was in Madrid," Nina's dad continued, "he kept looking for Caro. I was looking too, but it was impossible. Her parents were too frightened to help. Nobody heard a word about her till *Guerra Eterna*."

"Who told you? Nico?"

"About the book?"

Nina wiped her eyes on her arm. "Yeah."

"It was a high-school classmate of ours. Raúl Colinao. He moved to Mexico in 1978."

"Exile?"

"Grad school."

"You kept in touch?"

"He was an early computer guy. He looked me up."

"Did he try to look Caro up?"

"I asked him to, but no luck. Nina, I hired detectives. I begged the publisher, but nobody in their office would talk. The human-rights organizations were looking too, not just Nico, but the book made their search much harder. The bookstore in Mexico City isn't real. The detectives couldn't identify Graciela Brechner. It was—" He paused. A grackle squealed overhead. "Horrible. The worst time in my life."

The sky blurred and dazzled. Tears slipped down Nina's cheeks. "What else did you do?"

"What else?"

"To find her."

"Nico gave speeches. He asked on TV, on the radio, in the Chilean papers once Pinochet was gone. We thought—" He gave a rough, humorless laugh. "Given the content of *Guerra Eterna*, we thought it might be counterproductive for me to be the public face of our search."

"Bullshit." She heard her voice rear upward. "You were ashamed."

"Nina," he said. "Of course I was."

She wished he would lie. She wanted him to defend rather

than debase himself, to stop putting her in a position where she could pity him, or empathize with him, or forgive his enormous dereliction of duty. He was right: he was a failure. All his talk of privilege, all his efforts to teach her to use hers wisely and warily, and what had he done with his? He ran the family tannery. He lived in the suburbs. He'd curled up in his safe, soft version of tragedy and let his firstborn daughter vanish from sight.

She glowered at the ficus trees. She wanted to drop-kick their clay pots into the street, hurl her phone in their dirt-trailing wake, and let her dad express his regrets to the ether. Her sister—*her sister*—was born in a clandestine prison. Lived in exile. Bore God knew what marks of her mother's trauma. And Nina, selfish, unserious Nina, was furious not because her sister had suffered, not because her dad had failed to save his first daughter, but because his cowardice had denied her something she wanted. A female relative. A bigger family. Even now, beneath her shock, she was happy. She was excited. She was a little girl gearing up to ask her sister to braid her hair.

She let out a long, shuddering breath. Overhead, the sun loosed orange rays. A pigtailed Yorkie yapped on the next balcony, pressing its wet little snout through the bars. Very briefly, Nina permitted herself to close her tear-sore eyes and see her sister cradling a dog or holding a dog's leash in one hand and pushing a stroller with the other, buckling her baby into a playground swing and letting the child sail safely into the sky.

Somehow the image drained her. Never before had optimism exhausted her energy. She said, "I'm going to look for my sister."

"I know you are."

"And I'm hanging up now." She counted down from five. "I love you."

"Nina—" her dad began, but she lowered the phone from her ear. She muffled the speaker. Child that she was, she ended the call before he could say he loved her too.

NINA WOKE ON MONDAY filled with grief and resolve. Her brain seemed to contain only the looping words "my sister my sister my sister." She rescheduled her interviews, copy-pasting profuse apologies from one message to the next. She rain-checked drinks with Fabiana. She texted Ilán more Beyoncé. She booked a comically expensive Wednesday morning flight to Santiago, then emailed Nico saying she'd read *Guerra Eterna*, she wanted to find her sister, and could she please sleep in his guest room. She ate the strange foods of sadness: a half-wheel of smoked Gouda; seven of Paula's left-behind fiber crackers; two unspeakable bananas that practically melted when she opened their peels. She tried to find YouTube clips of Nico talking about Caro, but failed. She Googled Caro in all possible permutations—*Caro Ravest*, *Carolina Ravest*, *Carolina Ravest Giaconda*, *Caro Ravest daughter*, *Manuela Caro Guerra Eterna*, *Caro Ravest Guerra Eterna*, *Caro Ravest Graciela Brechner*, *Caro Ravest Gabriel Lazris*—and got only garbled, nonsensical hits. It was bizarre. How could a person be missing from the entire internet?

Nico responded in under an hour. He offered to retrieve her at the airport and to help in all possible ways with her search. *I remember how much you wanted a sister when you were little*, he wrote. *I can tell you now that it broke my heart*. It was a measure of Nina's inner state that the email made her burst into tears.

Once she finished crying, she proceeded to Twitter but found herself unwilling to ask the online world for help. She imagined the replies flooding in, the crackpots and conspiracists, the false leads—or, worse, silence. It had been less than a day. Nina couldn't handle that yet.

She locked her phone and laptop in her bedroom, knowing that if she had either in hand she wouldn't be able to stop Googling Caro's name. Without them, she settled on the fat velvet couch with *Guerra Eterna*, which she found she could neither read nor physically put down. She was treating it like a talisman, not a source of, what, facts? If Caro had a fake name, her employer didn't exist, and Graciela Brechner herself was unidentifiable, then how could Nina possibly trust a single detail the book had to offer?

She wished she could shake her academic training enough to temporarily accept a fictionalized truth, but she'd spent her adult life teaching herself to sort fact from half fact, then sweep the latter swiftly from her brain. Studying social media would be impossible otherwise. She'd go crazy, or get sucked into some Instagram sex cult, or wake up one day convinced the Jews planned 9/11 and she and her dad had just been left out. She couldn't reprogram herself to blur the line between true and false in a day.

She ditched the book and walked to the Disco supermarket on Calle Uriburu, where she bought a bottle of wine, a plastic clamshell of empanadas, and a fistful of yellow Bon o Bon candies. At home, she found herself with an appetite only for the wine, which she drank in the bathtub. She went to sleep mercifully early but woke at five thirty on Tuesday morning, slightly hungover and anxious to the point of physical dislocation. All day she tripped on carpets, banged her shins on tables, bit her tongue. She got distracted drinking water and dumped half a glass down her chest. She burned her ear with her blow-dryer—a foreseeable accident, given her current state, but what could she do? Left to its own devices, her hair separated into three distinct textures, like sedimentary rock. Not a good look for a potential date.

She still didn't know whether tonight's dinner was romantic or platonic, but the question was helpful to worry about. The more she fretted over Ilán, the less she fretted over how strange and possibly terrifying it would be to find herself in Santiago, or how many times she would cry in front of Nico, or how unfathomably hard it would be to track her sister down, or whether her sister would hate her for it if she did. Much easier to think about Ilán.

Nina told herself to relax as she finished her hair and did her makeup, as she debated sex bra vs. regular—she went with the latter, to avoid jinxing herself—and sent Hazel a flurry of texts. It was one dinner. She wasn't getting married. She probably wasn't even going to take her dress off. She certainly wasn't going to mention her discovery. No matter what happened between her and Ilán, it would be important to create separation between him and *Guerra Eterna*. Put them in two different buckets in her mind.

At first, she did an excellent job not talking about the book. Ilán had created a very calming atmosphere. Candles burned in his living and dining rooms, and soft folk music wafted from a wooden speaker set. Steaks hissed in a cast-iron pan on the stove, somehow not spitting their grease on Ilán's impeccable button-down. He had a blue linen apron tied over it, which Nina found both endearing and hot. No yarmulke, she noticed as he poured her a glass of Malbec. No yarmulke and no fringes. He offered her a bowl of wrinkled, oily olives, then instructed his daughter, who was already in her pajamas, to give Nina an apartment tour, which was ideal. It let Nina settle into her presence here, and let her assess Ilán via his house. He had overflowing bookshelves, ornate red rugs, and a leather couch, which Nina would have imagined she'd hate, but this one was a soft, battered mocha she loved. Maybe it appealed to the tannery heiress in her, or maybe she just liked Ilán's taste.

She certainly liked his child. Rebeca had the knowing eyes and pink cheeks of a child star and a comfort with adults that reminded Nina strongly of her own little self. Her tour highlighted five main attractions: the toy box, the windowsill herb garden, the spiral staircase connecting the apartment's two floors, the *Illustrated Encyclopedia of Whales and Dolphins*, and the gigantic Shepard Fairey print framed on the living room wall.

"That," Rebeca explained in lilting English, "is Obama."

Nina suppressed a laugh. "I know. I voted for him."

Rebeca nodded gravely. "You came from America."

"I did."

"Which is why I'm remembering to speak English."

"Exactly," Ilán called from the kitchen. "Very good." The scent of seared meat, mixed with the clean bite of cilantro, accompanied his words. Nina was, she realized, very hungry. Her lunch in San Isidro had been her last normal meal.

Rebeca seemed uninterested in positive paternal reinforcement. She hopped on her left foot as she informed Nina, "I have three American friends. Obama is one. Second Becca is two. And Lady Gaga is three."

"Second Becca?" Nina asked, and, in short order, discovered herself sitting on Rebeca's bedroom floor, solemnly shaking hands with the little girl's prized possession: a Jewish American Girl doll named Rebecca Rubin. According to the company-provided backstory in the book Rebeca showed Nina, the doll was the child of Russian immigrants. She spoke Yiddish at home with her parents, who called her Beckie, and at school, she used her full name. But here, in the Radzietsky household, she was Second Becca.

Nostalgia welled in Nina as she flipped through the American Girl book and admired Second Becca's wardrobe. She noticed the snarls in the doll's nylon hair, which matched those in her own long-ago American Girl doll's ratty braids. When Nina was little, the American Girl company hadn't yet introduced Rebecca Rubin, so she'd had Kirsten, a Swedish immigrant whose family homesteaded in—Minnesota? North Dakota? Somewhere in the Upper Midwest. Nina remembered the doll's backstory less now than she did her dad's efforts to use Kirsten to teach her about the hardships of farm labor and rural life.

It had been easily fifteen years since Nina had thought about Kirsten. Now, to her absolute mortification, she felt tears building at the memory of cuddling the doll. Kirsten was the only toy Nina never dropped down the laundry chute. Not because she was breakable, though she might have been, but because Nina was forbidden to drop herself down, and any rule that applied to her applied to Kirsten. For years of her childhood, Nina pretended—of course she did—that the doll was her sister. She wondered now if Rebeca did the same with her doll.

To stop herself from asking, she offered to do Second Becca's hair. Rebeca was so thrilled she leapt to her feet. As Nina began braiding, she heard Ilán's feet on the iron staircase, but she continued. He'd be charmed, she hoped, to find her cross-legged on his daughter's bright rug, tucking the doll's hair into place. When he entered the room, she smiled up at him, spinning the doll to display her half-finished handiwork.

"Welcome to the salon," she said.

Ilán beamed. "I think you just made a friend," he said, tipping his head at his daughter. "Much better than my braids, right, Rebeca?"

The little girl laughed conspiratorially. Behind her hand, she stage-whispered to Nina, "He only does really bad braids."

"I bet," Nina told her. "Know what?"

"What?"

"How old are you?"

Rebeca lifted a hand, splaying her tiny fingers wide. "Five!"

"When I was five, I lived with just my dad, and he couldn't braid hair at all." Nina screwed her mouth into exaggerated disdain. "He couldn't even do pigtails."

Delight spread over the little girl's face. When Nina flicked her gaze to Ilán, she saw that she had, in fact, charmed him. More than charmed. The look in his eyes tugged some string inside her. She stood as he said, in a voice calmer than his expression, "YouTube tutorials haven't gotten me very far." Then he switched to Hebrew, addressing Rebeca in a low, no-nonsense tone.

She scowled. "We said English for Nina."

"True."

"So tell me in English."

If Ilán was annoyed, he hid it admirably. To Nina, he said, "Our steaks are resting downstairs. And you"—he returned his attention to Rebeca—"should be resting upstairs. Your bedtime was half an hour ago."

Rebeca held up a finger. "One song?"

"One," Ilán agreed.

"From Nina?"

Ilán snorted. Rebeca looked longingly at Nina, who felt a full blush sweep her face and neck. She reached for her wine, thanking God she'd brought it upstairs. She knew acquiescing would both thrill Rebeca and up her chances with Ilán. She also knew she was brutally tone-deaf. She had never in her life been shy, but she'd started mouthing along to "Happy Birthday" in middle school. She wouldn't do karaoke unless she was blackout drunk. And yet, to her total astonishment and partial distress, she found herself Googling the lyrics to "Wagon Wheel," perching amid the stuffed dolphins on Rebeca's bed, and, in two verses and a chorus, singing Ilán's daughter to sleep.

Ilán and Nina waited a moment, listening to Rebeca's steady breath, before he ushered Nina downstairs, refilled her wine, and vanished to the kitchen to carve the meat. As he carried their plates to the table, he said, "Thanks for the lullaby."

"Thanks for tolerating my voice."

"Your voice?"

"It's awful."

"So?" Ilán shrugged. "You made Rebeca's night."

Nina tucked her hair behind her ears. The meal Ilán had cooked—gold-crusted potatoes and scarlet-centered slices of skirt steak, with oily green chimichurri drizzled over both— was beautiful. His red-patterned china was beautiful. His apartment was aesthetically pleasing from crown-molded ceiling to hardwood floor. Against her will, she wondered if he'd moved in here before, during, or after his marriage.

She returned her focus to Ilán. "Let me guess. Rebeca imprints on women since the divorce?"

"You could tell?"

Nina remembered the kindergarten aide she'd begged to be her stepmom, the third-grade teacher whose L'Occitane lemon hand cream she'd stolen, the two-doors-down neighbor whose graceless walk she'd copied, the soccer coach whose name she'd doodled in her diaries. She'd never been able to help latching on to women. On Sunday afternoon, she hadn't been able to help rifling through Fabiana's bathroom cabinets, and she knew perfectly well that tomorrow at Ezeiza Airport, she would struggle not to buy a duty-free bottle of Fabiana's perfume. If Nina ever found her sister, it would take exceptional willpower to avoid imitating her speech, her movements, her clothes.

"Of course," she said. "I did it too."

Ilán met Nina's eyes, and desire drifted through her. In a distant portion of herself, she was amazed she was capable of feeling it, or feeling any non-sister-related emotion. She banished the thought, then took a bite of meat, which was iron-rich and sweet with fat. The chimichurri was salty and herbal, mildly briny, almost unbearably good.

"Holy shit." Nina swallowed. "Ilán. This is delicious."

He grinned. "Welcome to Buenos Aires, steak capital of the world."

"Don't give the city credit. You cooked."

She wanted to ask if he'd always been a good cook, or if he'd learned post-divorce. Had he sought out perfect steaks while living in D.C.? Blown his PhD stipend on extravagant kosher meats? Was this steak even kosher? The inconsistencies in Ilán's performance of Judaism baffled her. He wore a yarmulke in the street but not the house; he taught his daughter Hebrew; he had a giant gelatin silver print of two Hasids in a chaste but plainly loverlike pose on the dining-room wall; he kissed her cheek in greeting; he'd brought a butter dish to the table, though mixing milk and meat was treif. Nina was stumped.

"Ilán, would it be rude to ask if you keep kosher?"

He pressed his napkin to his mouth. "Not rude at all. And I don't."

"Have you ever?"

"As a kid. My family is Orthodox."

"You're not?"

He hesitated. "Yes and no. I moved out of Once—the Orthodox neighborhood here—when I started university. I thought I would become totally secular."

"But?"

"But I never stopped wishing I believed in God. I'd still like to. And once Rebeca was born, I wanted her to have the option of belief."

"Is that why you taught her Hebrew?"

"In part. Also, Jewish kids here tend to learn it. Much more normal than in the States." He grinned. "Scared I was a Zionist?"

Nina blushed again. "Possibly."

"Hard not to be, in my family. Not as hard as atheism, though."

"You must have been so confused as a kid."

"Only about the rules." Ilán looked sheepish. "It made no sense to me that all the adults I knew acted as if some big man in the sky would spit on me if I ate bacon, or strike my mom with lightning if she forgot her wig."

Nina broke into laughter. Tears rose into her eyes, remnants of her Second Becca–induced swell of emotion. She willed them back, drank some wine, and told Ilán, "When we were walking to Rapanui the other day, an air conditioner dripped on my face, and I took it as a sign God didn't want me to flirt with you."

"God probably didn't," he agreed. Beneath the table, he brushed his knee against hers, which was the exact right mix of assertive and adolescent to set her scalp prickling with arousal. "But I did."

After that, Nina had to exert all the control in her body to eat her steak like the luxury it was, not wolf it down like a Whopper. She devoured her potatoes in six ravenous bites. She no longer noticed the chimichurri's complexity. The meal Ilán had presumably spent hours cooking was no match for her overwhelming desire to push his chair back and climb onto his lap.

But Nina knew the erotic virtues of stalling. She waited till Ilán was done eating, then bused the table and, over his objections, washed the fragile china and the battered tongs. She scrubbed the cast-iron pan with salt and oil, pressing her thighs together to better appreciate the warm pressure climbing between them. She kept herself at the sink until Ilán, finally, wrapped his arms around her from behind.

"Nina," he said softly. "Stop cleaning."

She turned. He bit her lower lip. Not a kiss: only a bite. Nina held still as Ilán moved his mouth—moved his teeth—to her earlobe, then the taut cords of her neck. His biting was gentle to the point of delicacy, and made her feel as if she were floating outside her skin.

Nina warned herself that he might not want to have sex. It was their first date. His daughter was sleeping upstairs. He might have lingering religious notions of propriety, which, if she wanted to be a good person, she knew she'd have to respect. Also, historically speaking, she knew that the more patient she was now, the more likely she was to have an orgasm later. If she obeyed her impulse to drag Ilán to the jute kitchen floor mat, unbuckle his khakis, and give herself rug burn sucking his cock, she would radically reduce her own chances of coming, but she couldn't help it. She hauled him to the ground.

Nina hadn't reckoned with Ilán's historical knowledge. Not until she was on her back, knees blurring in her peripheral vision, did it occur to her that she'd wasted a decade of her life not having sex with formerly married men. No think-tank Jared or grad-school Josh had ever—Jesus Christ—gone down on her this well. She felt as if she'd never gotten head before. She might as well not have. He made some new motion with his tongue, and her sight scattered into bright circles. She was coming before he could even get a finger inside her, which didn't deter him. Before the orgasm was over, he began working on the next one.

Eventually, he carried her to the couch to have penetrative sex, which, at that point, was a pleasant afterthought to Nina. She felt like a rag doll, though a rag doll who was still enjoying herself very much. She kept her sounds to an absolute minimum, conscious of Rebeca sleeping upstairs, but Ilán, she noticed, shivered at even her slightest gasp. After her trip to Santiago, she'd invite him over and be loud.

He rose almost the moment he came. Nina watched him peel off the used condom and take it to the bathroom. She felt as if her eyes had been pinned open. She was grateful he'd gotten up. She needed a second to settle back into herself. If Ilán were still on the couch, she probably would be offering to become his full-time sex prisoner—which, frankly, sounded ideal. She could renounce all deep thought. All thought, period. No sister search, no PhD, no nothing. She could become a career recipient of oral sex.

Ilán went from bathroom to kitchen, returning with the half-empty wine bottle, a fridge-cold carafe of water, and two clean glasses. He set them down and leaned over Nina for a kiss. "I hope," he said, "you enjoyed yourself as much as I did."

"Statistically speaking, I think I enjoyed myself more."

"Would you like wine?" he asked. "Water?"

The roof of Nina's mouth felt stretched dry. A faint cramp pulsed in her left calf. Sex dehydration. She asked for a glass of water, then, fearing a UTI, drained it in a single gulp and went to pee.

On her return, they sat quietly, Nina's legs stretched over Ilán's lap. Somehow he looked sturdier naked than clothed. He had thick curls of chest hair, a small divot beneath his sternum, the smallest possible layer of fat over his stomach and hips. His legs were corded with muscle; his feet turned nearly 45 degrees out from the ankles, duckfooted even at rest. Except for his forearms and hands, his skin was paler than hers, with visible veins snaking under his collarbone.

Ilán cocked his head toward her. "Looking at me?"

"Appreciating."

He laughed. "Good."

"I have to go out of town tomorrow."

"Already?"

Nina nodded. Her urge to resign from clothed life was gone, replaced by an impulse to tell Ilán about her sister. It was, she knew, oxytocin-based. After sex, she was hormonally disposed to be trusting and vulnerable. But not after all sex. Very little of the sex she'd had in D.C. inspired her to confide in her partner. Mostly, it inspired her to Uber home.

"Already. But only for five days."

"I thought you were going to the Nisman demonstration Thursday."

"I was. But I need to leave town."

"For research?"

"Kind of." She paused, waiting to feel daunted or agitated, but the anxiety that had dogged her all day barely surfaced. She liked the idea of testing her new self on Ilán. Not testing: she was someone's sister. That was a fact, not an experiment. And if she was truly committed to finding her sister, then why not tell him? He knew that her Nisman project was still nascent. He also knew the different pulls of academic and family life. She doubted he'd judge her for moving her attention from the former to the latter. It was a reasonable and adult thing to do.

"You don't have to explain," he told her.

"I'd like to."

She poured herself some wine. Ilán shook his head when she offered the bottle. A pair of thick white candles burned on the coffee table. Their warmth made the room seem soft and fuzzed at its edges. Out the window, she saw TV aerials framing a lone, blinking orange light. Nina watched it appear and disappear as she explained that the nameless daughter in *Guerra Eterna* was her half sister. Nina had had no idea. She'd thought she was an only child. Without Ilán's recommendation, she might never have learned that her sister existed. He had completely changed her life.

"No pressure," she added.

"Why would I feel pressure?"

"I—" She reached for her wineglass, feeling highly conscious that she was naked. Surely she should have realized before she began talking that this would be a shirt-on conversation. "I don't want you feeling obligated to me."

Ilán's face filled, swiftly and alarmingly, with mischief. "You mean I shouldn't feel obligated to date you out of guilt for accidentally changing your life, then having sex with you on my kitchen floor?"

Nina burst into astonished laughter, which made Ilán grin hugely. He looked like a hot Cheshire Cat. "Am I right?"

She nodded, helpless. "Completely."

"Well." His voice softened. "I do feel bad, but not guilty. Only sorry. And my feeling sorry has no bearing on my wanting to cook you dinner again. Is that all right with you?"

Nina sank as low into the couch as she could. Ilán's kindness made her feel like a small, exposed animal, a lost dog in a field far from home. "No," she said, doing her best to sound brave.

"No?"

"When I get back, I want to cook for you."

He cocked his head. "I thought you said you couldn't cook."

"You don't give a girl a break, do you?"

"Do you want breaks?" he asked. From his tone, Nina could tell that he knew the answer, which was that she did not; she never had. Instead of saying so, she twisted around for a kiss, which lasted long enough she thought it might turn into sex. Before it could, she straightened and returned to explaining her Chile trip. She had, she told Ilán, three reasons for buying a last-minute ticket to Santiago. First, she felt compelled to start looking for her sister immediately; second, she wanted to see Nico in real life, not through a screen; and third, her entire identity was scrambled, and she felt as if she had to take some decisive, dramatic action. She needed to create a point of visible separation between her only-child and sister-having selves, and, besides flying to Chile, what was there for her to do?

While she spoke, Ilán didn't move. He made no sounds—no little noises of agreement, no affirmations—but he didn't lower his eyes from her face. It was as if he were listening with his whole body. Nina had never felt so exposed.

He waited a moment after she finished. She braced herself for a big display of empathy, but all he said was "You come back Monday?"

"Tuesday."

"Could I pick you up at the airport?"

She blinked. "You want to?"

He squeezed her hip lightly. "I do. We could go out to lunch, unless you really do need to cook for me."

Nina smiled—a shaky smile, but real. "I can subject you to my cooking some other time," she said. "Lunch when I get back sounds great."

NINA BOARDED HER FLIGHT to Chile in a state of total psychic disorder. Her body buzzed with sex hormones. Her mind shrieked with fear. Sitting in her window seat for two and a half hours felt impossible. Sleeping was not an option. She tried to corral herself into finishing *Guerra Eterna* but couldn't stop wondering about the author. She understood why Paula reacted so strongly to the book's femaleness. Graciela Brechner devoted long passages to Caro's tandem struggle to trust day care workers and pay for day care; to her period, which vanished for months at a time; to her compulsive need to sweep and mop her apartment floor daily, even while dirty dishes overtook her counters and sink. It seemed highly unlikely even to Nina, child of a single father, that a male writer would evoke emotional distress via housework or childcare costs.

After two chapters, Nina quit reading and ordered a Bloody Mary from the beverage cart. In normal life, she wasn't a morning drinker, but this trip was several steps removed from normality, and her efforts to decode *Guerra Eterna* had not helped with her agitation. She could power the plane with the sheer force of her anxiety. The slightest shift in altitude made her stomach lurch. The smell of her seatmate's instant coffee made her want to puke. Possibly the drink was a mistake.

She spent the flight's second half watching clouds out the window, both eager and afraid to see Santiago take shape below. When the plane began to descend, she found herself illogically disappointed that the city, from the air, looked ordinary. Not special. Not like the site of great and imminent discoveries, or of terrible suffering whose full extent might never be known. It looked like what it was: a contemporary mountain city, like Denver but bigger, in which roughly 5.5 million people commuted on clogged highways and lived in plate-glass condos and shopped at malls and played soccer and led historically undramatic lives.

Nina disliked herself for her dissatisfaction. Did she really think she could spot four-decade-old suffering from a plane window? What did she want to see? An evil red aura? A *Harry Potter*–style Dark Mark over La Moneda? A giant neon sign above a former clandestine prison, flashing the news that CARO RAVEST WAS TORTURED HERE?

It helped, if only marginally, that the plane landed smoothly. No big bumps, no skidding, no delay pulling up to the gate. A crew member welcomed everyone to Santiago de Chile, where the temperature was 28 degrees Celsius and the local time was 9:57 a.m., and, moments later, Nina was at Passport Control, explaining to an immigration officer named Sepúlveda that she was here to see a family friend.

"You never visited your friend before," Sepúlveda noted, flicking through her passport. He spoke in English, though Nina had addressed him in Spanish. The Argentine immigration officer had done the same. Her passport must override her accent, or else her accent was worse than she thought.

"He always came to visit us," she said, switching to English. Signs affixed to the glass partition between them warned her not to smuggle fruits, cheeses, or seeds into the country; instructed all Mexican and Australian nationals to pay their reciprocity fees in cash; and gave her a number to call if she was or suspected she might be a victim of human trafficking.

"In"—Sepúlveda glanced down—"Washington, D.C."

"In Chicago. I only moved to D.C. in 2012."

"You like it?"

"I do," Nina said, a bit baffled. Was this small talk, or the start of an interrogation? Why did Sepúlveda care if she liked where she lived?

She knew it was absurd to worry. She was a white woman with an American passport. Sepúlveda wouldn't waste time interrogating her. He stamped her documents and, as he slid them under the glass, asked, "Have you ever seen Obama?"

"Not up close, but I was in the crowd at both his inaugurations."

The answer seemed to please Sepúlveda. He looked her over once more, then instructed her to enjoy her time in Chile. Before Nina could thank him, he leaned forward, beckoning the Mormon missionaries who had been behind her in line. "Next!" he called. Briefly, Nina wondered if he'd ask them about Obama too.

She emerged into an arrivals hall overflowing with families. Little kids jostled against the three-foot barriers separating travelers from greeters, or waved hand-crayoned BIEN-VENIDO signs. A shrunken grandmother in a neat wool skirt untangled the ribbons of two balloons that glinted over her head like silver suns. Nina was smiling at her, imagining the grandkids she might be here to collect, when she heard a familiar roar.

"Nina Lazris! My favorite American!"

She hurried to greet him, sandals slapping at her heels. Nico drew her into a shoulder-crunching hug. The linen of his shirt was soft on her cheek, and he smelled, as always, like St Johns aftershave and tarry dandruff shampoo. Nina squeezed him as tightly as she could with her carry-on bag still swinging from her arms, then stepped back to look him over: deeper crow's-feet, the occasional age spot, and higher peaks in his ever-receding hairline, but otherwise, he was no different. He had aviator sunglasses tucked in his shirt pocket and wore immaculate loafers and a cracking leather belt. His pockmarked cheeks were shaved cleanly. His chest was still broad, his belly still decently in check. He looked fundamentally like he had in her childhood; really, he looked like her childhood itself.

Nina hugged him again. She closed and reopened her eyes. Her bladder was throbbing and her eyes stung in the airport's fluorescent light, but she didn't care. She felt newly centered.

Into Nico's shoulder, she said, in the Spanish she always spoke with him, "You have no idea how happy I am to see you."

IN CHILE, NICO WAS FAMOUS. Not famous enough to get approached in the airport, but Nina saw people glancing his way. Over the course of his adult life, he had been a human-rights activist, a symbol of exile and grief, a symbol of return and reconciliation, a Socialist Party functionary, a one-term Socialist senator, and an activist once again. He'd drunk coca with Evo Morales and picked flowers with José Mujica. A few years ago, he'd founded an international watchdog organization, and both his car and his condo were filled with its signs and brochures.

The condo was, unsurprisingly, lovely. Sleek furniture, marble counters, giant windows overlooking a riverside park. Nico led Nina to the kitchen and poured her a glass of water, which she gulped gratefully. She was feeling a bit more human than she had on the plane, thanks mainly to an arrivals-hall double espresso, but her brain still seemed to be shrinking away from her skull. She refilled her glass and took it to the living room, where the ugliest cat she'd ever seen observed her from the metal-legged couch.

"That's my friend Héctor." Nico made a kissing sound at the cat, who yawned, displaying his toothless gums. "I found him in the parking garage. He was starving. Now look at him."

"Highly nourished." Nina scratched behind the cat's ears. He was endearing in his ugliness, she decided. Later, she'd send a picture of him to Ilán.

"You don't have to be polite," Nico said. "He's fat."

She laughed. "He is. How long ago did you find him?"

"A year."

Nina settled into the couch, which was much cozier than it looked. She stroked the soft place under Héctor's chin, and he purred, which she found very gratifying. "I like him."

"Me too."

"Why is his name Héctor?"

"Why not?" He sat beside Nina. "Andrés loved cats. He was always chasing strays around the neighborhood, putting out milk for them at night, even when milk was hard to come by. Drove his mother crazy." He tickled Héctor's ears. "I never liked cats before this one. But Andrés wouldn't have left him to die in a gas puddle, so"—he shrugged—"here we are."

Nina would have liked to hug Nico, but she didn't want to stop petting the purring cat. Instead, she said, "I'm really glad to be here."

"I'm glad too." Nico looked directly at her. "Nina, I owe you an apology. I should have told you about Caro. I'm sorry you had to find out from that book." His lip twisted on the last word. Nina added him to a tally she hadn't known she was keeping: Ilán and Paula were pro–*Guerra Eterna*; Nico and Fabiana, against.

"Don't be sorry. This is 100 percent my dad's fuckup. Not yours." She meant to keep going, but a photo on the end table distracted her. She scooped it up to examine it. Nico, Andrés, and her dad leaned into each other, smoking and beaming. They were at a party, probably drunk, given how relaxed her camera-shy father seemed. Nico was handsome behind his acne; Andrés shone with confidence. "Who took this?" Nina asked.

"A classmate of ours. Ítalo Ibáñez. He had a photography phase. After Andrés died, Ítalo went through all his film for me. We weren't even in touch. A boxful of pictures just turned up at my parents' house."

"Can I see them?"

"Of course." Nico stood. "Now or later?"

Nina took brief stock of herself. Her skin felt greasy and desiccated; she was either hungry or suffering from travel stomach; fear whirred somewhere deep in her chest. She wasn't at the box-of-pictures stage. "Maybe later. After we eat."

"Excellent. I thought we'd go out for lunch, see some sights, then come home, drink some nice wine, and have our talk." He tilted his head. "Good plan?"

Nina looked toward the window. Santiago stretched beneath them, earthquake-proof buildings mixed with Colonial clay roof tile. In her dad's adolescence, she knew, the city had been filled with holes from earthquakes and construction. Now the swath of Santiago she could see looked not only complete but perfect. Parks shone like green tiles set between buildings; the river shimmered comfortably between its banks; streaky pink mountains rose behind glass-black skyscrapers, reflected in story after story of windows. It seemed like a city designed from scratch, not created and re-created over centuries. Like an organized city, a city with answers.

"Great plan," she said, rising. "I want the full Nico Echevarría tour."

FOR LUNCH, NICO TOOK HER, with great fanfare, to a nameless downtown bar that looked as if it had been separated from a Gothic castle at birth. It had rough stone walls, little diamond-paned windows, a huge wooden door covered in scratches and soccer-team stickers, and a hip-height chalkboard on the sidewalk outside, alerting passersby to the availability of SÁNGUCHES SALCHICHAS Y CERVEZA. A cartoon hot dog danced beneath the text, waving its little arms like a vaudeville star.

Once inside, though, Nico told Nina that she was under no circumstances to order a hot dog or sausage of any sort. The sandwiches at this bar were the best in Santiago, which meant the best in Chile, which meant the best, naturally, in the world.

Nina struggled to imagine a sandwich competing in either quantity or quality with the lomito Nico had her order. Marinated thin-sliced pork spilled from the bun, which was slicked with golden homemade mayonnaise top and bottom, then laden with sauerkraut and mashed avocado. The combination sounded awful, but was perfect: salt and brine in one mouthful, garlic and fat in the next. Nina loved it. She watched in awe as Nico devoured his, then worked his way through both their sides of french fries while she, slowly but surely, ate all of her sandwich but its meatless crusts.

After the lomitos, Nico led her on a long walk through downtown Santiago, which was much less architecturally ornate than downtown Buenos Aires. There, buildings had curlicued balconies, carved doors, bits of mosaics, strange little peaks and gables and flourishes. Here, concrete and plate glass had, for the most part, taken hold, presumably thanks to seismic activity. Frilly buildings like Buenos Aires's would be at risk here. Occasionally, Nina spotted a surviving Colonial church or the whitewashed facade of an old mansion, but gray box-buildings outnumbered them ten to one.

Santiago struck Nina as a notch calmer than Buenos Aires, in the way D.C. was calmer than New York. It had fewer tourists, fewer speed-walking suits, fewer taxis honking their horns. The lone exception was the soccer graffiti, which, as in Buenos Aires, was omnipresent and relentlessly dick-swinging. Apparently, God had created the sky; Colo-Colo, the stars. Also, betraying the Universidad de Chile team was a fate worse than death. Nina liked it. She'd always envied sports fans, but, except her lifelong crush on Scottie Pippen, she'd never been able to make herself care.

Their meandering gave way to not the Nico Echevarría tour but the Gabriel Lazris one. Nico led her from landmark to landmark, starting with a plaza that had often been the site of Communist Youth marches, including one that had doubled as Nina's dad's first date with Caro. "He took her to a demonstration on their first date?" Nina asked, laughing.

"He did."

"Was that cool or lame?"

Nico's mouth twitched. "Caro liked it. Andrés and I thought it displayed his complete lack of game. Much too earnest, first of all. And who can get a real kiss at a demonstration?"

The plaza gave way to a pedestrian-only street that led to La Moneda, but an officious, mustached cop told them the MERCOSUR leaders were convening in Chile at present, and access to the palace was therefore blocked. Nico reversed course, steering Nina instead to a beige, satellite-laden building that had been the *Washington Courier* until Gannett bought the paper and axed its international coverage.

Nina studied the windows, which looked blankly back. Half reflected the sky, half the street. She waited to feel generational guilt. In the years her grandfather worked in this building, he committed crimes against both journalism and democracy. He developed a drinking problem. He tanked his marriage and nearly wrecked his relationship with his son. How betrayed had he felt when his former CIA handlers refused to help Caro? Had he expected them to help, or had he known he didn't rank highly enough?

"Did you like my grandfather?" Nina asked.

"Ray?" Nico shrugged. "Barely knew him. Gabriel never brought us over. He was embarrassed to speak English around me and Andrés. He'd do it as a joke, or sometimes to piss a priest off, but he didn't like us hearing him talk to his parents."

The ex-*Courier*'s glass door swung open then, discharging two skirt-suited women carrying identical nylon messenger bags. Nina's grandfather had probably never worked with a woman, secretaries excepted. He was a reporter, then a tannery owner, then the terror of the North Shore retirees' poker-and-golf circuit, then dead. He admitted freely, in his waning years, that he'd been a terrible husband and father, but he worked hard to be a good grandfather. He'd died when Nina was in high school, and she still missed him often. She always thought that if she ever had a son, she'd name him Ray. Ray Radzietsky, she thought experimentally. Horrible name. She banished it—banished all thoughts of Ilán—and tried to feel connected to her grandfather, but the only emotions that surfaced were curiosity and a distinct sense of satisfaction at having seen his old office, even if it looked exactly like half the buildings in downtown D.C., or downtown anywhere else.

From the ex-*Courier*, Nico took her to the Basilica de la Merced, the last Catholic outpost on San Pedro Nolasco's old block. "All this," Nico said, waving his arm to encompass two copy shops, a Chinese restaurant, a bank, and a store that seemed to sell only window air conditioners, "all this was our school."

Nina tilted her head up, examining the brick towers that had replaced classrooms and courtyards. Laundry danced from balconies; plump birds bickered and preened. The basilica's rose window cast shattered beams of light on the sidewalk. An oilcloth banner bearing a Renaissance Madonna flapped beneath it. The walls were heavy with graffiti—including, confusingly, two Stars of David and one swastika—but the stairs and sidewalk seemed recently power-washed.

Two women sold pinwheels and toys on the corner. Palm

trees rustled overhead. Nina was sweating, but only slightly. A meek little cloud drifted over the sun. She wondered if she'd remembered to put on sunscreen, then decided not to care. She stepped back to clear space for a man on crutches, followed by two mangy, fly-circled German shepherds. More stray dogs here than in Buenos Aires, Nina thought, but less dog shit. A mystery.

"Were your school Masses here?" she asked, indicating the church.

Nico shook his head. "We had our own chapel. Much less nice."

She surveyed the block once more, picturing a teenage Gabriel Lazris jogging toward her from the bus stop, polyester tie fluttering over his shoulder, school bag flying open at his hip. She imagined teenage Nico lighting an illicit cigarette, Andrés looking tragic and doomed at his side. Then she caught herself. Andrés might have always been doomed, but at fifteen he wasn't tragic. He certainly hadn't looked tragic in the picture in Nico's living room. He looked content to the point of cockiness. Had Nico not told Nina who'd taken the picture, she would have assumed it was a girl Andrés thought he could date.

They resumed walking, weaving through suited businessmen and red-vested PedidosYa delivery workers, empanada vendors, and Jehovah's Witnesses hawking their plastic-wrapped literature. The smell of candied nuts wafted over the sidewalk, the wrong kind of sweetness for summer. Nina fanned her neck with her hair. Andrés drifted through her mind, persistently tragic. Old habits, she figured, died hard. After Scottie Pippen left the Bulls in 1998, Nina had transferred some portion of her preteen sexual yearning from the basketball star to her dad's dead friend. Morbid in retrospect, and mortifying—he could have been her fake uncle!—but to eleven-year-old Nina, who apparently had come early to romanticizing trauma, Andrés's doomedness was extremely hot.

She cut the thought off. No self-recrimination now. She should enjoy the Nico tour. Tonight would almost certainly be difficult; no point ruining the afternoon by scolding her sixth-grade self. She stepped over a gas-laden puddle, which flashed violet in the sun. The sidewalk around it was littered with sunflower-seed hulls, thanks, presumably, to a snack cart down the block. The proprietor's Mets jersey strained to encompass his belly; his sneakers were toothbrush-clean. In addition to seeds, he sold popcorn balls, visibly salty peanuts, and what looked like individual Ziploc bags of Cheetos.

"Snack?" Nico asked, pointing his chin at the vendor.

"Are you kidding? After that sandwich?" Nina rubbed her stomach through her thin dress. "We better be eating salad for dinner."

"I was thinking sushi."

"Sushi, I could do."

Nico looked pleased. "You know Chile has excellent seafood."

"I seem to recall somebody telling me." Nina smiled up at him. "Possibly telling me while eating American seafood."

"Which"—Nico poked a finger in the air—"is inferior."

"You should have visited me while I lived in Providence. I could have taken you to the Oyster Festival."

Nina had always loved the Oyster Festival. In college, she and Hazel went yearly to flirt with the oyster shuckers and test their fake IDs at the beer tent. Their first time, both were tentative with the slippery shellfish; their fourth, Hazel bet a boy in Vineyard Vines shorts she could outeat him and sucked down two whole platters of dollar oysters in, as Nina remembered, a minute and a half.

"I should have," Nico agreed, in a tone that clearly contained a "but." Nina waited, and after a moment, he sighed and said, "I was in a fight with your dad."

"You were?"

"Gabriel's hard to fight with, but I pulled it off."

Nina forced a laugh. She thought of her many panicked calls home freshman year, the nights she couldn't sleep for worry about her dad. It had never occurred to her that he and Nico could be fighting, that he could be down for any reason beyond her departure. She had been completely convinced she was the center of his world.

Nico steered them onto a narrow side street. Its buildings were all old, pitted sandstone, with carved cornices and abundant graffiti. Shade fell across the sidewalk, making Nina's arms prickle with sudden chill. She rubbed them, asking, "Why were you fighting?"

"I told him it was wrong to keep hiding Caro from you. I'd been telling him, but I got"—he chuckled—"more forceful. You were eighteen! You had a right to know."

"I did." Nina bumped her shoulder lightly into Nico's arm. "Thank you."

"Don't thank me. It didn't work. I pushed him too hard, and he snapped."

Nina had seen her dad truly lose his temper only once, the day he caught her swiping his books. "I didn't know he could still do that."

Nico snorted. "Till it happened, I thought he couldn't."

The street narrowed further, its asphalt giving way to cobblestone. For the first time, Nina had the sensation of being in an old city, a city with secrets, not answers. To their right was a small, arcade-style bookstore, doors flung open to show glass display cases filled with books. A poster of a balding man in eighties glasses hung outside—the winner, apparently, of the

Premio Nacional de Literatura 2014. Nina had no clue who he was. He could be Graciela Brechner, for all she knew.

Her mood, which had been rising steadily, started to falter. She wanted to reemerge into the sun. As she picked up her pace, Nico said, "In fairness to your dad, I fought dirty."

"How?"

"I sicced Caro's cousin on him. Alejandra. We're having lunch with her tomorrow."

"We are?"

"Brace yourself. She's tough. She ripped your dad a new one."

"Seems fair."

Nico didn't comment. "She's excited to meet you," he said, "in her way. She likes getting to talk about Caro. They were joined at the hip. Caro loved your dad, I think, but she loved Alejandra more than anyone. She wanted to name the baby for her."

Instantly, Nina's spirits bounced back up. "So she'd be Alejandra Lazris? Or Alejandra Ravest?"

Nico shook his head. "The idea was Alejandro for a boy, but a different *A* name for a girl, to avoid confusion. She and your dad had a whole list going, but when the coup happened, they hadn't narrowed it down—which," he added, "is how you ended up named for me, not Andrés. Your dad got all paranoid about giving you your sister's name."

"Typical." The idea of her dad working himself into a neurotic baby-name frenzy was both easily imaginable and more endearing than she would have liked. Nico was right: her dad was tough to be mad at. Without warning, she was keenly sad to be in Chile without him. He had, once upon a time, loved it here.

A bike messenger jounced down the cobbled street, wallet chain—why did all bike messengers, across continents, love wallet chains?—clanking. Two long-skirted women gossiped outside a pharmacy. Sad piano music swam from an apartment window. Once the song receded, Nina said experimentally, "Ana Lazris."

"Adela Lazris," Nico offered.

"Aurelia Lazris."

"Artemisia Lazris."

"Ariana Lazris."

"Antonella Lazris."

Nina pulled a face. "Antonella?"

"Why not?"

"Sounds like an ugly stepsister."

"Half sister," Nico corrected, looking both mischievous and concerned. He was good at displaying contradictory emotions simultaneously—a disconcerting skill to Nina, who rarely felt more than one emotion at a time, except ones that were already neighbors: sorrow and anger, excitement and anxiety. Maybe Nico could give her lessons, help her expand her inner range.

It occurred to Nina that if she were capable of experiencing her feelings simultaneously rather than sequentially, she would be much more concerned for her academic career. She'd rescheduled all her interviews, which likely meant that some would fall through. She was skipping tomorrow's big pro-Nisman demonstration, which definitely meant blowing her best chance to interview outraged, infrequently politicized citizens about their trajectory from online speech to in-the-streets action. Kuiper would be unhappy. Brian Ryan would be unhappy. The entire Center for Media and Social Impact would be unhappy. *She* should be unhappy. Instead, she felt freed.

She was happy to see Nico and even happier to have him on her side. She understood how difficult it would be, even with his help, to find Ana-Adela-Antonella Lazris-or-Ravest, and that coming to Santiago had brought her no closer to her sister than she'd been in Buenos Aires, but she felt herself moving in the right direction. Her natural optimism was flowering anew.

Her buoyant mood, combined with a much-needed nap, carried her through the afternoon. In the evening, Nico ordered sushi and uncorked the promised wine—chilled red, biodynamic, very fancy—while Nina set up her audio recorder. It felt silly to use it, as if she were playing academic, but she knew better than to trust her memory.

She didn't start taping till the sushi was gone. "Okay," she said, wiping the last trace of soy sauce from her mouth. Her new notebook, filled with incoherent moral questions, lay open on the table. Her throat burned with nerves. Nico hooked his right ankle over his left knee, leaning slightly back in his dining chair. He still had on his linen button-down, and, like Nina's dad, wore loafers even indoors. His clothes and posture made him seem like a late-night TV guest, relaxed and ready to joke with Stephen Colbert.

Nina swirled the sediment in her wine but didn't drink any. She reminded herself that Nico was used to interviews. He'd appeared on news shows across the Spanish-speaking world. Also, he'd been waiting twenty-eight years to tell her what she knew about Caro. She might be frightened, but for him, this conversation would almost certainly be a relief.

"Okay," she said, fighting the urge to switch to English. The recorder blinked at her. Be an academic, it suggested. Who knows? This could be the last time. "Nina Lazris interviewing Nico Echevarría," she told it. "February 17, 2015. Nico, could you begin by explaining the context for this conversation?"

He lifted an eyebrow. "Very formal."

She shrugged. "For the record."

"Fair enough." Nico reached for his wine. "This conversation should have started, I'd say, twenty-five years ago. If your father—who, to be clear, I love like a brother, no matter how wrong I think he is—had listened to me, you'd have known you had a sister your whole life. But since he did not accept my sage parenting advice, the context for this conversation is that you, Nina Lazris, my beloved namesake, just learned, thanks to a moderately famous and more-than-moderately bullshit book by a person calling him- or herself Graciela Brechner, that your father has a daughter he's never met."

Nina thought again of her conversation with Paula. "'Him- or herself'?"

"Can't rule anyone out."

"Do you have a mental image of the author?" Nina asked. "A made-up one, I mean." As she spoke, she realized she'd been constructing her own Graciela Brechner for days. The woman she envisioned was slim, white, stern-looking. Dyed hair, reading glasses, non-designer leather purse.

Nico shook his head. "Impossible."

"Why?"

"Too many false leads. In the eighties, I talked to four or five Graciela Brechners a year. All liars, of course."

"How could you tell?"

He rubbed the side of his neck. "Caro had a birthmark. A huge one. None of them knew."

Nina mirrored his gesture. The recorder blinked at her, reminding her to keep talking. How many recorders had Nico spoken to in the past decades? How many people had sat, tapes and cameras whirring before them, while he described his trips to Pinochet's prisons, or recounted the hideous hour he'd passed with Andrés's body in the Hospital Militar morgue?

"What did the birthmark look like?" she asked.

"Reddish and uneven. She hated it, but we had consensus that it was"—Nico looked embarrassed—"sexy."

"Who's 'we'?"

"The boys of Vitacura."

"All the boys in Vitacura thought she was hot, and she ended up dating my dad?"

Nico rewarded her skepticism with a laugh. "She picked him out at a party. Gabriel never could have made the first move. He had zero game. Less than zero."

"Still true."

"Not for lack of my trying to teach him."

"Caro didn't mind, though?"

"Not at all. Remember, before the coup, Americans were glamorous. Your dad hated not being Chilean, but to everybody else, he might as well have gone home to Miami Beach after school."

Nina laughed. In her dad's version of events, his nationality made him a near pariah; his religion made it worse. "Were Jews cool too?"

Nico shook his head. "Anti-Semitism was a real issue. Gabriel tried to overlook it, but he heard some ugly stuff. Andrés and I should've been more sympathetic. We didn't get it."

"Did Caro?"

"No idea. I do know she liked that he was different, if only because it kept him from being full of himself."

"Were you and Andrés full of yourselves?"

"Absolutely."

"Who was worse?"

"Andrés," Nico said promptly. "Cocky little fucker."

"See, my dad would never say that. I've never heard him say a bad thing about Andrés."

"Have you ever heard him say a bad thing about anyone?"

"Sure. Himself."

Nina meant to be flippant, but the answer was true enough to shame her. She dug in her mind for a quick redirect. "Whose party did Caro pick my dad out at?"

"Ítalo's. The kid with the camera."

"How'd she know him?"

"He knew girls. We thought he had a gift. Turned out he was gay. But Andrés was the real connection. He lived next door to Alejandra."

"Is that why Caro went to his house after the coup?"

Nico scowled. "She didn't."

"How do you know?"

"I was there."

Fear spiked in Nina's chest. She knew it was decades too late to panic, but she couldn't help it. "Nico. You could've been disappeared."

"I was lucky."

She bit her lip till it leaked salt. It was awful to imagine a life without Nico; worse to think she'd never have been born. If Nico, Caro, and Andrés had all vanished, she didn't think her dad would have survived the loss.

She knew better than to ask Nico to explain his luck, or Caro's lack of it. Either it was money or it was random. Dictatorships worked by arbitrary violence. If there was a logic to Caro's disappearance, it was only state terror. Nina understood that. She had spent months studying the Pinochet regime's displays of power. She'd read, till she felt sick, about the clandestine prisons where soldiers abused women with such impunity that one such site was still known as Venda Sexy, or "Sexy Blindfold."

"Is any part of *Guerra Eterna* true?" she asked.

Nico nodded. "I know Caro was in a secret prison."

Instantly, Nina was relieved. She hated herself for it. What kind of monster wanted that? Why should truth matter more than pain? She should have hoped every bit of the book—except, yes, the fact of her sister—was wrong.

"I know she gave birth to a girl there," Nico went on. "I

can't find records, but that shit-heel Aldunante swore under oath."

It soothed Nina slightly to hear Nico insult Carlos Aldunante, whom in public he pretended to respect. Aldunante had graduated from San Pedro Nolasco with Nico, but while Nico had dropped out of college to oppose Pinochet's human-rights violations, Aldunante had skipped college to perpetrate them. He served in, then led, a string of military death squads. In the dictatorship's waning years, he was struck by contrition, deserted his unit, and fled the country. He confessed his crimes in horrific detail to Nico, who by then was living in exile in Spain. After Pinochet finally called a plebiscite and was voted out, Aldunante returned to Chile, served three years in prison, then moved to New York. He remained in the city even now, giving TED Talks and writing long, smarmy Twitter threads about the seductive nature of fascism. Nico hated him.

"You know," Nico added, "Aldunante was a major Jew-hater. Tormented your poor dad."

"Seriously?"

"Yep. He was a real little dick. Always drawing swastikas on the walls."

Nina rubbed her eyes. Her dad had never mentioned that. He'd sat quietly while Nico bad-mouthed Aldunante dozens of times. What was his problem? Why could he never admit to his own suffering? He'd been in visible pain for Nina's entire life, and yet he couldn't even manage to tell her he'd gotten Jew-baited by a famous ex-torturer?

She rolled her shoulders down. Get it together, the recorder suggested. Get me some more facts. She asked, "What else in *Guerra Eterna* can you prove?"

"Not much. I have Caro's Mexican asylum paperwork from 1975. No record of her moving elsewhere or changing her name, but she could've done either." He passed a hand over his face. "I persuaded *Guerra Eterna*'s editor to show me a release she signed, so I know she didn't write the book herself."

It hadn't occurred to Nina that she could have. "Too bad."

"I know. Would've been nice to look for one person, not two."

"Are you still looking?"

"I won't quit till Gabriel does." Nico sounded exhausted. "I wish he would. I think *he* wishes he would. He let the detectives go, which is a start. But Nina, it's a compulsion. You have to understand that."

Unwillingly, she nodded. "I do."

"You should know, also, he only took over the tannery to pay for it. He hated the idea of the job. Hates the job too. But he thought running Lazris Leather would guarantee he'd always have the money to look for Caro and the flexibility to be there for you."

"Here's what I don't get. If he's so determined to find her, why won't he look in public? Online? I mean, I Googled Caro, and—"

"And somebody's scrubbing her web presence," Nico said heavily. "Looking on the internet is no good. Her name lasts less than a day online."

"She's a hacker?"

"Or knows a hacker. Pays a hacker. We have no idea. But if I so much as tweet the name Caro Ravest, my account gets compromised. I have to delete it completely. Same on Facebook, YouTube, all of it. Somebody wants her name gone."

The roots of Nina's teeth hurt. She reached for her wine. She'd understood in the abstract that Caro wanted not to be discovered; that she was, functionally, in hiding. But hiring a hacker to get tweets erased was a level of commitment—or desperation—that Nina could not fathom.

"She hates us," she said quietly. "She hates my dad."

"She might. She might be afraid of attention, or retribution.

We have no real knowledge of what Caro went through, but Nina, we have to assume she's dealing with significant trauma. Probably PTSD. The way human minds reform themselves—" He shook his big head. Nina tried to concentrate on the gaps in his hairline, the wiry silver hairs curling from his eyebrows, the creases in his newly pendulous ears: signs of age, which so often heralds the decline of hope.

"We can't begin to understand," Nico continued, "why Caro wants so badly not to be found. We have no access to her thinking. We can only know that she's gone to great pains not to be discovered."

Tears pressed at Nina's eyes. She felt suddenly, powerfully drunk. "Tell me how."

"How?"

"I want to hear the ways she's avoided you."

"*Guerra Eterna* was released by an extremely small press, one that has very little money. Their employees signed Byzantine and highly punitive contracts prohibiting them from revealing both Graciela Brechner's real identity and Caro's. Getting out of those contracts would involve a legal battle the publishers can't afford and aren't willing to undertake. It would be very bad publicity, to be fair to them. Helping us might put them out of business, even though the book they published is, like I said, packed with misleading stories. Fabrications, exaggerations, total lies."

"What else?"

"If she's alive, she's underground. Aside from the online scrubbing, she's never had a Mexican bank account or driver's license. There are no leases or mortgages in her name. No car loan. Nothing."

"So she's got a fake identity?"

"Or she got married and has her husband do all the banking, though I can't find a marriage license with her name on it. If she has other children, she's not on their birth certificates. Her daughter—your sister—has never revealed herself publicly or tried to contact your dad, so if she knows who she is, which she very well might not, Caro has presumably been emphatic about keeping their identities secret."

"But you're still looking," Nina said flatly. It sounded like an accusation.

"Until your dad's ready to stop."

"Have you tried to convince him to?"

"I try every time we talk."

Nina had never seen Nico look this sad. She wanted badly to look away, but she remembered how Ilán had kept his eyes on her, how present he'd been. She wanted to offer Nico that comfort.

"I love your dad. You know that. I love you too. I want to give both of you hope. But"—he spread his big hands on the table—"it wouldn't be right. I would be lying. Finding Caro isn't possible. Not unless she decides she wants to be found."

He broke off. Nina looked at her recorder. It gave her a callous LED wink. She hit STOP, then pocketed the device and stood. Blood whirled between her temples. She was sleep-deprived, drunker than she should have been, dizzy with grief.

Nico rose. "Nina."

"It's okay. I'm okay." She steadied herself against the table. "We can talk more tomorrow. I just need to go to sleep."

IN THE MORNING, NINA REMAINED in bed longer than she would have permitted herself in either her real or temporary home. She had left the blinds up, and sun sank into every surface in the room. She felt hazy, sub-hungover. In the kitchen, she heard Nico making coffee—Nico or, she supposed, his housekeeper. She had no idea if he employed one; it seemed un-Marxist to pay somebody to clean your apartment, but also, he was a rich single man who, surely, hadn't seen a broom once in his childhood.

The thought sparked a pang of guilt. In imagining this trip, she'd neglected to add a stop at her dad's housekeeper's grave. His grief when she'd died was no less strong than when his mother had. A visit, with some flowers, was in order.

Nina had never had a relationship like Gabriel had with Luz. In his commitment to parental presence, her dad hired only undergraduate babysitters, transient twenty-year-olds whose main role was to feed Nina snacks and keep her from physical harm. After the Philip Roth incident, the babysitters ended. From then on, her dad picked her up at school, then finished his workday from home. In her early teens, she resented his constancy. By college, she knew enough to love it. Thought she knew, rather. She never imagined that being present for one daughter could have been an oblique way of making amends to another.

She hauled herself upright and reached for her phone. Too many notifications. She deleted an email from Kuiper without reading it, then wrote to tell her dad she was in Santiago and wanted to know where Luz was buried. The sentences emerged stiff and odd-sounding, like a robot impersonating a daughter. Nina sent the message without fixing it, then tapped her way to her overflowing Twitter inbox. So many rescheduled interviews. She must have always planned to postpone some. Had she genuinely believed she would be able to interview thirteen people this week? And if so, why hadn't she written questions to ask them? Why hadn't she prepared?

She knew why. She hadn't prepared because she didn't give

a shit. Pre–*Guerra Eterna*, she had been faking. She might have convinced even herself, but a successful pretense was still a pretense. She hated her PhD. She didn't care about writing a good-according-to-Kuiper dissertation. Worse, she didn't care about Alberto Nisman, though his death was an outrage and a tragedy. She'd been fully prepared to exploit his story for her own professional advancement.

Nina pulled the fat feather duvet over her head. She was, even now, pretending. She was displacing her self-loathing. Distracting herself from the new and terrible understanding that had led her to cut short her interview with Nico, then lie awake, tormenting herself, till dawn: it was not ethical to look for Caro. It was not right or even acceptable, and no matter how badly she wanted a sister, Nina had to stop before she started. She had to leave Caro alone.

But if Nina refrained from searching for either Caro Ravest or Graciela Brechner, she had no possible route to her sister. No clues, barring the likelihood that her name began with *A*—and what was Nina going to do, scour the globe for women in their early forties with *A* names and birthmarked moms? She had no real leads. No imaginable path to take.

Nina dragged herself from bed. She showered, drank some coffee, apologized to Nico for cutting last night's conversation short. She told him she was, on top of her other troubles, having serious professional doubts. Her dissertation was failing. She wasn't sure academia was the right place for her. She'd lost her purpose, her sense of self was unprecedentedly wobbly, and she didn't know what to do.

Nico tried his best to be comforting, but Nina knew she was, for the moment, beyond comfort. She was sad, and she hadn't slept enough. She spent the morning sorting silently through the box of Ítalo's pictures, photographing each one so she wouldn't have to think about it. She felt listless and smudged, like the blurred afterimage of a body moving too fast for a camera's shutter. She wasn't adapted for negative emotions. She was, at her core, a chirpy little optimist so accustomed to having the world organized in her favor that she'd genuinely believed she could find a woman who'd been in self-imposed hiding for thirty-three years.

She considered telling Nico to cancel lunch but saw no point. It would make him feel bad. Besides, she should be interested in Alejandra for Alejandra's own sake. She'd lived through a seventeen-year dictatorship. Surely Nina could stand to hear about that.

In the car, Nina did her best to chat, trying to warm herself up for lunch. Nico, clearly pretending to be deceived by her talkativeness, steered their conversation to her nonacademic, nonfamilial life: How was she liking Buenos Aires? How was D.C.? Her love life? Her Hazel?

"Hazel's good. Still doing design at Simon & Schuster, and getting married next year. I miss her," Nina added, which was true. She needed to call her. She and Hazel kept each other rigorously, ritually updated on the developments of their lives. No experience except sex made Nina feel more seen or more real than a catch-up with Hazel. She had never been more honest with anyone, even her dad, and she knew that the honesty went both ways.

On the sidewalk, an aproned man winched a restaurant gate open. A red-and-black soccer ball shone, impaled, on a TV aerial above him. Could that happen by mistake, or had somebody stuck it there? Bizarrely, Nina found herself envying the soccer ball. She'd like to be perched above the world.

It took nearly half an hour, with traffic, to get to La Reina. The neighborhood's major streets held a mix of European-based banks, international schools, and glass-balconied apartment buildings that looked to Nina like cruise ships, or how she imagined cruise ships: she'd never seen a real one up close. Once Nico turned onto a more residential block, the big construction vanished, and the Andes reared behind every house.

"Not a bad view," Nico said, pointing his chin at the mountains.

"Beautiful," Nina agreed.

"Alejandra knows her real estate. She sold me my condo."

Nico eased the car to the curb. The block ahead was filled with long, whitewashed ranch houses. The one before them, which Nina assumed was Alejandra's, had a high iron fence surrounding its plush lawn. The front door was painted the same glossy forest shade as the surrounding cypress trees. The landscaping was plainly professional-grade, but Nina didn't see a single flower. Maybe Alejandra kept them in the back, for herself.

Nico buzzed them through the front gate, and Nina trailed him up the cement walkway, her stomach restless with unhappiness and nerves. She'd tucked a full sleeve of individually wrapped Lactaid pills in her jeans pocket, but still, she hoped lunch would be dairy-free.

The door swung open before Nico could knock. Alejandra regarded them coolly. She wore straight-legged khakis and a knit red shell and had the immaculately preserved skin and hair of an aging newscaster. Her posture was Pilates-perfect, her biceps and deltoids distinguishable at a glance. Small opals winked in her ears as she kissed Nico on the cheek, then extended a hand to Nina. "You must be the American daughter," she said.

Alejandra escorted them straight to the dining room, which looked staged for a magazine shoot. A pitcher of water stood, not sweating, on the table runner, flanked by platters of salad: tomato and avocado, corn and cucumber, mixed greens. Nina's dairy worries had been unnecessary: Alejandra was vegan. Also nondrinking, non-coffee-drinking, and non-soda-drinking. She offered iced herbal tea, which Nina accepted and Nico declined.

"All your tea tastes like grass," he said cheerfully.

"You're welcome to add sugar," Alejandra told him.

His eyebrows shot up. "Sugar? In your house?"

"I keep some." She moved toward the kitchen doorway. "For guests."

Nico snorted. "For pigs like me, you mean."

Alejandra didn't reply. She fetched a jug of tea—which did, in fact, turn out to taste like yard clippings, though not in an unpleasant way—and served herself salad, which she ate with admirable neatness, never dropping a leaf or having to indelicately shove an arugula stem between her lips. She sliced her tomatoes into perfectly triangular wedges, like Trivial Pursuit pieces, before eating them, and replenished her water when the glass was still half-full. Nina would be willing to bet that Alejandra tracked her daily water intake, counted her steps, wore sunscreen even if it was raining, took the skin off her chicken—no, she was vegan; what did sober vegans do to limit calories? Ration their nut consumption?

The water pitcher shone in the sunlight. The cut-glass chandelier refracted bright little squares onto the table. Nina had grown up in a world of hired cleaning crews and stay-at-home moms, and she wasn't sure she'd ever been in a room as spotless as this one. Maybe Alejandra, as a real estate professional, kept her home in a state of constant readiness for sale. More likely, her house and body reflected an overriding, perfectionist need to be in control.

In contrast to Alejandra, Nico seemed even more relaxed

than usual. He chatted about Santiago real estate trends until Nina gathered herself enough to ask, "How long have you been a real estate agent?"

"Since 1992. I got my license after the return to democracy."

Nina very much hoped the oblique invocation of dictatorship was an invitation. "What did you do before?"

"Tried not to attract attention."

"Would that have been different if Caro hadn't been detained?"

"Of course," Alejandra said sharply.

Nina blushed. She took an acidic bite of tomato and pressed her knees together till the bones hurt. "Sorry," she said. "Bad question." Then, before Alejandra could either accept or reject her apology, she asked, "But could we talk about Caro now?"

"I thought that was the reason Nico brought you here."

Nico smiled. "It is."

Alejandra set her silverware down, and Nina followed suit. She wished she'd brought her audio recorder so she could hide behind it. Let it steer the conversation. Briefly, she considered recording on her phone, but there would be no real point, and Alejandra struck her as an enemy of the pointless.

She took a deep breath. No vagueness, she decided. Ordinarily she liked asking broad interview questions, but she doubted that Alejandra would react well to imprecision. Besides, her dad struggled to recount painful memories in any form of detail. It would be hard to conjure herself a Caro from what he managed to say. If she wanted specificity, Alejandra was likely her only shot.

"Okay," she began. "When did you last talk to Caro? Or hear from her?"

"September 10, 1973."

"When was the last time you tried to contact her?"

Alejandra pressed her lips together, thinking. Nina felt a childish pleasure at having stumped her, though she recognized "stumped" wasn't the right word. "Her birthday," Alejandra said eventually. "I always write to someone about her on her birthday."

Nina tilted her head. "Who's 'someone'?"

"It varies."

"I'd like to know."

Alejandra took a sip of water. "Are you asking how I've tried to find my cousin?"

"I am."

"Since *Guerra Eterna* was released, I've written consistently to its editor." Alejandra splayed her hands on the table. She wore no rings. Her nails were buffed but bare. "I write to every relevant refugee and asylee organization in Mexico City. I send letters to newspaper editors in Mexico, Chile, Argentina, and Spain."

"Why Spain?"

"Wide circulation." Alejandra paused. "In the years immediately after Pinochet was ousted, I spoke regularly on the radio, including radio call-in shows, which I found humiliating. I made two TV appearances. All, as you can probably guess, now scrubbed from the internet."

"Does that upset you?"

Alejandra held Nina's gaze. Her face and voice were devoid of pain or aggravation. "I find it very hurtful."

Nina suppressed the impulse to say she did too. "Hurtful in what way?"

"I take the digital erasure to mean Caro is alive and has seen some quantity of my messages but is refusing contact with me. Nico likes to remind me that trauma works in complicated ways, and that Caro may find it psychologically impossible to communicate with me or anyone in Chile, but what he forgets"—she shot Nico a sharp look—"is that the Caro I knew would have understood that those of us who lived through seventeen years of dictatorship experienced trauma ourselves." She drew herself even straighter, somehow. "That Caro," she added, "would have wanted to know the version of me that survived."

New misery rushed through Nina. The sparkling table blurred before her. Caro was unfindable. If Nina looked, not only would she fail, but in her failure, she would reactivate or worsen Caro's post-traumatic wounds. If she renounced looking, as she'd already decided to do, she could feel pleased with herself for making the morally correct call, but she'd never meet her sister. Her family—she herself—would always be incomplete.

She redirected her attention to Alejandra. Without Caro, did she feel incomplete? She seemed so whole in her terseness, her forthrightness, her dietary and domestic restraint. She had the bearing of a school principal, or a reformist politician, or a Suze Orman–type life-skills guru. Nina would take her life advice. If Alejandra told her to finish her dissertation, she'd do it; if Alejandra told her to set her laptop on fire and go picket the Pentagon, Nina would paint some protest signs.

"Alejandra," Nina said, seized by impulse, "should I look for Caro?"

"Only if you like wasting time."

Nina flinched. Alejandra didn't blink. Nico, who had stopped eating and moving, reached for Nina's hand. "It's all right," she told him softly. To Alejandra, she said, "I appreciate that." Through her knee-jerk hurt, she felt soothed but not comforted. She had never known there was a distinction before. Her unhappiness spread into a physical weight. Though she'd eaten only tomatoes and roughage, her stomach felt densely, unpleasantly full. Somewhere in her sorrow, she knew, relief was hiding. She always liked having her choices confirmed.

Nina's eyes ached. She assessed the risk of tears—medium to high—then stood, excused herself, and beelined to Alejandra's front-hall bathroom, which was too perfect to cry in. The mirror was streak- and dust-free, and the conch-shaped soap had plainly never been touched. The hand towels were fluffy enough to look blow-dried. Nina couldn't wipe tears on them, let alone snot.

She tiptoed through the living room, then down a clay-tiled hall where she opened three doors in turn: linen closet, home gym, bedroom with en suite bath. Nina slipped inside, taking a moment to survey the new terrain. Alejandra had thick white bedroom carpet and a heavy bronze bed frame. Her sheets were pea-shoot green. She had a real, old-school vanity, the kind Nina remembered from her grandmother's house: travertine top, curling legs, hair appliances and perfume bottles arrayed neatly before the mirror. At the vanity's back corner stood a silver-framed photograph of two high-school girls in navy pinafores.

Nina moved closer, letting her feet drag across the soft rug. She lifted the frame and examined the print with its washed-out colors and soft 1970s edges, its fuzzed halos of fading light. The girls in it looked equal parts glad to be photographed and impatient to be elsewhere: school, a party, someplace without the parental surveillance a camera then implied. In an equivalent picture today, they would be preening, sucking their cheeks in, pouting and arching their backs and pressing their nascent tits to the sky. Here, they slouched together, blond-brown hair comingling on their shoulders. Both had gapped teeth, upturned noses with scattered freckles, brows plucked with comic severity. One had a birthmark climbing her neck, reaching a reddish tendril under her chin.

Sweat collected under Nina's arms. She could feel her heart beating. She looked again at the girls in their jumpers, starched shirts tucked neatly underneath. Catholic-school uniforms: had to be. Carefully, Nina turned the frame over, swiveled the backing's anchors loose, and lifted it to reveal spidery brown script on the photograph's back. *Caro & Ale. 1r día Sta. Ursula. Feb. 1971.* Though Nina had known—of course she'd known—the name still sent her pulse skittering anew.

She replaced the backing and flipped the frame to examine Caro. Nico was right: she wore the birthmark well. Nina imagined, with a horrified little lurch, her adolescent father kissing the birthmark's wings and lines, tracing it with a finger. She could not and did not want to envision this girl going further than kissing. She looked so much like a child. She would have been, if this was the first day of school in 1971, fourteen. Two years later, in October 1973, she would be pregnant and locked in some secret detention center—Venda Sexy or one of its evil equivalents—subject to tortures and assaults that Nina could not stand to contemplate. Even the abstract thought defied her understanding. It made fourteen-year-old Caro almost unbearable to look at.

Nina screwed her eyes shut. Red webs of light danced beneath her lids. She tried to merge the Caro in her hands with the teenage Gabriel she'd studied at every opportunity, to conjure how her sister might possibly look. Fewer freckles than Nina, though not none; thinner cheeks than hers; roughly the same quantity of nose. She'd be in her early forties, which meant she'd have more delicate skin than Nina; some wrinkles, some age spots, a decent amount of gray hair if she didn't dye. Or, depending on the life she'd lived, she'd be leather-skinned, face creased from forehead to jawline, hair silvered and frizzy and wild. She could have full-sleeve tattoos and ears gauged to her collarbone, or Botox and a boob job, or a soldier's scraped-back hair. She could be trans. She could be Hasidic. She could be almost anyone.

Slowly, squinting, Nina reopened her eyes. The bedroom was dazzling. Sun shot through the curtains, landing in wide stripes on the carpet and catching dust motes—it pleased Nina to see dust here—in their eternal dance. She clenched her free hand into a fist. A small beam of hope shone in her mind. Knowing what her sister looked like now was not possible. Knowing what her sister looked like at fourteen? That could be done. Nina wasn't best friends with a graphic designer for nothing. Hazel knew how to merge faces. She could help.

The question was whether Hazel could create a computer approximation that Nina's sister, wherever and whoever she was, might plausibly recognize as herself. If yes, then Nina had a shot. She could attract her sister's attention without disrespecting Caro's privacy. Nico had said the only way to find Caro was if she wanted to be found. Well, what if Caro's daughter did? What if she would leap at the opportunity to know her sister, or her dad?

Nina knew how bad the odds were. She knew the power of virality too. Social media could destabilize leaders. It could block highways. It could fill parks with camped-out activists. Surely it could change one family.

Moving quickly, she took her phone from her pocket and photographed Caro, zooming as tightly as she could on her face. Then she scrolled through her shots of Ítalo's pictures, choosing one of her dad in a laughably tight red-striped ringer shirt. He looked so skinny, so hopeful. Nina couldn't help thinking, Poor kid.

She resaved the image, then created a new version cropped to show only his face. Her hands and armpits were damp. Optimism pulsed through her limbs. She texted the two faces to Hazel, writing, *Huge huge favor. Can you Photoshop-merge these? Into a girl? Thank you thank you I love you!* Then she returned to the lunch table, shaking slightly. Nico and Alejandra regarded her with visible concern. She took a deep breath, then a gulp of water. Her phone vibrated in her pocket, but she left it there. She wanted to be alone when she read Hazel's reply.

Nina had never worked harder to control herself than she did for the rest of lunch. She felt ready to levitate with excitement. She imagined physically reaching inside her chest and squashing her eagerness with a flattened palm as she helped Alejandra bring out dessert, which was—what else?—a platter of gorgeously arranged fruit. Between bites, Nina asked, finally, what Caro was like. All her dad had said was that she was curious. Alejandra agreed: Caro was overwhelmingly inquisitive, extremely smart, sometimes self-absorbed, and often irrational, but always conscious of her own irrationality. Nina, through her jitters, couldn't help thinking she and Caro had some traits in common. She wondered if her dad had, in fact, raised her in his disappeared ex-girlfriend's image. The prospect struck Nina as plausible, even likely, but too fucked up to consider in her current disarranged state.

Not until Alejandra was walking Nico and Nina out did she explicitly mention Gabriel. She put a cool hand on Nina's arm and said, "Your dad did a good job raising you, didn't he?"

"He did."

Alejandra nodded. In the front hall's glittering light, Nina could see the bleached fuzz above her upper lip. "I always thought he would make a good father. He knows how to love people. He loved Caro very much."

Immediately, Nina's eyes filled. She hugged Alejandra hard. It wouldn't have occurred to her to ask how well, or how plainly, her dad loved Caro. She'd assumed and been right. Her father was so reliably affectionate. Even in his worst times, he was, in that one way, steady. His unchanging love was the bedrock of Nina's life.

DRIVING HOME FROM LA REINA, Nina barely spoke. She wanted to be alone. Only by herself could she start picking hope apart from fear, fear from guilt, guilt from relief. She couldn't tell if, by texting Hazel, she'd made a choice or simply offered it to herself. Was she really going to post a fake picture of her sister online? Was that crazy? Was it immoral? Did it make her a stalker, or an asshole, or just a person who wanted to know her whole family?

She didn't decide that afternoon. She didn't even open the file Hazel emailed her, subject line *your wish is my command*. For three days, she left it sitting ignored while she brought flowers to Luz's grave, roamed Vitacura with Nico, wept at the Museo de la Memoria, wept more on the riverbank where her dad and his friends once drank and smoked. Sitting in the warm grass, breathing the Mapocho's green smell, all she wanted was to spin time back, to pass a flask of pisco with her fifteen-year-old father, tease Nico, flirt with Andrés. She wished so badly that she'd known him. That she could have met him even once.

It was noon on her last day in Chile. Nico had gone to a morning meeting but was meeting her for lunch in half an hour. He'd made a reservation at a place that specialized in barnacles. Nina dried her face on her dress. She took a picture of her surroundings and texted it—*Look familiar?*—to her father. Across the river, neat stucco houses climbed into the hills. For a moment, she let herself pretend Caro lived in one. She could be mopping the tile on her patio now, smoking a cigarette in the sunlight, finishing a crossword, reading a book. She could be here or anywhere. She could be nowhere at all.

Nina closed her eyes. She didn't need to look to find her way to her email. She opened the app reluctantly and scrolled to Hazel's message. It had no body text, only an image of a girl who looked like a younger, blonder Nina. She wore Gabriel's ringer shirt and had Caro's loose, chest-length hair. Hazel had erased the birthmark and added gold hoops. Absurdly, stupidly, Nina's whole self leapt toward the girl on her screen. Her fake sister. Her real sister, she knew, was a forty-one-year-old stranger—Nina had worked her age out by now—but maybe, if Nina was lucky, a forty-one-year-old who'd once looked enough like this wide-eyed, big-nosed teenager to spot the picture on Facebook or Twitter and think, baffled, Is that me?

Nina's phone was hot in her hands. She needed to start walking to the barnacle restaurant. She had no indecision left. She wanted her sister. She wanted to believe that the real woman hiding behind this mocked-up girl would like a sister too. If that made her selfish or bad, so be it. She would rather be a sister than be good.

She promised herself she was ready. She had learned from her dad how to love. In the months to come, Nina would grow only more confident that she could be a solid foundation for her sister. For Ilán and Rebeca too. At Nina and Ilán's wedding— beach ceremony, barefoot, very small—Rebeca, in a toast Ilán helped her write, would inform the assembled guests that marriage meant that Nina was officially her other mom now.

It took Nina only a moment to find a free photo editor online. She plugged the composite into a square black frame, writing beneath it, *HAVE YOU SEEN MY SISTER?* Energy burned in her fingers. She needed to pick a name. Who would trust a missing person ad without one? Nina rocked in the grass. She squinted in the sunlight. She wrote, *ANA LAZRIS RAVEST. 41 Y.O. TELL HER I WANT TO TALK.*

A hot breeze blew from the water. Nina saw herself as if from above, hair swirling in the wind, phone clenched in her hands. Her whole body was tense. She'd be sore later. Her jaw would hurt. She opened Facebook, Twitter, Instagram, cuing her newly created image on each. She had left something out, she realized. On all three platforms, she wrote, *Tell my sister I love her.* It was the only truth she had to offer. She sent it into the online world.

DECISION

\\\

Silver Spring, Maryland, USA, April 2019

I knew Nina long before she knew me. Knew *of* me. She does not know me in the slightest, though her viral summons certainly sounded, to the outside world, as if she did. She received a whole greeting-card aisle of sympathy after sending that Photoshopped pseudo-me to circulate online. I did not participate beyond reading the reams of comments that accrued beneath her various posts. It was entertaining to see how many strangers thought I deserved to be found. Irritating, also. Still, when Belton asked if I wanted him to do the usual, I told him to leave the graphic-designed me alone. *Ana.* Only off by one letter. Not bad.

Belton has been very useful in the years since our breakup. We met in the mid-nineties, shortly before he took up recreational hacking. Not long after I moved out, he became a full-time hacker for hire. I know he offered me his continued assistance primarily so he could remain in my life, but I also know he would have hung around—or, rather, snooped around—regardless. It is difficult not to imagine that Belton, a professional cybercriminal who has spent two full decades providing me with my birth family's passwords, does not also gather my passwords for himself. Not a thought I relish, but it would make me a hypocrite to protest.

It was Belton who first suggested attempting to erase my birth mother from the internet, which I would not have guessed was remotely possible. He thought doing so, even incompletely, would improve my state of mind. He was right. Unfortunately, erasure was not his only idea. On my twenty-sixth birthday, he gave me a teal iMac accompanied by an index card on which he had written the email address gabriel.lazris@hotmail.com and the password "colocolo." I should have shredded that card. I waited less than an hour to use it.

Counting the iMac, I have owned five computers. Belton equipped each with an anonymizing onion browser through which I observe my birth father and sister's digital lives. I imagine that he also infected each with various forms of malware. Occasionally, he informs me that he will be remotely accessing my server on a given day, or that he is temporarily storing code on my hard drive. I suspect that this is his way of reminding me that by hiring him I have compromised myself, which is not something I tend to forget.

I recognize that I have made my birth family vulnerable to Belton. It is part of our contract—which is heavily encrypted but does exist—that he may not attack or steal from them. Presumably I would notice if he did the latter, since, in addition to reading their emails, I pay close attention to their many financial records. You can learn quite a lot about a person by reading their bank statements. eBay is also revealing, especially in Gabriel's case. His nostalgia for Socialist Chile has only seemed to grow through the years. Nina has less informative shopping habits. Her overall online presence has become significantly less revealing since the 2016 election, after which she became disillusioned with social media and ceased to post. Presumably she would have deleted her accounts were it not for the digital version of me still circulating on Twitter and Instagram. On Facebook, these days, no one seems to care.

My sister is not at all like me. She is an optimist, if no longer blithe. She claims not to deserve the comforts of her life. She has spent her career pursuing a shifting array of ideals, thinking hardly if at all about stability. Our similarities are rare and incidental: we have the same father, vote for the same candidates, suffered the same number of miscarriages last year. Hers came as a surprise. Mine did not. I am, after all, forty-five. My odds were always remote.

I did not explain my two absences to my employer, but he handled them graciously nonetheless. They were my first prolonged sick leaves since 2001, when I became a hygienist in his dental practice. I enjoy being seen as dependable. Certainly I depend on Dr. Levin. His pay scale is generous, his benefit package unrivaled. It is possible that if I worked for another dentist, I would not have been able to afford two IVF cycles or a home. My ability to get what I want has not been a constant over the years.

Upon enrolling at American University eight years ago, Nina moved into an apartment three Metro stops from my house in Silver Spring. Not convenient to campus, but I was unsurprised that she chose a trendy neighborhood rather than a logical one. At the time, her part of Columbia Heights was what certain people call transitional, meaning that it had three bars for white people but was also home to a gas station that served as a hub for prostitution. I assumed that Nina was pleased with herself for living there.

I also assumed that I would see her in my own territory before long. On Instagram, she documented her love of ethnic food, though she would never use such a term. I expected her to be drawn to Silver Spring's multinational dining scene. Guided by the blogs she trusted, I created a dinner rotation. I ate Ethiopian at Lucy, Burmese at Mandalay, and Chinese at Hollywood East Café. Once a week, I got Jamaican carryout from Negril. I thought Nina might share my love of their red snapper, but of the restaurants I selected, Negril is the only one that, to this day, has never appeared in her Wells Fargo transaction history. Her loss.

During Nina's graduate studies, I encountered her once at Hollywood East Café, two times at Lucy, and three at Mandalay. My first sighting, though, took place at the Quarry House. I was sitting at the bar with a Dogfish Head. She was under the neon-markered shots-and-specials sign, eating leaden tater tots and drinking National Bohemian beer. Her companion was a bearded, ratty-looking man in Doc Martens. I correctly predicted that I would not see him again.

I felt neither satisfaction nor accomplishment that evening. My main reaction was irritation that I had not thought to add the Quarry House to my rotation. In her own neighborhood and the ones near it, Nina frequented the Red Derby, the Raven, and Looking Glass: bars with canned beer, bad lighting, and regulars who are either lifelong Washingtonians in their forties or transplants in their twenties. I should have realized that the Quarry House suited her taste.

My frustration, to be clear, had less to do with my incomplete guesswork than with my dislike of surprises. I was not prepared to see Nina at the Quarry House. Frankly, I felt that she had intruded, illogical though that response was. It was my bar. My sanctuary, in a small way. I do not keep alcohol in my home; the Quarry House, until I saw Nina there, was the only place I drank.

When Nina arrived in the District, Belton offered to guide her to Dr. Levin's practice, which he said would not be difficult. One of his skills is tricking search engines. He has spent years burying all mentions of my birth mother's name in washes of false information and badly indexed data. If I wanted, he said, he could manipulate Nina's search history such that no other dentist seemed like a viable option. I had him do the opposite. I wanted to choose our encounters, not wait for her to land in my chair.

Nina moved to D.C. in August 2010. She left in February 2015. During that period, I sought her out once every three months. In between, I took precautions against accidental run-ins. I wanted to keep her from recognizing me, and I am not visually nondescript. At fourteen, I committed myself to the District's hardcore punk scene. My devotion, which ended seven years later, left me with slight tinnitus, a lingering distrust of my own impulses, a decently valuable collection of Fugazi and Minor Threat records and flyers, and forearms scattered with stubbornly unfaded tattoos.

My precautions were simple. I consulted Nina's Google Calendar before making plans. I monitored her credit- and debit-card statements and avoided places she habitually spent money. I would like to note that I never used either her credit cards or Gabriel's. Nor did I withdraw cash or transfer stocks from their various accounts, although, once I began paying Belton, I certainly could have used a second income stream. His retainer is

$12,000 a year. No ex-girlfriend discount, though if he had of-
fered one, I would have refused.

I had both moral and practical reasons for not stealing from
the Lazrises. Belton promised that using the onion browser
made my presence untraceable, but siphoning their money
would have alerted them to the compromised nature of their
online lives. It also would have made me a thief. A self-evident
point, but worth making. I have often been murky on the questions of what the Lazrises owe me and I them, but I have never
lacked clarity about who I am. I am Ada Sophie Goldman,
daughter of Nancy Beth Goldman, and Nancy did not raise me
to steal.

In my adolescence, I often defied and upset my mother.
Take the tattoos. Not many of the District's punks were prone
to getting tattoos at that time, but my hardcore period coin-
cided with her religious one, and I enjoyed flouting the Jewish tradition of not marking one's skin. Also, Nancy was softhearted and symbolically inclined enough that she couldn't
bear the thought of a Jew tattooing herself after the concentration camps. I dismissed her objections. Worse, I laughed at her
for them. I am not prone to regret, but I regret that.

Around that time, she bought a triple plot in the Judean
Gardens Memorial Cemetery, having confirmed with her rabbi
that, tattooed or not, I could be buried there. One spot is now
hers. One is waiting for me. I sold the third. I never knew who,
if anyone, she intended it for. My eventual husband or wife, I
suppose, or my birth mother, whose ashes were long buried in
a flowerpot on Nancy's balcony. I transplanted the ficus tree
growing from them to my own yard several years ago. It suffers badly in winter but lives on.

My birth certificate was Belton's first erasure. Caro's death
certificate was the next. She had been dead over a decade when

the internet entered ordinary life, and Nancy had ensured that the record of my adoption was sealed, but I still felt calmer knowing that the only proof of her death was garbled beyond recognition. It was a relief not to worry that if somebody found it, the do-gooders, reporters, and historians who wasted their time looking for my birth mother would—as Nina did—turn their attention to me.

Without Belton, I imagine, I would have been found years ago. I can see the irony here: he has invaded my birth family's privacy, and almost certainly mine as well, but he has also helped me live a private life. In his way, he has tried to be a good friend to me, though he still has ulterior motives. When we talk, he drops his voice half an octave, as if to convince me he has become more masculine over the years and as if I would care if he had. When I called on Sunday to tell him I would no longer be watching my birth family, his voice leapt right up to its usual pitch.

As previously stated, I am not prone to regret, but I regret both dating and employing Belton. I also regret my actions this weekend, but I am not sorry. I would not apologize to Nina or her husband if confronted. Nor am I apologizing to myself. I will benefit from having broken the one-way mirror through which I long studied my family. I may be unhappy now, but I know that I set myself free.

Nina returned to the United States this winter. She and her husband bought a $765,000 row house on Shepherd Street, six blocks from her old apartment. Her husband is on the tenure track at Georgetown. Nina works at the Central American Resource Center, coordinating visa and green-card applications for Spanish-speaking immigrants. Her nine-year-old stepdaughter, Rebeca, attends the Milton Gottesman Jewish Day School, which is barely over the District line from Silver

Spring. I pass it on the bus to and from work, though I take the Metro more often these days.

I never imagined feeling connected to—or jealous of—Nina's child. Stepchild. Before our shared year of miscarriages, I never felt connected to Nina herself. My reactions to her, up to that point, had included envy, curiosity, loathing, resentment, and amusement. Gabriel once triggered dizzying hatred and grief, but, lately, provokes pity. My hiding has hurt him badly. Damaged him, possibly. Again, I am not apologizing. I have a right to my anonymity.

Nina tried to get pregnant after she got married. I tried after Nancy died. I missed her so much my body felt overtaken by it. I also missed the comfort of belonging to a mother-daughter dyad. It was stabilizing to slot myself into her. I knew better than to hope to re-create that sensation for myself, but my child, I thought, could slot him- or herself into me.

Adoption seemed beyond my emotional capacities. Pregnancy, less so, though I worried. Still, I put my doubts aside, found a fertility specialist willing to take me on, and consulted the man I was dating, whom I had met at the Capital Area Food Bank, where I volunteer. He had all the right qualities: kind, smart, no major disorders, not an Ashkenazi Jew. I didn't want my child to have Tay-Sachs. I do not mean *our* child. He agreed to be a sperm donor, not a co-parent. My baby would have been mine alone.

He was present through both miscarriages. He drove me to the clinic. We saw a small body the second time. I do not want to go into detail. We broke up shortly after. I couldn't afford a third round of in vitro. Nor could I stand the thought of it. Nina lost a pregnancy at three months that winter, another at five in the fall. I read the emails she wrote after. I could have written the same words myself.

When I imagined having a child, I saw myself not with an infant but with a little girl. I envisioned picking her up from school, kneeling so she could run to me. I would have checked the knots in her shoelaces before we walked home. I would have carried her book bag, held her hand not only when we crossed the street. Every Friday, we would have stopped at Tropics Ice Cream on Georgia Avenue. On Saturdays, we would have eaten corned-beef sandwiches at Parkway Deli. I would have let her refill her plate at the pickle bar as many times as she wanted. It would have been a ritual and a treat.

Nina seems to know the importance of rituals. She and Rebeca have established several since their move. Wednesdays are library days; Sundays, indoor pool. On Fridays, Nina picks Rebeca up and drives her to the kosher butcher on Massachusetts Avenue to select the meat for Shabbat dinner, which Ilán cooks. All very cozy. Very familial. Nina and Ilán are working hard to ease Rebeca into her new existence. I envy their efforts. I would like to help Rebeca too.

Rebeca, who is not a Lazris, is the only Lazris I have ever felt capable of meeting. She is certainly the only one to whom I could offer something other than the fact of myself. Rebeca is roughly the same age now as I was when Nancy and I moved here from Mexico City. Different circumstances, but a similar transition. I could provide perspective that would be useful to Rebeca. Comforting, even. I could tell her I remember how homesickness feels.

We moved to Maryland in 1983. Caro was dead. *Guerra Eterna* was a hit. The three Uruguayans who contributed their life stories to the author-character of Graciela Brechner were extremely satisfied with my mother's work, and rightly so. Graciela Brechner was a highly effective screen. That false identity, created at the request of the real people behind it, enabled them to tell their stories safely. The pseudonym generated interest in the book while protecting them from scrutiny. It also protected me. It would have protected my birth mother, had she lived long enough to see the book in print. She did not, but that was her choice.

You might assume that Nancy adopted me after Caro killed herself. Not true. Nancy got to know Caro when I was five. When I was a feral, unschooled seven-year-old, Nancy suggested that I might spend the occasional night at her apartment, where I could eat meals and take a real bath. Caro one-upped the offer. I didn't protest. According to a letter I wrote in red crayon and hand-delivered to Nancy the day of my adoption, I was very excited and glad.

Nancy never regretted me, but she did regret *Guerra Eterna*. It ruined her ability to relax in her Mexico City social circle, where the author's identity was a source of constant gossip, speculation, and debate. Nancy was terrified that she would be exposed and judged, though, to my knowledge, nobody ever suggested it was her. This strikes me as remarkably unimaginative. Should it not have been evident that the woman who adopted Caro Ravest's daughter—itself a subject of gossip, especially in the year between my household migration and Caro's death—was likely to have also adapted her story? But Nancy was not a native Spanish speaker, which seems to have meant she was above—or not worthy of—suspicion.

We left Mexico eight months after the book came out. Later, she said she would have liked to leave earlier, but she'd felt I should finish the school year. Why, I have no idea. School was not teaching me the skills necessary to soften the move to suburban Maryland. In retrospect, neither of us could have guessed what skills those might have been.

Neither Nancy nor I thrived in Chevy Chase. Nancy grew up there but had no remaining relatives or friends. She also had no source of income. *Guerra Eterna*'s underground success did not translate into significant royalty payments, and Nancy considered herself bound to split what she did earn with her three Uruguayan collaborators. Though she had supported herself in Mexico by freelancing for various American, British, and Australian news outlets, no newspaper or magazine in the District would look at her clips. She applied for work as a paralegal, a secretary, an entry-level bureaucrat. No luck. In greater Washington in the eighties and nineties, the received image of a welfare recipient was a Black woman living east of Rock Creek Park, not a white Jewish one living in wealthy Montgomery County. Nancy and I disproved many stereotypes in our day.

It seems fair to add that I severely hampered her job hunt. In Chevy Chase, I became a very difficult child, prone to night terrors, temper tantrums, vandalism, playground violence, and sudden disappearances from class. A social worker was in order. I was never assigned one. Nancy missed interviews and left temp shifts to beg the school system not to expel me. In my adulthood, she told me that when she introduced herself to administrators and support staff as Ada Goldman's mom, the kindest reaction she could expect was "God bless."

Rebeca is handling her move much more gracefully than I did mine, which is not surprising. She has no major preexisting psychological trauma, but she still has the therapist I needed. She Skypes with her mother daily, and her father and stepmother seem to have unlimited time and energy for her. Nina has arranged her work schedule around Rebeca's days. In her emails, she writes that she and her stepdaughter are closer than ever. She recently told her friend Fabiana that if she can never have a child of her own, she will still be happy. She has Rebeca. It was a challenge not to wonder if Nancy would have said the same about me.

Nancy never spoke of wanting a biological child. I imagine I would have resented a sibling if I had had one. "Resent" is not a strong-enough word. I needed Nancy. I was rooted to her. It is not hyperbolic to say she was my only source of stability until I was well into adulthood. Bear in mind that in my first decade of life, I was Chilean, Mexican, and American. At seven, I acquired a new family and new name. Before then, I thought I was, variously, the daughter of a disappeared Chilean leftist; a rich Chilean human-rights advocate; a Chilean Jew who dumped my birth mother upon learning she was pregnant; and a Chilean prison guard about whom I should never think and of whom I should never speak. Caro told me the latter when she gave me to Nancy. She promised it was the truth. I obeyed her injunction not to repeat it. I learned that it was a lie only when, at thirteen, I demanded to read *Guerra Eterna*. Nancy, unhappily, let me. She had decided years before to trust me when I told her it was time.

I should describe Nancy more fully. She is the reason I live a life I enjoy and possibly the reason I am alive at all. She was an unfailingly kind person. She had a strong sense of morality, loved children, and always followed her instincts. Nobody is selfless, and Nancy never tried to be, but without effort, she came close. She moved to Mexico in 1968, having dropped out of college after sustaining a serious concussion at the riots surrounding the Democratic Convention. She did not want to live on the domestic front of the Vietnam War. In Mexico City, she worked as a waitress, nanny, bookseller, and writer. She was quite gifted, though only in English. Critics have noted that *Guerra Eterna* is syntactically stiff and formal; tonally, it tends to be brusque. Nina calls it bitchy. Nancy was anything but. She was an ex-hippie, casual and warm to a fault. Her Spanish, however, was imperfect, and though her Uruguayan collaborators edited the manuscript heavily, they chose to let her linguistic oddities shine through.

Although Nancy allowed me to read the book, she worried openly that it would inflict more psychological damage. It did. I had never told her I thought my father was a prison guard. She had no idea how violently I hated him. Reading *Guerra Eterna* made no impact on that hatred. I wanted it to. I told myself to be happy that I was an American Jew by birth as well as adoption. I had been the same person, in that limited sense, my whole life. It didn't matter. I still hated my father, and now I hated my birth mother too. Caro told me an unspeakable lie. She sent me into the world believing I was the child of rape. You can choose whether to forgive her for that. Please trust me when I say I have tried.

You may have realized that, in erasing Caro from the internet, I have effectively erased her memory. She has no grave. Nancy left me the rights to *Guerra Eterna*, which means I can arrange for it to enter the public domain as a novel. I am aware that Chile's Pinochet apologists—there are many—will crow over this choice. I regret giving them ammunition, but not enough to change my mind. I intend for "Manuela" to become a character, not a woman who lived, gave birth to me, and died. Slowly, the public will forget her. I wish I could do the same.

I remember loving Caro. Being her daughter. We used to lie on our bellies in the sun, pretending to be sleeping lizards. We took daylong walks that made my feet swell. We went to synagogue. Ate grasshoppers. Cooked cereal for dinner. Shared a bath every Sunday night. She always detangled my hair first, yanking till the knots gave way. She cried if I told her it hurt.

I was a child when Caro gave me to Nancy. She told me it would be a simple reversal: I would live with Nancy and she, Caro, would visit. How could I have known she was lying? How could I have guessed that if I had refused to leave her, she might be alive today?

None of this was Gabriel's doing, but I still blamed him

for many years. It was easier than blaming either Caro or myself. At this point, though, I hold very little against him. I can even accept that his search for me and my birth mother, unwelcome though it may be, is morally necessary. Intermittently, I wish I could let myself be found. I suppose that route is not yet blocked. I could decide someday to accept his affection. It would be both a disappointment and a relief.

At the National Zoo on Saturday, I took away my other options. I made myself visible to the Lazrises. On Sunday, I called Belton. On Monday, he sent Nina, Gabriel, and Ilán personalized emails containing each one of their passwords in plain text, suggesting that they change them immediately. For good measure, he forcibly logged them out of their bank accounts. I paid him to never offer me their new passwords. Belton knows me well enough to take me at my word, which means I will never again have access to my family online or anonymity with them in person. After twenty-four years and many failed efforts, I am cutting myself off, or cutting myself loose. Unless I decide to become one of them, my time with the Lazrises is done.

IN MY MOST SENTIMENTAL IMAGININGS, the ones I tried hardest to banish after ending fertility treatments, I took my daughter to the zoo. We parked in the lower lot and walked upward, stopping to see the flamingos, the prairie dogs, the chimpanzees. We visited the chittering bats in their dark mansion, the snakes in their bright one. We looked at the small African deer, the rhinos, the hippos yawning in their fetid bath. We always checked on the pandas, but in my imagination, as in life, the enclosure was surrounded by tourists, the bears themselves nowhere in sight. My daughter was disappointed—Mei

Xiang and Tian Tian are major attractions—but I promised we could try again next time.

After the pandas, we turned downhill. We passed the American bison and the Andean bears. Sometimes we paused to watch the keepers feed the seals and sea lions, but usually we kept going. I wanted to reach Amazonia, which I have always loved, before my daughter burned through her energy.

Amazonia is not a traditional zoo exhibit but a unified tropical scene. On the first level, zoogoers walk between enormous tanks filled with cruising arapaimas and pacus. Red-bellied piranhas float near the surface, and beige rubber eels wriggle like strippers at the glass walls. On the second, the tanks become dark slices of river in a damp, hooting jungle. Birds flutter overhead, and snails ooze across the wooden footpaths. In my imagination, we sometimes caught sight of a titi monkey on the second level or saw a painted turtle trundling into the trees. I wanted my daughter to be enchanted. Even in fantasy, I wanted to know she was happy we came.

After the Lazris-Radzietskys moved here in December, I began casting Rebeca in my zoo scene. It was slightly less awful to imagine her than to imagine my fictional child. I tried telling myself that step-aunt would be a satisfying role; that it would be rewarding to develop a relationship with Rebeca. I knew Nina would let me. I also knew it would be buy-one-get-one. It would not be possible to invite Rebeca into my life without Nina tagging along.

All winter I considered it. Never before had I been open to the concept of sisterhood, but it had been months since I had talked about my miscarriages. None of my friends knew I had been attempting to get pregnant. Neither does my current girlfriend, whom I began seeing not long after ending my relationship with the would-be sperm donor. I keep my family life, such as it is, separate from my social life. I saw no reason to mix them before it was completely necessary. I certainly see no reason to mix them here.

I knew I could have described my loss to Nina. She would have understood. At times I imagined that hearing about my grief would help her process her own. I disliked—and continue to dislike—that the idea appealed to me. Nina has plenty of support. Offering mine would only have encouraged her to ask more from me. She would have asked too much regardless. She would have wanted to know about my childhood. About Caro. She would have wanted my memories of Chile, which do not exist. She would have tried to give me money. She would have wanted my forgiveness for Caro's kidnapping, torture, and death.

I resent that Nina holds herself accountable for my birth mother's fate. Her logic offends me. If she, as Ray Lazris's granddaughter and as an American taxpayer, is guilty of the atrocities committed by Augusto Pinochet and his CIA-backed regime, then so am I. Her concept of historical responsibility would have me shoulder the blame for my mother's suffering, or else identify myself strongly enough with that mother and that suffering to become a victim of harm perpetrated against a body that is not mine.

I know how Nina's mind works. I have read her emails, her texts, her search histories, her bank statements, her drafted but unsent tweets. I was the accidental audience of the Google Doc diaries in which she held two years of internal debates after Donald Trump's election crushed her faith in social media and made her feel even more ashamed of America than she had already taught herself to be. In the years immediately after the election, Nina wanted to atone for every American misdeed since our great-grandfather immigrated in 1929. She still does, though her new job at an immigrant-services nonprofit seems to be making her feel more purposeful, which is her code word for "virtuous." If she's lucky, it will eventually teach her the lesson she needs, which is how to feel small.

From the privacy of my living room, I have often found it entertaining to watch Nina writhe on her own hook. In person, I cannot see myself tolerating it. If I met her, sooner or later I would begin to hate her, which she does not deserve. I mean that in two senses. She is, first of all, a good person. Second, I have spent my adult life working not to hate Gabriel. Hating Nina would undo that effort. It would be a large step down the wrong path.

You may be thinking I have traveled far down that path already. You probably consider my behavior illegal, obsessive, and alarming. I certainly do. I understand the concept of stalking. I know I have devoted years of my life to committing cybercrimes, aided by an ill-adjusted, narcissistic creep. It is the one piece of my life that is wrong. I could have invested the tens of thousands of dollars I gave Belton over the years. I could have traveled, paid off my mortgage, or helped my mother pay hers. Instead, I hired my ex-boyfriend to help me spy on a pair of strangers. You think I think that's normal? Good behavior? A reasonable way to spend my money or time?

I have tried to quit watching my family, with the help of psychiatry and religion. I got hypnotized twice. I joined Obsessive Compulsive Anonymous. I filled my evenings and weekends with choir practice, marathon training, pottery classes, volunteer work. I let my worst-ever girlfriend persuade me to take a guided peyote trip, which she claimed would unlock my emotions and which I privately hoped would unchain me from my fixation. I vomited for three hours and, while hallucinating, hit the so-called shaman hard enough to break his nose. I knew he was blameless, but I was angry. I couldn't contain my-self. I felt something had to be done.

I CAN IDENTIFY THE PRECISE MOMENT I departed from the correct path. It was years before the birthday card with Ga-briel's email and password. I was twenty and in crisis. I had just left the hardcore scene, which for years had provided me with meaning, friendship, and an outlet for rage. At the time, my reasons for quitting were murky. Belton, who had then been my boyfriend for two years, was not part of the scene, but he never pressured me to leave it. He claimed to be con-cerned when I did.

Nancy was genuinely worried. She liked my punk friends, if not my punk aesthetic, and she thought I would be lonely without them. It was difficult to explain how lonely I had al-ready become. My scene had coalesced around an activist col-lective called Positive Force. I belonged, and contributed to its various projects and actions, but I was faking. Nothing in me was positive. How could it have been? I hated myself. I needed some kind of reinvention. For the first and only time, the pros-pect of becoming Ada Lazris appealed.

Belton had already begun erasing Caro, but I did not ask him to find my father. No need. Nancy had told me Gabriel's name. At the library, I searched it in newspapers and found his grand-father's obituary, his wedding announcement, and a quotation in a two-year-old article about pollution and the leather industry that told me he lived in or near Chicago. After that, all I had to do was call 411. I correctly guessed that his number and address would be listed. He would have wanted them available to me.

I bought a plane ticket to Chicago, which was a major expense. I knew perfectly well that I wanted access to Gabriel's wealth. I had spent years telling myself that my Lazris blood meant I was part not only of the Jewish religion but of Jewish history. I decided that the same principle applied to wealth.

On the flight, I rehearsed what I knew about Gabriel. His wife was a home stager. He had switched Lazris Leather from chrome tanning to vegetable tanning. He had an MBA from the University of Chicago. I imagined he would not be proud that I had an associate's degree in English from Montgomery College, though Nancy and I were both impressed I had seen it through.

It did not occur to me to wonder if he had children. I learned later, through Belton, that Nina was seven then, and that Gabriel was divorced. We are a family of only children and single parents. I do not ill-wish Nina and Ilán's marriage, but I do not expect it to hold.

Reciting Gabriel's wedding announcement to myself in the air did not comfort me. I was very nervous. I sweat so much that the flight attendants started bringing me airsickness bags. My self-loathing came in waves, like exhaustion. I called myself a sellout and a hypocrite. A doubly bad daughter. I had told Nancy I was visiting a friend from the hardcore scene, a lapsed punk like me. She was too relieved by the idea to question it. I have always known how to tell strategic lies.

I arrived in the late afternoon. Gabriel lived in Evanston, on Chicago's North Shore, and in a fit of unusual optimism, I had booked three nights at the suburb's cheapest hotel. I had planned to introduce myself to him in the morning, but sitting in my polyester-curtained room, I saw that stalling would be unwise. I had reached the edge of my courage. I put my bag down and went for a walk.

Gabriel and Nina were playing in their front yard. At first

I didn't understand who she was. A neighbor? A relative? She was small and sturdy, with round pink cheeks and a little belly beneath her green dress. She had jammed a lopsided crown over her curls and was clutching a glitter-filled wand. Gabriel brandished a wooden sword and shield. He wore a plastic knight's helmet with the visor lowered, but I could still see that he looked like me.

Nina was the narrator of their game. As I approached, I gathered that she was a princess. An evil wizard had imprisoned her in a tower, represented by the tree stump on which she stood. Her wand couldn't save her. Only Daddy could come scoop her up.

I kept moving. It seemed impossible to stop. What would I have done? Planted myself on the sidewalk and watched? Offered to join the scene as an ogre or a witch? Announced that the princess's sister was here to claim her rightful throne? I was, I thought, a grown woman. A stranger. Their game was fine without me.

For miles I walked blindly. A cool wind blew from Lake Michigan. My heels blistered and leaked. I could not join that family. Could not approach them. I would die before I subjected myself to this level of envy again. To be jealous of a child—of my sister—was humiliating. Worse than humiliating. I hated her. I felt contaminated. I promised myself that I would not return.

At dusk I boarded an El train into the city. The empty suburbs were not comforting me. I wanted grime and sound. Moving bodies. Not a show necessarily, but at least a crowded room. I rode the Purple Line until I saw neon signs and badly preserved buildings. Then I disembarked and walked directly into the rattiest bar on the block.

I never knew the bar's name. I know it had a glowing Old

Style Beer advertisement over the door, smoke-stained linoleum ceiling tile, and not a single punk in sight. In D.C., I had
never been to a bar that contained only non-punk white people. I had also never been to a bar to drink. I became straight-
edge when I discovered hardcore. In that ugly, tobacco-hazed
room, three months after I turned twenty, I ordered my first
beer since the summer before ninth grade. Also my second.
Also my first through fifth shots. I understood in theory that
getting drunk takes time, but in practice, I either misunder-
stood the process or was not willing to wait. In under an hour,
I was on my knees in the bathroom, vomiting Jim Beam–
smelling foam.

My binge had no serious consequence. I was not harmed. I
did not embark on a full bender. The bartender, perhaps realizing that it had been an error not to card me, eventually collected me from the handicapped stall, brewed me coffee, and
hailed me a cab. In the morning, I took an early bus to the
airport, bounced a change-fee check to Delta, and flew home.
When Belton picked me up at National, I asked what he could
learn about a person named Gabriel Lazris. Information, I
thought, would shield me. Give me power. After all, my greatest misery had come from not knowing his identity; my humil-
iation had come from not knowing he had a second child. Now
I wanted all the knowledge I could get.

I WOULD LIKE TO SHARE a second memory. A counterpoint. I
was unhappy throughout my childhood, adolescence, and early
adulthood, but I was always conscious that I was deeply loved.
Nancy was a persistent woman. Demonstrative, too. She never
let me turn away from her warmth. It never seemed possible.
Nor could I ever persuade myself, even in my worst times, that

I had no human value, if only because every time my mother saw me, she lit up as if she'd just been plugged in.

I never told her the true reason I went to Chicago. She still guessed that it had gone wrong. At that point, she had worked as an administrative assistant at the Department of Agriculture for six years. She owned a small condo in College Park. She could shop at Yes! Organic, dye her hair at a salon rather than in the bathroom, and, when she detected burgeoning distress in her only child, impulse-book a weekend at the beach.

I told her it was too indulgent. A waste of money. I didn't own a bathing suit. I didn't like the sun. She laughed in my face and handed me a Speedo one-piece in a Filene's Basement bag. It was electric purple. I accepted my fate. We drove to Delaware on a Friday evening. Bugs streaked themselves over our windshield as we cruised through farmland in the dusk. I remember red silos and golden-beige corn silk. Green tractors. The occasional coveralled man. Our motel was on the beach in Lewes, with a view that stretched to Cape May. Fat trumpet-shaped flowers bloomed everywhere. Instead of having dinner on arrival, we ate banana splits at King's. Nancy loved an elaborate sundae. If I had thought to get pregnant in time, she would have loved taking my daughter out for ice cream, urging her to order sprinkles, chopped peanuts, hot fudge. Both of them would have returned to me with chocolate stains on their shirts. Nancy was a messy eater. I remember her blotting maraschino-cherry juice from her mouth like lipstick, then dropping the napkin to catch a firefly.

I suspected that she had brought me to Lewes to force a discussion of my mental and emotional health. I tried to evade the conversation. On the beach, I pretended to be fascinated by washed-up jellyfish and horseshoe crabs. I went for long solo walks. I read crime novels. I submitted to her cocktail-mixing experiments. I went to sleep early and woke up late. Only driving home did I appreciate the trip's purpose. My mother had wanted me to relax, and I had.

Nancy taught me how to slow myself down. She identified my desires for control, stability, and simplicity long before I did. I doubt I ever would have recognized them without her; I certainly would not have attained them. Nancy knew how to help me, even when I resisted. She was never afraid to override my authority over myself. I would be more willing to meet my birth family if I thought them capable of learning that skill.

Gabriel, I am confident, would be tentative with me. After years of pursuing me, he would be too frightened of scaring me away to ever press an issue. He would let me reject whatever he offered, up to and including love. Nina would be more tenacious, but also more apologetic. She would turn every conversation we had into a favor I had done her. I spent this whole winter reminding myself that I am not patient enough to put up with that. Would not have been patient enough. The issue is not open now.

On Saturday I ended my debate over whether to introduce myself to my family. It was an accident. I accompanied them to the National Zoo because my imagination took me over. I did not have the will to fight it. Also, although I reject the concept of fairness, it struck me as immensely unfair that, after all the nights I lay awake thinking about it, Gabriel should fly in for the weekend and take Rebeca to the zoo. I didn't even know he was visiting until last Tuesday. I missed the ticket purchase. I knew he was coming only because Nina emailed him a weekend plan. Zoo Saturday; Baltimore aquarium Sunday. A very animal-oriented trip.

I knew instantly that I would join them at the zoo. I did not otherwise know my agenda. Maybe I would introduce myself. Maybe I would trip Ilán in the dark and crowded bat house. Maybe I would snatch Nina's purse. I promised myself, as I showered and dressed, that I would permit my impulses to guide me. Not standard procedure, but I was already deviating from personal norms. I had not seen Nina since her return. During her last D.C. stint, I passed her on Metro platforms, or nursed a beer on the Red Derby patio till she walked by, or, once, ate dinner at Lucy while she and Gabriel split a meat combo platter on the far side of the room. I had never shadowed her before. I understood that I was taking a new and unwise risk, but I couldn't help it. I have no better explanation than that.

I began my day at Timber Pizza, Nina's preferred breakfast spot. I ate quickly, then stirred my cooling coffee at the back bar until I heard her voice. She was in the snaking front-counter line, simultaneously collecting her family's orders, telling Ilán to save seats at a patio table, and asking, already, whether her dad was having a nice time. He walked in sixty seconds ago, I wanted to tell her. And he's in line behind a hungover couple with a three-year-old. The answer could only be no.

I couldn't hear Gabriel's reply. His voice didn't carry like Nina's. I am, however, strategic even in my less logical moments. I picked my bar seat because it was opposite a mirror. I could, therefore, see him clearly. My first sighting since the Ethiopian restaurant in 2014. His most striking visual trait, then and now, was a plain and elemental harmlessness. He was thin and stoop-shouldered in his worn, nubby fleece. His hairline receded in peaks that mirrored his aquiline nose, which I inherited. It looks better on me than on him. He wore a mild, hopeless smile, and though I cannot read lips, I was fairly sure he was telling Nina he was enjoying himself very much.

I waited in my car while my relatives ate their breakfast

sandwiches at a picnic table on the restaurant's front patio. Timber makes excellent if untraditional wood-fired bagels. The adults, however, opted for biscuits and ate them sloppily. Rebeca chose a bagel, which she ate slowly and cautiously, as if the egg and cheese inside were still steaming hot.

Ilán was the family driver. I tried to keep at least one car between their newly purchased Chevy Bolt and the Subaru Outback I inherited from Nancy. She died two and a half years ago, but, somehow, the upholstery still smells like her signature mix of spilled Whole Foods French roast and eucalyptus Dr. Bronner's. I will be bereft when the scent fades.

If Nancy had been in the car with me, she would have been appalled. She knew I paid Belton to remove Caro from the internet, and supported me in doing so, but that was it. Nobody wants to reckon with their grown child's worst habits. Nancy thought I was an unmitigated success story. I was well employed, well adjusted, a loving daughter. I prayed with her on Rosh Hashanah and fasted with her on Yom Kippur. On Mother's Day, I brought doughnuts and flowers. We got our hair dyed together. I rebooked our Lewes trip yearly. I brought my friends to meet her. I introduced her to every person I ever dated except the peyote-trip girlfriend, who I knew from the start was full of shit. Nancy worried enough in her first two decades mothering me. Once she stopped, I never wanted to give her even the smallest reason to restart.

Ilán parked in the zoo's Beach Drive lot. Tourist season hadn't quite begun, but the day was unseasonably warm, and so the route to the primates and big cats was dense with Washingtonians taking advantage. It was barely ten o'clock, but high schoolers were already kissing on half the benches. Toddlers' shrieks filled the air. Elderly women took morning constitutionals. I heard families speaking languages I took to be

Arabic, Amharic, Hindi, and Korean. Also, three varieties of Spanish: Dominican, Salvadoran, and the Argentine-Chilean blend into which the Lazris-Radzietskys sometimes lapsed. I have long been irritated by Gabriel's activist accomplice Nico Echevarría, but I will give him credit on this front: thanks to him, Gabriel still sounds like a native Spanish speaker. Nina does not. Neither do I, though I am one. Though Nancy tried to persuade me to keep it, I let my Spanish go. In middle school I started pronouncing my name the American way. I took French in high school. I still understand Spanish when I hear it, but I can't communicate anymore.

Unlike the adults, Rebeca confined herself to English. She had the piccolo voice of a smaller child, which, surprisingly, did not make her seem immature. She looked like Ilán but carried herself like Nina. Both she and her stepmother kept their shoulders back and heads forward, as if always straining for a view. When not walking, they turned their feet out and cocked their left hips. Their thick, woolly sweaters corresponded. So did their Adidas sneakers and pinned-back hair. Rebeca wore small silver dolphins in her ears. A dainty gold one leapt in Nina's right lobe. Anyone would have taken them to be mother and daughter. I wondered if, to Rebeca, they were.

I kept several yards from the Lazris-Radzietskys for the majority of our time at the zoo. This was harder than you might think. They did not move in a tight pack. I imagined that Nina would hover, but she and Ilán let their daughter roam. I watched Rebeca linger, nose wrinkled, in front of a dung-smelling elephant asleep in a pile of hay. I listened to her chirping at a cockatiel, which did not chirp back. I saw her beam at the charming, foxlike red pandas, then return to beam at them again. She was significantly less interested in the actual pandas. I heard her tell Nina she would wait in line to see a dolphin but not a bear.

It seemed to me that Rebeca was in a good mood. Nina was anxious. Ilán and Gabriel worked visibly hard to connect. The trip was only their third in-person encounter. At the tiger enclosure, I saw Gabriel attempt to clap his son-in-law on the back. The gesture was delicate to the point of clumsiness, but Ilán received it well. I wondered momentarily how Gabriel would react to me physically if I introduced myself. I doubted either of us would initiate a hug, though I was sure Nina would.

I did not think I was planning to talk to them. I had entered a state of concentrated observation. Involved but separate. Not invisible, but not present. The sensation was both awful and powerful. I recognize now that it was also false. A self-protection. Had I truly believed that I was disconnected from my family, or that it was impossible for them to notice me, I would have had no reason not to follow them into Amazonia. Instead, I let them vanish into the humid building without me. Then I walked to the outdoor stingray pool, where I pretended to be absorbed in the rays' fluttering motion until Rebeca approached.

I omitted the stingray pool from my earlier description of Amazonia. I should not have. The pool is physically removed from the exhibit but visible through a glass wall opposite the first-floor tanks. A large glass door leads directly from the science hall to the stingray pool. In the hall, large plaques break down the differences between the three species on display: vermiculate river rays, white-blotched river rays, and ocellate river rays, also known as peacock-eye rays. A lone ray floats in an open indoor tank, waiting forlornly to be touched. I anticipated the possibility that Rebeca, having petted the inside ray, would come outside to see the rest, and that she would do so alone. As I said, Nina and Ilán let her wander. Promoting independence, I assume.

For a moment, she stood beside me. She came roughly up to

my elbow. Above us, Amazonia's cultivated trees rustled, and a roseate spoonbill emerged. It had very pale pink feathers, with the exception of a fiery chest tuft and a fuchsia band on each wing. Its legs looked like pink pear stems. A tracking band rode above its left knee.

"Pretty bird," I said.

She cocked her head. So did the spoonbill. "It has a funny beak."

I touched my nose. "I do too."

Rebeca turned to appraise me. I had dressed not to be noticed. Baseball cap, crewneck sweatshirt, worn corduroy pants. The hat covered my highlighted hair, which is my main vanity. Under her scrutiny, I took it off and tucked it in my back pocket, then released my hair from its bun.

"Better," she told me.

I smiled. "Yes?"

"Yes. Your nose is big, but your hair is nice."

"It costs a lot."

"Your hair?"

I nodded. "I get it dyed every month."

"From gray?"

"Half gray, half brown. Not a good mix."

Rebeca examined me once more. I held still. An onlooker would have thought I was indulging her. After a moment, she said, "Nobody ever tells me what stuff costs." Pride moved briefly over her face at her colloquial phrasing. What stuff costs. I knew that a construction like that would have real value to her.

"Do you ask?" I said.

"All the time."

Not once in my childhood had an adult refused to discuss prices with me. I knew Nancy's bank balance most weeks. If

I'd had a daughter, she would have learned how to budget not long after learning how to count.

"Maybe," I said, "I could help."

Rebeca moved closer. She smelled like bacon and pencil erasers. The spoonbill flapped its wings and returned to the trees. "How much does it cost to fly to Argentina?" she asked, pronouncing the country's name with a hard English *g*. "From here, I mean."

I recalled the Radzietskys' tickets: Ezeiza to Miami International, Miami to Dulles, purchased three months in advance. "Eight hundred dollars," I said. "Give or take."

She sucked her cheeks in. "That's expensive."

"It is."

A ray swam near the pool's edge, cartilaginous tail ticking in its wake. Rebeca peered at it. My scalp prickled with nerves. Our conversation could end at any moment. I wanted to keep her engaged. I wanted to feel proud, later, that I had offered her knowledge nobody else would.

"Which stingray is that?" she asked, pointing.

I knew the species' names, but not their markings. Still, I could guess. "Peacock-eye."

Rebeca nodded, still examining the ray. As if addressing it, she said, "How much time does saving eight hundred dollars take?"

"Depends."

"On?"

I recognized that I had to be careful. I could not show that I knew why she was asking, or that I empathized. At ten, I had scrounged up change to fly home. I once snuck out of my elementary school and ran a mile to the Metro, planning to ride to National Airport and cry at a ticket counter till somebody put me on a plane to Mexico City, but a transit cop caught me at the turnstile. At dinner that night, Nancy asked whether I was fleeing her or her city, and I didn't know how to answer. I had assumed she would come after me. She'd never failed to before.

"Depends on the person," I told Rebeca. "It depends how much money you make, and what your bills and expenses are."

Rebeca lifted her chin. Her eyes glittered with daring. "How long would it take you?"

"Not long."

"That's an answer like my mom gives," she said scornfully.

I rocked back on my heels. It took great effort not to ask her which mom. For the first time, I imagined Nina monitoring our exchange through the window. "Well," I said. "I make $80,000 a year before taxes. I have no kids, which means that after I pay my bills and my mortgage, I can spend all my money on myself. Usually, if I have some left over, I put it in my savings account, which means that, if I really wanted, I could buy a ticket to Buenos Aires right now."

The answer left me short of breath. Sweat collected under my arms and in the cups of my bra. I would have liked to add that she, too, would be an adult soon enough, and, considering her background, she'd have plenty of money to spend on herself. Instead, I watched her metabolize my answer. I saw that it had earned me her trust.

"How long would it take a kid?" she asked. "A kid with no allowance?"

I could no longer look directly at her. "For a kid with no allowance," I said softly, "eight hundred dollars is very, very expensive. Saving that much money would take a long time."

She was silent. A second stingray approached the pool's rim. It had umber spots with black rims, like eyes. Had she asked, I would have called it a vermiculate river ray. I would have added that "vermiculate" means wormlike, and that I learned the rays' names at roughly her age. I would not have said that memorizing trivia was a strategy I devised for combating tantrum-inducing anxiety. Nancy was proud of me for it. She bought me an atlas, an encyclopedia, and the 1985 *Guinness Book of World Records*. All three helped.

I had wanted to help Rebeca, not to upset her. I understood that I had done both. Her bottom lip shook. Her cheeks were wet. Never in my imagination had I made any child cry. I would not have been a comforting mother. Regret overwhelmed me. She covered her face with her hands. It was not appropriate for me to console her, but it would have been cruel not to move close enough to give her a hug.

She nestled into my rib cage. I patted her thin, heaving back. Ferns rustled gently above us, sun shining through their damp fronds. My eyes started to ache. I smelled stagnant water evaporating from the rays' pool and felt my sweatshirt growing damp. Dark blotches radiated over the gray cotton. I was surprised Rebeca could cry so hard without sound. Also that she could cry so hard into a stranger's torso. I know her world has trained her to be trusting, but her defenselessness both frightens and touches me still.

Soon I heard the glass door swing open. I could not turn fully without dislodging Rebeca, but I twisted my head enough to meet Nina's eyes. She was unaccompanied, though I assumed Ilán and Gabriel were watching through the window. Her expression held more concern than fear. I tried to project kindness and safety, which worked. She, too, had learned to be trusting. She flashed me a resigned smile, then said quietly, "She's going through a tough time."

Rebeca stiffened but did not otherwise move. I wondered if she could feel my heart rate speeding. I had delivered myself into a moment of truth. After this, Nina would recognize me. She was already learning my face. From now on, if she happened to encounter me on the street or the Metro, I would be visible. I would be the Amazonia Woman, to whom she owed gratitude and an abstract favor. She'd stop and chat. Might eventually ask for my number. She wouldn't allow herself to let go of me.

Or she would recognize me in the other way. Our resemblance was not striking, but it was plain. So was my resemblance to the Ana Lazris Ravest she'd mocked up and circulated. She could take one step closer, cock her head, and say, with halting excitement, Are you—?

I had three nested decisions. I could introduce myself or not. If I did not introduce myself but she identified me, I could tell the truth or not. If I did not tell the truth, I could be the Amazonia Woman or vanish from her life. The choices came with their own clarity. I was holding on to her child. I was in control. I would never have this much power over my family again.

I rubbed Rebeca's back. Nina put a hand on her shoulder. "You're very kind," she said to me. "I'm sorry if—"

I shook my head. "No need to be sorry. I understand."

Nina nodded. Perfume wafted from her. Rebeca still hadn't stirred. Nina knelt on the concrete, which rendered them roughly the same height. She wrapped her arms around her daughter. I moved my hands free. For a moment, we leaned together like dominoes. Then Rebeca shifted backwards, into Nina's body, and I stepped clear. The ache in my eyes had worsened. The sun seemed exceptionally bright. Rebeca wiped her face, looking embarrassed. Our moment had ended. I put on my baseball cap, then, absurdly, gave the brim a Clint Eastwood tug. Nina began to thank me, but I could not bear to listen. Before the words were out, I was walking away.

REFERENCES

Short War is the result of nearly a decade of reading and research. I could not possibly have written it any other way. Consider this list—which is Greatest Hits; it's far from exhaustive—equal parts recommended reading, works cited, and a moment of gratitude and appreciation for the journalists, memoirists, and scholars whose writing I relied on. All mistakes are not theirs but mine.

I am not including novels, though reading them can certainly be research, because if I started listing the fiction I'm grateful for, I wouldn't know where to stop. But I will say that without Roberto Bolaño's *Distant Star*, *By Night in Chile*, and *The Secret of Evil*, this book would be nothing and nowhere, and, as a writer, so would I.

Inside the Company: CIA Diary, Philip Agee

Although Agee was posted in Ecuador, Uruguay, and Mexico, never in Chile, his diary gave me a much-needed window into the mindset of Cold Warriors operating in Latin America. Agee, famously, became an anti-covert-intelligence activist and dissident; in his *New York Times* obituary, his friend William Schaap called him "the first person to do whistle-blowing on the C.I.A. on the grand scale." I tried to keep his spirit present during my research.

El Infierno, Luz Arce

Arce was a Socialist militant who served as one of Salvador Allende's guards during his presidency, then fought against Augusto Pinochet's regime. She was then incarcerated, tortured, and forced to collaborate with military intelligence. Her memoir is utterly harrowing and is required reading to understand both Allende's time in office and the horrific abuses that Pinochet and his soldiers perpetrated. Stacey Alba Skar translated it into English in 2004.

La CIA en Chile 1970–1973, Carlos Basso Prieto

"The CIA and the Media," Carl Bernstein

If you are wondering how plausible it is that a journalist would have collaborated with Richard Helms's CIA, let Bernstein tell you: very.

Allende's Chile: An Inside View, Edward Boorstein

Boorstein, an American Marxist economist, worked for Allende's government. His perspective, as both an insider and an American believer in the Chilean road to Socialism, was invaluable to me.

A Nation of Enemies, Pamela Constable and Arturo Valenzuela

Conversations with Allende, Régis Debray

The Condor Years, John Dinges
Dinges worked as a journalist in Santiago in the 1970s, and his writing on that time, as well as memories he shared with me, both gave me insight into the political moment and helped me build a detailed vision of Allende's Chile through North American eyes.

"La crisis de la interpretación," Alejandro Grimson
Like Nina, I paid obsessive attention to the case of Alberto Nisman. Grimson's essay helped me understand the news I was consuming more than any other analysis did. It also gave me the titles of *Short War*'s first two sections.

Story of a Death Foretold: The Coup Against Salvador Allende, September 11, 1973, Oscar Guardiola-Rivera

The Pinochet File, Peter Kornbluh
If it's declassified, it's here. I could not have researched my book without Kornbluh's, or without the online National Security Archive at George Washington University, where he works.

Predatory States: Operation Condor and Covert War in Latin America, J. Patrice McSherry
If you choose one book from this list, make it this one. (Well, this one and *El Infierno*.) *Predatory States* is necessary reading if you want to understand U.S. intervention during the Cold War not only in Chile, but throughout Latin America.

*El camino de la memoria: De la represión a la justicia en Chile,
   1973–2013*, Carla Peñaloza Palma

Condor, João Pina

I first saw Pina's profoundly moving photographs at Santiago's Museo de la Memoria, which is a museum I cannot recommend highly enough. I feel the same about the images in this book, which I looked at every day for many months while I was writing.

Beyond the Vanguard: Everyday Revolutionaries in Allende's Chile,
   Marian E. Schlotterbeck

The Black Book of American Intervention in Chile, Armando Uribe
Uribe was a Chilean poet, writer, and diplomat who went into exile after the coup. He worked in Chile's U.S. embassy and studied military relations between the two countries as an adviser to Allende, and his understanding of U.S. imperialism and interventionism had a massive influence not only on my writing but on my sense of what it means for me to be American. I read this book in Jonathan Casart's very good 1975 translation.

ACKNOWLEDGMENTS

Writing *Short War* was not a short process. I am profoundly grateful for my agent, Sarah Burnes, whose patience and belief in me—and in this book, even when it was a mess—I do not take for granted. Sophie Pugh-Sellers has been helpful and encouraging from the moment she arrived at the Gernert Company, and Nora Gonzalez gave me absolutely vital feedback along the way.

I feel so lucky to be part of the Deep Vellum universe as both a writer and a translator and luckier still to join A Strange Object's phenomenal list. It is a dream to be edited by Jill Meyers, whom I cannot thank enough. Will Evans is a king of enthusiasm and advocacy, and Sara Balabanlilar and Walker Rutter-Bowman are publicity and marketing champions.

Short War took shape through reading and archival digging, but also through interviews. John Dinges and Bill Knox both spent afternoons telling me about their years in Chile. Annie Dean, Tony Dean, and Meredith Burns talked to me many times, shared their written and recorded memories with me, and read drafts. I cannot say how much I appreciate their trust—or that of my beloved friend Maddie Johnston, who helped me swipe her family's stories and helps me understand my life.

My obsession with U.S. intervention in Chile started when I was a sixteen-year-old exchange student in Quillota, not far from the small towns where Gabriel goes to do volunteer labor. My host family, the Mercado Laferttes, were unfailingly generous, fun, and welcoming, and have—of course—remained so when I've gotten to visit. Also a queen of welcome and generosity, and a person I want to grow up to be: Elena Iglesias, whose apartment on Calle Azcuénaga I lived in in 2011. I dream of our next Rapanui outing.

I began writing *Short War*, or a version of it, during my MA at the University of East Anglia, where Henry Sutton and Andrew Cowan could not have been more supportive. Joe Banfield, Jacqui Landey, John Patrick McHugh, and Sophia Veltfort have remained key readers, correspondents, and confidants. Eliza Robertson and Kim Sherwood, my witches of Ten Bell Lane: no Norwich without you.

I finished *Short War*, or a version of it, during my PhD at the University of Cincinnati, where Chris Bachelder, Michael Griffith, and Leah Stewart steered me out of years of creative chaos. Leah's novel workshop was especially transformative. Both the Taft Dissertation Fellowship and the University Research Center Summer Fellowship helped me concentrate on my work, and my classmates, especially Alida Dean, Anessa Ibrahim, Maia Morgan, and Natalie Villacorta, made my writing better and made my life in Cincinnati fun. I would have suffered without them and without both Downbound Books and its excellent owner, Greg Kornbluh.

Between my times in graduate school, I mainly worked on *Short War* while also working on the Politics and Prose events team, which is to say while guided and supported by the iconic Liz Hottel, my friend far beyond any bookstore or greenroom. Events also gave me the great Jonathan Woollen, key book- and translation-world gossip-mate. Chase Culler and I started discussing books many years ago, and his reading—of my work and in general—is a source of great happiness to me.

For years, I have written freelance book criticism, a practice that has shaped my fiction writing. I am grateful to all my editors, especially Petra Mayer, who took a real chance on me and whom I miss deeply, and Jane Kim, who has done more than anyone to sharpen not only my sentences but my ideas. (Arguing with Julia Fisher over the years has helped too.) Mary Kay Zuravleff has been my professional fairy godmother throughout.

My paternal grandfather, Bunny Meyer, was the source of the toast that gives *Short War* its title. I apologize to my family for hijacking it, even in a spirit of tribute. My birthday cousin Julie Cutter did some very helpful steering and fact-checking along the way. Nina's relationship with Ray is modeled on mine with my maternal grandfather, Nate Rosenbaum, who I truly wish could read this book.

I cannot begin to say how thankful I am for my parents' and brother's unshakable faith in me. Your support, curiosity, and combined model of commitment and tenacity motivate me to write. My husband, Will, is my moral compass, my bullshit detector, and my favorite person to talk to in any language. I love you all very much.

ABOUT THE AUTHOR

Lily Meyer is a writer, translator, and critic. She is a contributing writer at the *Atlantic*, and her translations include Claudia Ulloa Donoso's story collections *Little Bird* and *Ice for Martians*. She lives in Washington, D.C.

ABOUT A STRANGE OBJECT

Founded in 2012 in Austin, Texas, A Strange Object champions debuts, daring writing, and striking design across all platforms. The press became part of Deep Vellum in 2019, where it carries on its editorial vision via its eponymous imprint. A Strange Object's titles are distributed by Consortium.